Ballantine/31682/$2.95

A DEL REY BOOK
SF

For 2000 years Mankind had returned
to the Middle Ages. If Ormson was defeated
it might never progress...

# A DARKNESS UPON THE ICE

a novel by
## WILLIAM R. FORSTCHEN

DKS

## TO THE MANNER BORN

The seven-year-old slowly raised his head to examine the new presence in his life.

Only long training prevented Nathan from revealing his shock. There was so much of Michael Ormson in the child—Thomas was pale and slender, with a high forehead and blond, nearly white hair. But his eyes were the eyes of an old man who had seen too much. Like his father's they were of two different colors—one pale blue, the other a dark steel gray

"Who are you?" Thomas asked while his small hands pushed the game pieces into position.

"My name is Nathan. I am to be your bodyguard and trainer."

"Trainer in what?"

"Dueling with weapons and defense against attack."

"Will you teach me to kill?"

# A DARKNESS UPON THE ICE

## WILLIAM R. FORSTCHEN

A Del Rey Book

BALLANTINE BOOKS • NEW YORK

For my father, who first pointed out the stars, and for my mother, who taught me to imagine what was beyond them.

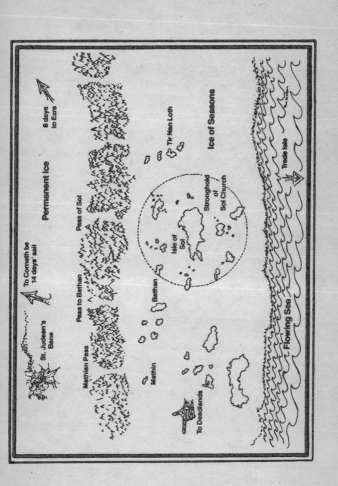

# PROLOGUE

Seven years have passed since the taking of Cornath by the followers of Michael Ormson. The forces of the Cornathian Church have abandoned the East and, to the surprise of many, retreated to the forbidden Dead Lands, where, building new bases, they wage a protracted war against Ormson's followers.

Many dreamed that with the coming of the Prophet the New Age would arrive. But rather than an ending has come yet more war—a conflict apparently without end, dividing family against family, friend against friend, in a struggle to the death.

For some it is the year 1037; for others it is the thirty-seventh year of the Prophet. But for a small group, hidden from all the others, it is at last time for the Fulfillment— the completion of the long-cherished dream.

# BOOK V

**Ice Cruiser**

# CHAPTER 1

*So look to us now, Michael Ormson, and see what we have become. We denounced the fear and called it blindness, and in the end we have embraced that fear, and called it our own.*
—ANONYMOUS

"BACK. STAND BACK, YOU SCUM. GIVE THEM ROOM TO TURN!"

Reluctantly the ice runners edged away, watching in silence as two fur-clad warriors maneuvered in the dance of death.

"Cut 'em open, Eldric. Slice the liver out of the pig."

Fighting down a cough, Norn looked across the circle of men and stared down the Mathinian who had shouted the advice. The combat was a death challenge, and by all the mandates, no one was to offer weapon, encouragement, help, or advice until one of the two men in the circle had spilled his life's blood onto the ice.

Eldric edged to the left, looking for an opening. The challenger waited for the rush—his two-handed battle-ax held back in preparation for the death swing. The challenger's tunic was open, revealing taut, sinewy muscles that shone softly in the frigid cold. A thin wisp of steam rose from his sweaty body and the bloody gash that trickled a scarlet river across his stomach. Eldric was yet unmarked, his face alight with a sneer of contempt, as if the challenge to his command was more a joke than a life-or-death struggle.

The two combatants stood poised and ready, looking for an opening. With a defiant shout Eldric swung his scimitar back, opening his defenses with a taunting disregard for danger.

"Come on, you bastard," Eldric whispered, "you think you can take me. What are you waiting for? *Take* me, you whoreson—kill me!"

The challenger was motionless, breathing hard.

Eldric laughed softly and, with a lightning sweep of his left hand, pulled a razor-sharp poniard from his boot top. Raising the blade to eye level, Eldric quietly cursed his young opponent.

The ice runners and freebooters watching the fight quietly mumbled bets to each other while awaiting the outcome. Most were indifferent, but some watched with fervent interest, since the death of Eldric would spell a shift in their alliances and fortunes.

With a sudden shout the challenger closed. Feigning a stab to the eyes, Eldric stepped back and with a deadly slash cut the air at knee height, his scimitar whistling a high-pitched song of death. The challenger jumped lightly but continued to more forward, his ax slashing in a series of short, deadly arcs. Eldric pulled back, ducked low, and started to advance, but the challenger stepped back again and, with a quick spin of the ax handle, cut across Eldric's face. Eldric was stunned and blinded as the cold steel blade smashed his cheekbone and came within an inch of carving out his right eye. A spray of blood arced away from his body and he staggered from the impact. Despite. the rules, a roar went up from the crowd, which was steadily growing, as news of the fight echoed down the narrow, filthy streets of Bathan.

The challenger spun quickly on his heels and went into a backhand sweep. But Eldric anticipated the move and dived to the ground, the ax blade cleaving the air just inches from his head. Still half blind, Eldric lashed out wildly, trying to cut his opponent's legs, but the ax wielder jumped over the blade and with a shout of triumph smashed Eldric's scimitar against the ice, severing the blade from the hilt.

An expectant hush fell over the crowd as the challenger screamed with joy while raising his ax for the death blow. But with a serpentine movement Eldric's left hand whipped out and the wild shout of triumph died, changing into a strangled scream. The challenger tottered above Eldric, the ax slipping from his trembling hands. He looked down at his chest and weakly fumbled at the hilt of the poniard, already red with blood. He looked at Eldric with a curious distant gaze, as if by throwing the knife an unspoken rule had been broken, and then, with an almost graceful ease, the young warrior fell to his knees and collapsed by Eldric's side.

Trying desperately to conceal the trembling of his limbs, Eldric got to his feet and fumbled for the ax. He picked it up and with a single blow decapitated the body. A scarlet river flowed briefly across the dark-gray ice. Dropping the ax, Eldric wiped the blood from his face and through a dim red haze looked out at the silent warriors.

"Ten have challenged my right as captain of the freebooters' guild," Eldric cried. "Is there an eleventh?"

No one answered and the crowd looked away from its leader. Several men broke from the crowd and hurried to Eldric's side. Wrapping their arms around him, they started to lead him away. The crowd parted to let him pass, but one did not step aside.

Eldric squinted at the aging warrior whose flowing gray beard reached halfway to the ground. "Norn, it was his challenge; I asked not for this fight."

Norn was silent.

"I did not want this; it was he who challenged me. You were there to hear it."

There was no answer, only a sullen look of defiance.

"He'll be buried with honor. He served me well at the Cornathian gate."

"I'll bury my own son as I please. He would prefer my rites to the heretical ones that you practice and try to force on the rest of us."

A man stepped out from behind Eldric.

"Idol worshipper!" the man screamed, waving his sword. "Ours is the one true belief. You and yours must see what folly Sol's teachings are. Kill him, Eldric, he and his scum should be wiped out. They're vermin, they are, worshippers of the Sun."

Without looking back Eldric extended his hand in a soothing gesture. "Abelsson, enough blood has run today."

Norn did not answer, nor did he move. In a surprising act of deference, Eldric stepped around him and went on.

"Those followers of Sol are trouble, Eldric," Abelsson whispered. "We should kill Norn before he causes more trouble."

Eldric looked back at Abelsson and shrugged. "He is dying of the lung fire; leave him be. Besides, Michael demands a full acceptance of all religious creeds, and, of course, we must obey our Prophet." Eldric gave a sad, sarcastic smile to his lieutenant as they pushed through the cheering throng of ice runners, freebooters, harlots, and relic sellers that were the flotsam of the free port of Bathan.

No one else dared be first to the body, and an unmoving cloud of metallic-smelling vapor had enveloped the chilling corpse by the time Norn finally approached and knelt beside his son in a slushy pool of blood. "Sedmath, why were you such a fool?" he whispered. "There was no need to challenge him openly. We had the men, we had the ships; why couldn't you wait?"

Norn wept silent tears of rage over the body of his youngest son, the last of five. All the rest had died in the wars of the Prophet. No one would mourn him now, nor pray for him as the lung fire drained away his life. Michael had done this, Michael and Eldric—they had slaughtered all that was his, slaughtered his dreams along with the dreams of thousands of others. He knew now, at last, where he would go and what would have to be done. And as he bent over the body, washing it in tears, he silently called to Zimri. Zimri would listen to him. Zimri would understand.

"Oh Saints above..."

"Look down upon us in our hour of need" came the chanted response.

Sigurd Wulfson of the Cornathian Missionaries slowly stood and turned from the altar to face the gathering that waited in the icy darkness of the chapel.

"Oh Saints above!" he suddenly cried, raising his hands in a gesture of supplication and despair. "Ye who did guide our forefathers, hear us now in this, the hour of trial."

"And guide us back to the Light of Grace" was the whispered response.

"So that we may be judged worthy to enter into the Everlasting Feast, where at the Long Table of the Saints, bathed in warmth and light, we shall await the day of the Return and the resurrection of the Garden forever."

"Amen."

A faint rustling echoed in the darkness as the faithful stood and quietly stretched while the choir of initiates started its chant.

*"O feag Athar, direah Aig em beil fearg e."*

"Oh angry Father, Whose wrath is just."

Taking the gilded image of the sacred Arch, Wulfson thrice blessed the assembled crowd, and while the deep basses of the choir chanted in the background, he held the image aloft and called out with a full passionate voice.

"For is it not written that there shall come the time of the heretic, the bringer of false doctrine? And he shall be the snare of the Evil One, sent to lure us into darkness eternal.

"Look around you, oh my children, look around you and remember. Remember fair Cornath, and the Night of Death, remember always that it came from his hand. There are some here who might say that he lets us live and keep our faith, and I cry out to such as they and tell them to leave our presence. For Ormson is the Dark One. Ormson slaughtered the innocents of Cornath. Ormson is the force sent from Frozen Hell to curse us. And yet you, all of you of North Prydain, have swallowed his words and allowed his noisome presence to pollute this Earth. But I for one shall tolerate no longer the cursed stench of a heretic breed. For if I allow it to exist here on our sacred soil but one more day, then I am cursed by the very words of Ragnarson who said 'suffer not a heretic to live!'"

Holding the sacred Icon over his head, Wulfson swept away from the altar and, with eager steps, rushed down the aisle of the church. In the darkness he could hear the congregation stirring, shouting, and pushing to follow.

The doors of the church swung open to reveal a torchlit courtyard packed to overflowing with the faithful who awaited him. A cold, delicious chill ran through his body and he could feel the pounding of his heart. The tension was electric, all-encompassing. The feeble voices of the choir were washed away by the swelling chant of the multitude—and it was a chant of awakening fervor, a call of bitter defiance and religious hysteria—ready to explode.

He led the procession down the narrow, garbage-choked alleyways, and it seemed that from every hovel, from every tavern and hidden refuge emerged others eager to join the faithful in midnight procession. Even the roar of the wind, as it echoed through the city, could not overwhelm their chant. They came at last to the harbor gate and the hated citadel of stone. Atop its high pointed spires the pennants of Mathin and of the Companions flew, illuminated by the shimmering green of the aurora. And drawn up across the ice was a thin line of white-clad forms, shields up, swords and crossbows drawn.

The crowd hesitated, but Wulfson stepped forward and pointed with an accusing finger.

"There is the creation of our anguish!" he cried. "There is the reason for the darkness that is still upon the Ice. For it is written, 'suffer not a false believer to live, for he is an instrument of the darkness, his presence dooming all to the wrath of the Father and the Ice Eternal.'"

An expectant hush fell across the square as one of the white-clad warriors put aside his shield and, with empty hands extended, walked across the open, windswept ice.

Approaching Wulfson, he pulled aside his mask. "Wulfson, not this way. You know as well as I do that only the innocents will be slaughtered. Haven't you had enough of death? We must live together. It's the only way both of us can survive."

"Cowan, it is beyond that now," Wulfson said softly. "You've known that from the beginning, the moment you came to us sword in hand, you became like us. It was then that we knew we could beat you. That mob behind me could have been yours, but now it is mine, and they're ready to act on my command."

"We give you the right to worship as you please. Why bring this to blood? Hasn't enough been spilled already?"

Wulfson looked at his old friend and smiled. "Your Prophet is dying, and your cause is dying of its own corruption. The people will follow me, for ours is the One True Faith."

"You don't really believe that!"

"For the moment I do. And for the people there is no greater fear than religious fear, no greater hatred than religious hatred."

"Don't force me to act."

"But I must. It is my mission to make you act."

A voice called from behind Cowan. "Cowan, let's have at the filthy Cornathian scum. They're pox-eaten idol worshippers."

An ugly roar rose from the crowd behind Wulfson. The priest smiled at Cowan.

Cowan turned to his men. "Silence! By the law of the Prophet they are entitled to their holy rites."

But his men were beyond reason. Years of mutual hatred and misunderstanding had come at last to the flash point.

"Death to the Cornathians," one of the Companions shouted, his voice breaking with hysterical rage.

Cowan faced Wulfson, his hands extended in a gesture of despair.

For several seconds a strange, dreamlike silence held, until suddenly, from the shadows, a rock caught Cowan on the side of his head and sent him staggering.

A wild cry of rage came up from the line of Companions. Unordered, the first rank dropped to its knees and swept the square with a ragged shower of bolts. An arrow caught Wulfson in the leg, spinning him around so that he landed next to Cowan. A wild, explosive rage ignited the mob, which swept forward screaming words of hate. Cowan, regaining his balance, tottered back to the protection of his men.

Wild cries of pain and rage echoed in the night. Wulfson watched as old men, women, and even children rushed the wall of heavily armed troops and died by the hundreds in a vain attempt to destroy the followers of the heretic.

"Wulfson, are you badly hurt?"

He looked up to a young monk kneeling at his side, while all around him was chaos.

"No, I'm fine. It is nothing; just help me to my feet."

He turned away from the square and limped off into the darkness. The fighting would rage through the night, and by morning a third of North Prydain would be in flames as neighbor turned against neighbor. But Wulfson would not be there to witness it. The task set for him by Zimri was accomplished.

"Bring it closer to the wind, damn it. Closer, I say!"

"Down, Grimath—*incoming*!"

With an instinct born of forty years on the Ice, Grimath dove for the scant protection offered by the foremast. The wheel behind him exploded in a shower of deadly splinters—the pilot's body disappearing in a bloody spray that drenched the deck in scarlet. Grimath looked to his chart reader, who had shouted the warning. Miraculously, the young boy was still on his feet, but his tunic was torn open from throat to groin, his abdominal cavity slashed out by the passage of the ball. Regaining his footing, Grimath struggled over the wreckage to help the young monk, who tottered toward him. The boy collapsed into Grimath's arms, his internal organs spilling out in a slimy pool of steaming blood. In shock, Grimath laid the body down and returned to his duties. The ship was heeling away, her steering cables severed. Another shot slammed into the deck amidships, sending a deathly shudder through the craft.

"Hook up the steering cables from below!" Grimath shouted. "Keep on her, damn it! Move lively, you men, lively now."

He suddenly remembered his first responsibility and with a wild panic looked across the shattered wreckage of the foredeck. Where was he!

He suddenly saw the purple and gold robes standing next to a twenty-four-pounder amidships. By all the Saints, he was safe. With a curt nod of recognition, Grimath strode forward to get a better view of the enemy. The corsair was trying to pinch closer into the breeze, its downwind escape cut off by the *Braith du Mor*. Another volley rang out from the Morian ship and half a dozen holes appeared in the enemy's sails, while one shot plowed into the deck, dismounting a stern chaser.

"Not the deck, damn it, not the deck!" Grimath shouted. "I'll flay the next gun captain who hits it!"

"Another volley!"

Grimath looked up in time to see the smoke from the enemy's guns as the wind whipped it away. He braced for the impact.

The deck rocked beneath his feet and wild cries of anguish echoed up from below.

Damn it, how much longer can we take this? He struggled with the desire to go astern and demand the right to fire for the hull, but it was useless, the orders were explicit, and he gritted his teeth with rage.

"The cables hooked up below," a blood-smeared deacon shouted.

"Good, bring her back in on line, two points to starboard."

"Two points to starboard it is."

"Another shot coming in," the forward gun spotter cried.

Grimath didn't even bother to look up as the ball cut through the maintop and hummed across the ice.

"Bowchasers ready, stand clear."

Grimath quickly stepped back as the two long eighteens fired, and as the shots hit, a wild cheer went up from the monks on deck. The enemy's mainmast slowly leaned over to port, her backstays snapping under the strain, sails collapsing and tearing free. Toylike figures tumbled out of the rigging, and Grimath could imagine their wild cries of terror as they fell to their death upon the frozen sea.

The corsair, its balance between blades and sails destroyed, started into a wild skid as the mainmast collapsed onto the deck. The maintop smashed into the mizzen and carried it away. The chase was nearly over.

"Close in!" Grimath cried. "Boarding crews stand ready."

In response to his command, heavily armed monks poured up from below and lined the starboard rail, ready for the assault.

"I'm bringing her in fast," Grimath shouted. "Ease off the fore and main. Bayran, take command and put her in close; I'm going in with the assault team."

With every second the heavy frigate closed on its target. Grimath slid down to the outrigger and eyed their prey, half expecting one last defiant shot. The monks around him checked their equipment and lowered the slides that would allow them to drop onto the ice while the ship was still in motion. It was a dangerous maneuver, but it allowed a ship to drop off an assault team without having to stop.

They came abreast of the ship and Grimath, leading the way, jumped onto the slide and tumbled down to the ice. Hitting the frozen sea, he rolled away from the ship. As his momentum slowed he gained his footing and led the mad dash toward the enemy ship, his men falling in on either side. There was no fire, no final broadside or shower of bolts—all was strangely quiet.

The *Braith du Mor* drew away and turned across the bow of the crippled opponent, where it drifted to a stop. His heart racing from exertion and fear, Grimath gained the outrigger of the corsair. He let his men go forward to take the first shock of boarding, but all was quiet, as if they were boarding a phantom ship. Cautiously, he went up over the side and gained the deck.

It was empty, except for the dead. His men spread out and, tearing off the deck hatches, went below. Grimath turned to one of the monks and nodded. The monk touched a smoldering taper to a heavy wooden tube and then tossed the flare over the side. A cloud of red smoke billowed out, signaling the flagship that all was secured.

"Grimath, here, below."

There was a strange note of urgency in the call, and he ran to the ladder that led below deck. As he leaped down the stairs he came upon a circle of dead—his men standing back from the corpses as if a spell had been placed upon them. There were twenty bodies, still warm and oozing blood, all dressed in the dreaded black robes. Each had cut his own throat and lay back to die, so that it appeared as if there were twenty spokes formed around a blood-red wheel. Grimath looked to his men.

"Inys Gloi," one of them whispered. "Grimath, you said it was a Bathanian smuggler, but it's not. Saints preserve us, it's Inys Gloi."

He could sense the men's panic.

"Silence!" Grimath shouted, "Not another word of Inys Gloi. Is the magazine secured?"

One of his men pointed forward and Grimath walked away from the awestruck men. As he approached the oaken-walled chamber amidships, one of the monks came running to him, wild with panic.

"Someone's alive in there—someone's in the magazine!"

The monks around Grimath turned and with cries of fear started toward the hatchways. It was not uncommon for a survivor to wait until the enemy was aboard before touching off the powder reserve, thereby taking his foe with him in a blinding flash of light.

Racing up to the door, Grimath kicked it open, ready to strike with his drawn scimitar.

A black-robed shadow stepped out of the darkness.

"Grimath of Mor," a voice whispered.

Stunned, Grimath stepped back. He knew that voice. "Nathan of Mord Rinn," he whispered.

"Yes, Nathan of Inys Gloi," the shadowy form replied. "You got my message then."

"Obviously."

"Where is Zimri?"

"Aboard our ship; he awaits you even now."

"You know what has to be done?"

Grimath nodded, trying to conceal his disgust and rage.

Nathan looked at Grimath and smiled, while from under his robes he produced a smoldering taper and held it up.

"They know it's a ship of Inys Gloi," Grimath said softly.

"I realize that. And you already know what we have to do in order to keep this meeting secret."

Grimath, suddenly sickened with what was to happen, turned and left the magazine. After a brief delay, Nathan followed. Reaching the bright, sunlit deck, he surveyed his boarding crew of twenty men. These were some of the best; several had been with him since the Ezrian wars.

"I'm taking the prisoner back to our ship," Grimath growled. "The rest of you stay here on deck and guard this vessel."

The men looked at him, torn between their fear of the

secret brotherhood and the unusual severity in Grimath's tone. Grabbing hold of Nathan, Grimath scurried down the outrigger support and jumped onto the ice. Breaking into a trot, he started back to the flagship. They had barely crossed half the distance when a thunderclap knocked them to their knees. A blinding flash filled the sky and, turning, Grimath watched in cold, silent fury as the corsair's magazine exploded.

"I've just helped you murder twenty of my own brothers. You better be worth it."

"The secret had to be kept. Inys Gloi has spies in your ranks as well. And remember this, Grimath, they were once my brothers also. Now take me to Zimri. What I need to tell him cannot wait."

"Oh Saints above, as I call to thee, heed me in my hour of need."

Bowing low to the small gilded icon of Saint Mor, he lit a taper of incense and knelt in silent prayer. He was alone, the strain of command lifted away; now only the waiting remained, the hoping for what was to come. He looked into the tormented eyes of his patron Saint, longing with all his heart for a measure of comfort, but he found none—only the cold, forbidding gaze of a long-dead legend, and the altar wreathed in smoke.

"Seol mi, Naomhi Mor, Seol mi."

No voice, no response came to still his quiet, aching fear.

A rolling boom of thunder washed over him, shaking the icon, and for an instant, a stunning flash of light was reflected through the frosted windows. Above him came cries of dismay, which slowly drifted away.

Soon now, soon he would know if this was the portent of disaster that haunted his dreams. He waited, the sweet incense weaving about him in a seductive, enveloping cloud. He tensed, waiting for the moment.

A knocking sounded at the door, and then a voice not familiar.

"My lord, may I enter?"

"You have my permission."

The door swung open to reveal a gaunt, fur-cloaked ice runner dressed in black—his face concealed by a wind mask and goggles. The chill of the ice still clung to him and crept into the room like an invisible harbinger of death. The ice runner bowed low, his extended hands touching the floor.

"My lord Zimri."

Yes, it was he. Zimri could remember the man's face now, the one who at one time had stood by Madoc's side. But that was a lifetime ago, lost forever in the past.

"I believe your name is Nathan. You may enter, Nathan of Inys Gloi, formerly of Mord Rinn."

The ice runner stepped into the room.

"Be seated, Nathan. I've already prepared a goblet of Yarwinder for your refreshment."

Zimri stood and walked to a simply carved sideboard where two goblets stood with the traditional drink of greeting.

The ice runner took the goblet proffered and sat on the stool that faced the Holy See's desk. Nathan looked carefully at the drink, and Zimri laughed softly.

"No, there's no poison. I trust you. We knew the risk that some of our agents would truly convert to Inys Gloi, but we trust you."

"And why do you trust me?"

"For several reasons. First, your sister and mother reside in one of our convents. Of course, for a man such as yourself, that is no final hold. But when you were selected seven years ago as a plant in the ranks of Inys Gloi, we already knew your character and designs. If you succeed, and if our cause wins, an archbishopric will await you—that is far more than Inys Gloi can ever offer. No, Nathan, we choose our spies well."

"Archbishop of Mord Rinn?"

Zimri hesitated for a moment, but knew that the man was too important to be trifled with.

"Of Mord Rinn, if that is your wish."

Nathan settled back in his chair and offered Zimri a soft conspiratorial smile. He knew he had the advantage for the moment. Over a hundred had been sent out by Mor, the Black Brothers, and Mord Rinn as agents to infiltrate the ranks of Inys Gloi. He alone had succeeded.

"I was hoping to hear you say something like that since my actions do bear a certain degree of risk." Smiling, he raised the cup of Yarwinder and downed it in one gulp.

Sensing the mockery in Nathan's tone, Zimri nevertheless suppressed his anger. He decided to change the topic. "How came you to get the message to our agent in Cornath?"

" 'Twas easy. I went there myself on a mission."

"A mission?"

"Yes, the Master sent me to kill someone."

"Who?"

"A Morian who was trying to infiltrate our ranks."

Zimri felt himself bristling with rage. Nathan was talking about one of Zimri's own. "Go on, tell me."

"It was an easy kill—a cup of poison, a day of cramps from 'a bad meal,' and then the frozen grave. I daresay no one ever suspected. Before returning I saw my contact in Caediff and let him know of the sailing of that vessel over there." Nathan waved vaguely to starboard in the direction of the burning ship.

"So why did you advise this attack? This taking of a ship of Inys Gloi."

"Because, my lord, that was the task that you set for me. To penetrate Inys Gloi. Over a hundred have tried so far, and I alone have succeeded to the middle circle."

Zimri nodded slowly in response to the boast. "Go on."

"My mission was to penetrate, to report, and, finally, to disrupt. It has come time, my lord, for me to apply the third directive. You see, Inys Gloi is about to implement its ultimate plan."

Zimri was silent. Now he had to suppress all feeling. He had feared this moment for the last seven desperate years. He had fought his way back from the edge of oblivion, knowing full well that Inys Gloi was perhaps using him for its own ends and, when finished with him, would destroy Holy Church once and for all.

"Do you know that Michael Ormson has a son?"

"What!" Zimri rose to his feet in astonishment. But he had killed the only son, eight years ago. That is what had provoked the war, had brought Michael out to do battle on the Ice, and had set the seeds for Michael's defeat.

"Yes, surprising isn't it?" Nathan said softly.

"Explain."

"There was another woman. An agent of Inys Gloi. She was planted by Seth Facinn, Michael's advisor, and she seduced Michael."

"Seth Facinn?"

"He's of Inys Gloi as well, my lord. Didn't you know that?"

Zimri waved that aside.

"Tell me about this boy."

"It is definitely a child of Michael Ormson. He was born six months after Cornath fell."

"And their plans for him?"

"It's quite simple, my lord. You and Michael are in a deadlock. Neither has the capability to totally destroy the other, but both of you have the capability to continue the deadlock. Michael's original intent was to end the cycle of religious wars. That was the motive that perhaps appealed most to the common people. Those hundreds of thousands who died for the two of you. The son is the answer. When the time is ripe—and from what I can gather it will be soon—Michael Ormson will die. It will appear to be a natural death. At that time, the son will be revealed. Of course, the boy is only seven; he will need a regent."

"And the regent will be the Grand Master of Inys Gloi."

"But of course."

"However," Zimri ventured, "he will still be of Ormson, and those who oppose Michael, what reason will they have to follow him?"

"Quite simple, my lord. This son of Michael will proclaim an allegiance to the old teachings of Holy Church. He will be the compromise impossible while you and Michael live."

"While we live, you say."

"My lord Zimri, can't you see that when the time comes, you will die as well? This son of Michael will be the avenue to bring together the two sides, both of them burned out by this war. The old brotherhoods will remain but mere shadows of their former selves. Inys Gloi will reign supreme. Her people will occupy the key posts. Michael will be acknowledged as the Messiah, the fulfiller of prophecy, and Inys Gloi will fulfill its own prophecy—to rule over all the Ice."

"But not all the Ice," Zimri said softly. "What of Ezra?"

"Ah, my lord, of that I am not sure."

Zimri could sense that Nathan was holding back, that there was something more, but he felt it would be senseless to press the issue.

"Is there anything else?"

"Yes, my lord. The taking of this ship was necessary for your cause. You killed thirty-five agents—men who were to be plants in Michael's ranks; you've also taken the documents that can prove what I said. However, my lord, I must advise you that you will be able to conceal what has been done for only so long. Once Inys Gloi knows that you know, I can assure you that your death will be swift and painful."

Zimri looked closely at Nathan. Just how loyal was he? Had he turned on his former master? Was this a plot of Inys Gloi to unnerve him? He knew that the answer would never be clear.

"What shall we do with you, then?" Zimri asked quietly.

"I've already worked that out. As soon as your ship

sails, I'll go over the side. A week from now I'll report back to Inys Gloi."

"I shall say that we were attacked at night, that I was knocked overboard, and the ship was destroyed."

"Wouldn't they suspect?"

"But of course, my lord. They aren't naive. They might kill me, but most likely they will hold me in the fortress and not send me into the field. For your cause, sire, that would be far preferable to my wandering about the Ice assassinating Morian priests."

Zimri eyed Nathan coldly. Why not kill the man now? There was a risk in letting him go.

"You're considering killing me, aren't you, Zimri?"

There was no sense in hiding it. He nodded his head slowly in reply.

Nathan laughed softly. "I am the only plant in the middle level. Kill me and you lose that advantage."

Zimri stood up and walked over to the window to gaze at the flaming wreck.

Turning, he stared at Nathan. How he hated this man. He knew that Nathan could control him. And that was the one position never to place one's self in. But he needed Nathan. For the moment.

"Leave the documents on my desk. I shall go topside and order our immediate departure. Once we are underway, slip out the window. I shall make sure that there is no watch astern."

"Before I leave, my lord, a simple bit of advice."

"That is?"

"Your guard on the second watch, Hayset I believe is his name. He's an agent of Inys Gloi. I would recommend that you kill him, make it look like an accident."

"How do you know that?"

"I know and that's all that's required."

Without another word or gesture of dismissal Zimri walked from his cabin and slammed the door behind him.

Nathan smiled quietly to himself. Pulling the folded parchment out of his tunic, he looked at the bloodstained papers. This brief written report would shake the very foundation of the two surviving churches, and the power that was Ormson. It was the proof necessary to break the deadlock between Michael and Zimri.

A shudder ran through the vessel and distant commands echoed down from above. The frigate, catching the morning wind, started forward and quickly gained speed as it ran close-hauled to the west.

Nathan took the papers and tossed them on Zimri's desk. The mission set for him had been successful.

The cabin was empty, as he knew it would be. Throughout the day he pondered what was before him and the means that had brought them to his attention. Were Nathan and the documents part of an elaborate trap set by Inys Gloi? Would they sacrifice a ship and crew just to deceive him? He could not shake the fear that thought produced, but he had to play the information. Michael had a son, this one beyond any dagger or poison that Zimri could produce. This was the way to bring Michael into open conflict with Inys Gloi, that brotherhood which had created him. Somehow he would send the damning evidence to Michael. Let Michael see what Inys Gloi had planned for him.

And there was the other information as well—the reports out of North Prydain and the envoy from Bathan. The operation was coming together at last. The power of Ormson had reached its peak and was poised for complete victory, or collapse. Only one factor remained to be dealt with—would Michael perceive the threat and react in time? Once he had underestimated Ormson—he would not again. But with every day his suspicions grew that the days of Michael Ormson were growing fewer as the so-called Messiah lost control of the revolution that was now leaving him behind.

"Guard!"

The door opened and a hooded Morian priest filled the entry way.

"Your wish, my lord."

"Bring Hayset to me. I wish to talk with him."

# CHAPTER 2

THEIR WILLS HAD BEEN JOINED AS ONE—THE BROTHERS WERE gathered in the ancient ritual of collective meditation—when a distant shudder, a gentle warning disturbance cut into his thoughts. Riadent, Grand Master of Inys Gloi, opened his eyes, cutting away from the chanted pattern—but the rest were intent, lost in the whole. It disturbed him, and he felt a cold chill of fear. Was there some danger out there that he alone was sensing, or was the premonition yet another game of imagination? For the remaining hour his thoughts rode along and finally, without a word of explanation, Riadent left them at the start of the morning mass.

As he climbed the spiral staircase that led to the high chambers, he could hear the low bass plain chant of the morning service, its dissonant chords echoing softly down the cold torchlit halls.

"To the One above, who has guided our paths."

"We offer our prayers, our lives, our sacred destinies."

"As it has been in the beginning, is now, and forever shall be."

"Amen."

He whispered the words in gentle counterpoint, responding to the sacred liturgy of the mass. He felt the brief moment of comfort, the soft flow of contentment that the words offered. But, after all, they were only words, and for the Grand Master such things were long lost. He followed the prayers in his mind until the final door atop the long staircase was reached. The four guards, brothers

25

of the inner order, bowed low at his approach and stepped aside to allow his entry. To the gentle creaking of iron hinges, Riadent entered the north chamber—the suite of rooms permitted to fewer than a dozen.

"So, my lord has decided to honor us with a visit."

She stepped out of the shadows, her long burgundy gown shimmering softly in the candlelight. She nodded in acknowledgment and bent slightly one knee, nothing more.

Damn this bitch! Riadent thought. She knows her power and states it whenever she can. She should prostrate herself in my presence; anything less is an insult.

"Varinna, your courtesies are, as usual, a pleasure to receive," Riadent responded with a note of threat to his voice. "The boy, where is he?"

Varinna stepped closer and a warm scent of perfume and femininity swept over him, tingling his nerves. All his life he had lived in cloister, away from women, except when in his climb upward he had gone on missions. For ten years he had not stepped foot off the holy island of Inys Gloi, and Varinna was the only woman he spoke to. He had once thought that his control over himself was complete, but the fear that this might not be so had surfaced more often of late, and he sensed that Varinna knew it.

"He is taking his lessons with the brothers. Shall I fetch him?"

Riadent turned from Varinna and, walking over to a chair, sat down.

"No, that can wait. We've had a situation turn up and I want to discuss it with you."

He could sense her curiosity. Varinna had been kept out of the council from the beginning for she had but one purpose—an action of biology that none of them could have fulfilled. Bearing Michael Ormson's child, she was needed only for the raising, until such time as the brotherhood would take him. Then she could be quietly disposed of.

"Go on, then, my lord. What is it that you wish to know?"

"There's been an incident. We aren't sure yet, but I think something more is behind it. One of our agents returned this morning. Two weeks back he sailed with a ship bearing a number of our brothers on a mission."

"What mission?" Varinna asked quietly, feigning indifference.

"Most of them were to be infiltrated into Ormson's ranks, some were destined for the Church of Ezra. The ship was set upon at night; only one man survived."

"How?"

"He claims that he was swept overboard and then saw the ship go up. If that is true, then the master of the ship followed standard procedure and destroyed the vessel before capture. But something more I cannot be sure of."

It was a most unusual admission coming from the Grand Master, Varinna thought. Inys Gloi never admitted doubt, all paths were always assured.

"The men know their orders," Varinna replied. "Never be taken alive; what cause is there for worry?"

"There is more," the Master said quietly. "The ship carried important documents, some of which were destined for Seth Facinn."

"What were these documents? And, might I ask, why would you risk placing valuable information in writing?"

"We thought the shipping lanes secure. Ormson's fleet controls the Ice for two hundred leagues out. Somehow, and I am not sure if it was by accident, the ship was taken. If it was attacked, and even if it was destroyed, I must assume the possibility that the documents were found. To do otherwise would be foolish."

"So, my lord," Varinna said softly, while offering him a glass of Yarwinder, "I can't help but ask why you are telling me? You've kept me from your council ever since I delivered to you what you and your—forgive me—*our* order wanted."

Riadent looked at her—her slip was intentional; she

was stating a dissatisfaction with Inys Gloi, and she knew she could get away with it. He let the rebuff pass.

"I have to assume that the documents have survived and fallen into the wrong hands. Therefore, the plan has been changed. Your son Thomas must be prepared immediately to assume his father's position."

"You seem disturbed by this move, otherwise you would not have come to tell me. This does not fit your plans at all."

Damn you to hell, he thought quietly, I should have strangled you with my own hands years ago.

"I had hoped that our original plan could be followed—that Ormson and Zimri would destroy each other. After all, it was we who quietly helped Zimri in establishing his base in the Dead Lands. It was we who fanned the embers of the war so that Ormson and Zimri would exhaust each other. I had hoped to have another five years at least, before our time came to act. But my heart warns that time is running out, and we must strike soon if our plan is to be fulfilled."

"Of course, this means you will have to kill Ormson," she said quietly. "And knowing Michael, I daresay that will not be easy."

"That is already half completed. Michael has languished for years, a victim of a strange illness. Already he walks near the border of death, where he can hover for years yet to come, slowly draining the strength of his cause in endless fighting."

He hesitated for a moment and smiled a strange, distant smile, and then looked back at Varinna.

"And besides, that is not your concern. Your duty is to service Inys Gloi, and Inys Gloi demands your complacent role as the new Prophet's mother."

Varinna knew further questions about Michael would be useless, so she tried another tack.

"What about Zimri? He will not sit by idly while you plan his death, and Michael's as well, for that matter. I heard rumors of a meeting between you—surely something must have passed between the two of you to prevent your striking him down earlier."

Before Riadent could answer a gentle knock sounded at the door. It could only be the boy, the son of Michael Ormson, whose blood had finally brought Inys Gloi to the edge of power.

"You may enter, Thomas," Riadent called in an authoritative voice.

The door swung open to reveal a slight form that did not have to bend low to cross through the low, round doorframe. He was dressed in the dark robes of an Inys Gloi initiate—his sandaled feet concealed beneath a billowing robe of dark, coarse wool. The hood was pulled back from his head, showing pale-blond hair cut square at the shoulders. Already he showed the slight frame, high forehead, and thin pale lips that were characteristic of the Ormson line. But it was the eyes that held Riadent's attention. They were like Seth's descriptions of Michael's. Of mismatched hues, deep and penetrating, they spoke of a control far beyond his scant seven years. He displayed none of the actions characteristic of a small boy confronted by an imposing elder, and for several seconds he held Riadent's gaze without a flicker of emotion. As if a distant voice suddenly reminded him of the proper rituals, the boy went down on his knees and bowed his head, awaiting Riadent's blessing.

Riadent turned away. Let this one wait a moment. Unlike his father, he must always know who is the complete master of his fate.

"My lady Varinna," he said in a nearly pleasant voice, "it's time that I leave. Brother Bartram will keep you posted in the days ahead as to what will be expected."

Riadent rose from his chair and turned from Varinna without the usual blessing. As he reached the door he looked down at Thomas, who still awaited his benediction.

"You may rise, Thomas," he said sternly.

Thomas stood and, raising his head, looked at Riadent.

"Master, your visit comes as a surprise," Thomas said in a high clear voice. "Is something wrong?"

Is this mere childish curiosity? Riadent thought quietly.

"It is nothing, Thomas. I just wanted to pay my respects to your good mother, but other matters call me. Soon I shall invite you to visit me and we shall have a long talk together about many things."

"Such as my father?"

He stared down at Thomas. So much depended on one boy. "Yes, Thomas, we shall talk of your father, but now I must go."

The boy knelt for blessing, and with a vague wave of his hand marking the sacred sign, Riadent left the room.

Thomas looked into Varinna's eyes and could read the worry that was washing over her.

"It's nothing, child, nothing important." She tried to veil her emotions. In many ways he was indeed his father's son, and part of his inheritance was the ability to sense the emotions of others.

He stood silently, appraising her, and she quickly looked away. When the child was born she had felt that her duty was complete; motherhood was the last thing in her plans for the future. But the Master had insisted, so she had nursed and raised the child. And in that process had come something she had never expected. With the passage of years, she had come to love Thomas, sensing that perhaps he would be the only thing of hers to last. But with that love daily came the disturbing reminder of the withdrawn, angry leader who now ruled half the Ice. Through Thomas the memory of Michael Ormson returned again and again to haunt her.

The soft childish voice interrupted her thoughts. "Mother, you're not telling the truth. I can tell."

She looked away.

Thomas walked toward her and slipped his hand into hers. "He came to talk about my father, didn't he? Mother, why do you never talk about my father? My teachers mention him all the time, and say that I am destined to rule when he is gone. Did the Master say that it is time for my father to die?"

She swept him into her arms and hugged him. Damn them all, Michael, Zimri, and Inys Gloi as well. How did she ever allow herself to get tangled into their game? The life of a courtesan was what she had wanted, and Inys Gloi had allowed her to consort with the wealthiest and most powerful. But now they had sunk their barb in her flesh, and she could not escape. Damn them all, and Michael Ormson most of all.

"What was her reaction, my lord?" A tall, shadowy form stepped out of an alcove and fell in alongside of Riadent.

"What I expected, Jeremiah ... All that I expected." Riadent looked to his short, heavyset assistant, Master of the Knife and second only to him in power. Jeremiah's hawklike visage and dark penetrating eyes were concealed beneath the folds of his hood. He walked with a sensuous, almost feline grace that betrayed the easy movements of a born killer. He had once been of Cornath, and was proud of the fact that he had personally trained Ulric, who was considered by many to be a Saint. Now Jeremiah assigned the assassins of Inys Gloi when a killing was necessary.

"I still cannot understand why you told her anything about what was coming. She raised the boy—her task is complete; it's time to kill her."

As he spoke Jeremiah looked sidelong at Riadent, trying to gauge his response. "There's trouble in that woman, Riadent, or haven't you seen that?"

"She's no problem yet. Besides, we still might need her. Remember, this boy is all that Michael Ormson failed to be. We got to Michael too late, that was our biggest failing. We got to him too late because of that damned traitor Rifton, who knew that young Ormson fit our prophecies. But remember, Michael was raised in a monastery, removed from all contact with women, and therefore was more susceptible to the first women he came into contact with. Michael never had a mother, and at the key moment, when all was ready, he was lured away by Janis. We've paid for that mistake a thousand times over. Michael should have been the one, but he was already too far beyond our control. We shan't make the same mistake with Thomas. Through his mother we can mold him to our needs. She lives until all is ready, and then, if need be, we can deal with her—once Thomas has taken control."

Jeremiah looked at Riadent, his eyes concealed beneath the shadows of his robes. He sensed other reasons behind Riadent's desire to let her live, but he would not press the issue. Time enough in the future for that. Time enough for his plan as well. "Shall we call the meeting of the inner council now?" he asked, changing the topic of their discussion.

"Yes, I think it is time. I want a full report on the dispositions of Michael's and Zimri's fleets. We must send word to Seth that his presence is needed, and we must know of his progress in preparing Michael."

"As you wish, my lord."

"You feel uneasy about all this, don't you, Jeremiah?" There was no sense in lying, the Master could tell.

"I feel that we are acting too quickly. So what if the documents were lost? The chances of their being found are one in a million. I fear that if we strike too soon, while Zimri and Michael still have some strength, we might undo a thousand years of planning. I counsel a cautious approach. If it takes another five years, or ten, so be it."

Besides, he thought, you will be too old at that point to rule, and it will be I who takes control in your place.

"You know my decision on this, Jeremiah, and I am the Master."

Jeremiah gave a slight nod of acknowledgment at the reproach in Riadent's voice.

"By the way," Riadent asked as they turned into the final torchlit corridor that led to Riadent's high chamber, "what of this Nathan—do you trust his story?"

Jeremiah had recruited Nathan out of the gutters of Caediff and had made him his protégé. A slight against Nathan could be a veiled attack on his own judgment.

"I stand by his report."

"Nevertheless, I want it checked out."

"I'm working on that now. A team has been sent out to examine the wreckage and to make the usual inquiries. Hayset, who is with Zimri, should let us know if anything unusual occurred on that side. In the meantime, where shall we assign him?"

"Wherever you want—but he's not to leave Inys Gloi."

"Might I suggest as a guard to Thomas then. The man is a Cornathian, he knows the people and the commoner dialect. He can teach the boy the language and the customs of his future subjects."

"Fine, go ahead. You have my permission."

And he can also keep me posted as to your actions concerning Thomas and that woman, Jeremiah thought quietly.

"You may leave me now," Riadent said quietly, "and summon the council for a meeting at sunset. We have much to plan for in the days ahead."

"As always, my master, your word is my command."

With an absentminded wave of blessing, Riadent, Lord Grand Master of Inys Gloi, retired alone to his study, where in meditation he would chart his plans for the final triumph of the hidden order of Inys Gloi.

# CHAPTER 3

DAMN, HOW HE HATED ALL THIS FOOLISH FANFARE. BY ST. Wright's loins, he could remember when the only salute he received in this town was the laughing jeer of a pox-eaten harlot.

Daniel Bjornson quickly surveyed the orderly ranks of the Companions, who waved their scimitars and chanted his name as he crossed the great square of Cornath and approached the steps of the old Morian cathedral. He was their captain, the commander of the elite guard, and many of the old veterans in the ranks had served with him since the beginning. There was a time when he relished the glory of it all, but it had become all so tiresome. Now he suffered through the rituals and the never-ending calls for battle. As he walked toward the high-towered church, his thoughts raced back to another time, nearly a decade in the past, when he had fought his way through the square at night and stormed this same building—the stairway approaching the nave choked with dead and dying, and the city around him consumed in flames.

Michael, was it really so long ago? he thought sadly. And I had thought then that the dream was true, that there would be an end to the violence. Now look at us—still we fight on, and I simply get older, slower, somehow out of touch with this nightmarish conflict that appears to have no end. He absently stroked his beard, which was now streaked with gray. It was a bitter-cold day and he could feel the chill in his bones and the old wounds that crisscrossed his body.

A familiar voice cried out to him and he stopped for a moment. It was Ulthar, commander of a hundred. As a survivor of the Mathinian Pass, he wore the silver helm of honor. Daniel knew the men were watching, and, putting aside his thoughts, he gave Ulthar a playful cuff across the shoulder and mumbled a gentle curse. The Companions roared their approval and chanted his name even louder as he ambled up the steps and passed into the darkness of the cathedral.

After the wild shouts of the assembled guards, the silence of the cathedral was almost unnerving. The stained-glass windows admitted a soft rose and amber light that bespoke tranquility. But the building was a haunt of memories. It was here that he had first cried "no prisoners"—a call that spread throughout the flaming city of Cornath, triggering the massacre not only of a city but possibly of the Prophet's cause as well. He avoided the building whenever possible, but he could not today; Seth had called for a council meeting, and, damn him, it was time the issues were finally confronted.

With a weary shuffle Daniel walked down the apse of the cathedral, occasionally stopping to examine the fine wooden floor and the bloodstains of the hundreds who had died in the storming of the citadel. Seven years and they had not been able to scrub out the blood. It remained, a silent reminder of the fury of battle that had swept Cornath in the Night of Tears, as it was now called.

His staff marched behind him but he paid them no heed. There was a time when his thoughts were like theirs—one in a dream of glory and war. But the glory of war had begun to fade with age, and now Daniel fought more from habit and tradition than out of a zeal for the shock of combat. Their hobnailed boots echoed against the vaulted ceiling, so that Daniel turned and gave his men a look of reproach, as if demanding that they walk in silence in what was once a holy shrine. The men were used to his sullen moods of late, and softened their pace.

He passed behind the high altar and entered the door

that had once been secret, concealing the chamber where Zimri had sought refuge in the final hours of the siege. Leaving his staff behind, Daniel Bjornson climbed the narrow circular staircase that rose a hundred fifty feet above the city of Cornath. He had to stop once to catch his breath and calm the pounding of his heart. He was getting old, and the thought made him curse the fates. *Perhaps I should have died in battle long ago,* he thought. *Died for Michael when the dream was young and still alive, rather than live until this slow fading into the night.*

The trap door was open, and putting on the usual show of bravado, he vaulted up the last dozen steps and landed with a jump on the high platform that looked out over the city.

"You are late, my friend. We've been waiting for you."

Daniel looked at Seth Facinn. "A discipline case that had to be attended to first," he growled softly. "One of my men murdered a mendicant friar of the silent brotherhood of Cornath."

"Such things happen all the time," Seth replied absently. "It should have been no concern of yours."

"I remember the words of Michael," Daniel replied, concealing his hostility. "Our Prophet said that all religions are to be treated with fairness. Based on his words I had to order my man to be put to death."

Seth turned away from him and looked out the window to the city below.

"It is only a minor question," Eldric replied softly. "Perhaps the friar provoked your man, but after all, we must remember the teachings of the Prophet. And of course, Daniel, your men are yours to command."

Daniel looked at Eldric and the half-healed scar that twisted his features. Eldric had not said a word about the wound and turned aside all questions concerning it with a smiling gesture of disdain.

"Let's not waste our time on this petty matter," Cowan said softly from the corner of the room. "I've important information to discuss. After all, I did ask for this meeting."

Daniel looked at his old friend and could sense the agitation. Cowan had arrived the hour before dawn, his light frigate having run close-hauled through the night. A quarantine had been placed on the heavily guarded ship and a rumor of plague circulated so that the curious would not go near. But knowing the ways of command, Daniel was ready to hear the truth.

"Go on, then," Daniel said gruffly, while fixing Seth with a malevolent gaze, as if to tell him their argument would be picked up later.

"When I left North Prydain, two days ago, the city was in flames," Cowan said softly.

"North Prydain in flames?" Daniel cried. "How can this be?"

Seth leaned back in his chair and looked at the ornately carved ceiling. "Continue please, and no interruptions," he commanded with a tone of harshness.

"The city is consumed by the flames of rebellion. A Cornathian monk arrived in the city six months ago, and in a short time he gained quite a following. He never openly made any hostile statements against us, but his words could often be interpreted in more than one way. Minor incidents soon started between my men and his followers until, two weeks ago, a band of Companions on leave attacked his church in the middle of the night and killed a deacon. I publicly disciplined the men, but the damage was done. This monk, whom I had come to know and in fact came to respect, made a public declaration that the deacon was now a Saint, martyred in a holy cause."

"Why didn't you just quietly murder the bastard and be done with it?" Eldric growled.

Cowan shook his head sadly. "You know Michael's injunction: preachers of all faiths are to be held sacred. I would have needed permission from Michael himself to do that, and besides, I hoped that I could reason with the man." And so saying, Cowan extended his hands in a gesture of despair.

"I'd've done it, and be damned with the permission," Eldric replied.

"The chance is passed. What I'm concerned with now is the danger of this rebellion," Daniel interjected.

"It's bad, very bad," Cowan stated, fixing Seth with his gaze. "It seems as if every man, woman, and child in the city has taken up arms and turned on each other in a frenzy of killing. The followers of Cornath are shouting ''tis better to die than live under the hand of the heretic,' that 'death in battle is the road to salvation and Sainthood.'"

"So what are we to tell Michael?" Seth asked quietly.

Cowan's question was greeted with grim, tight-lipped silence. Each waited for someone else to broach the difficult topic of how best to deal with their distant, charismatic leader. The only sounds in the room were the shouted commands of warriors practicing in the square and, almost beyond the range of hearing, the drifted plain chant of a Cornathian church service.

How totally removed each is from the other, Cowan thought. The warrior-crusaders were preaching an end to religious war, yet the old Cornathian church still survived and even now was flourishing in their midst. Yes, how to tell Michael? How to tell him that the multitude had not flocked to him as the savior, but clung instead to the old beliefs, perhaps even more fervently than before? They might have had a chance, long ago, if Michael had acted more mystical and linked himself somehow with the old church. But in his fervor he had severed all links to the old religion and preached an entirely new way. That decision and the massacre of Cornath had either driven most into an even more fervent devotion or at best into a watchful neutrality, where they waited to cheer the winning side.

Cowan looked to the other three and wondered what they were thinking, and knew that they were still following the old path—answering war with yet more war.

"There's only one answer," Eldric said with a malevolent smile. "Dispatch ten cohorts of the Companions using my fleet as transport. They can be at North Prydain in three days' time. In four days the last of the rebellious scum will be dead, and all will be settled."

"And of course your men get the loot of the city!" Daniel shouted, barely concealing his hatred. "You're talking about *my* city, *my* home, you freebooting scum."

"They are in rebellion against our lord the Prophet," Eldric said easily. A vicious smile lit his face.

"It's not that easy," Daniel grumbled, and Cowan looked at his old friend with surprise.

"What are you going to do once you get there?" Daniel asked, slowly placing a soft cadenced emphasis on each word. "Just what in bloody hell are you going to do? Massacre the entire city?—'cause from what Cowan has said, half the city is in arms against us."

"Then you see the crisis after all!" Cowan cried. "Can't any of you see what has happened? We were never enough—even in the beginning, we were never enough—and our only strength was in the surprise with which we struck. We've taken Cornath's cities but can we continue to hold them? For that matter, are they *worth* holding anymore?"

"What are you saying? Just what do you mean with that statement, 'Are they worth holding anymore?'" Seth looked carefully into Cowan's eyes.

"Precisely that, Seth. The statement is obvious. We should have followed Michael's original dream and stayed in the Southward Isles. Within a generation—at most two generations—the churches would have collapsed of their own corruption. The people would have flocked to us and created an age free of religious persecution and fear. But no, not us, instead we played straight into Zimri's hands."

"And what about Janis and Andrew? Are you saying their murders should have been left unavenged?" Cold challenge was obvious in Daniel's voice.

"No, my friend, you don't understand. I'm simply stating that by attacking we fell into Zimri's trap. He knew the people who were leaning toward us would rally to their old church if attacked. Provoking Michael was a master stroke on Zimri's part, and now, as a result, North Prydain is in rebellion."

"Damn it, Cowan!" Eldric shouted. "You're making an ice mountain of a single crystal! Send the Companions and a fleet of frigates. Within a week the scum will scurry back to their holes where they belong."

"I have to agree with Eldric," Seth said quietly. "This is just a minor outbreak. We shall send ten full cohorts of the Companions. The important thing is to quarantine the rebellion before it spreads. Cowan, you are making far too much of this little inconvenience."

"Little inconvenience! You weren't there, I was. Those people are fanatics, fired by religious frenzy. Some of them attacked my men with their bare hands. My men were in full battle armor, and they with nothing more than their bare hands. We slaughtered them in the hundreds and still they came on, chanting for the Saints to aid them. I tell you, Seth, those people are every bit as devoted as we are, and that frightens me, for they outnumber us, and in this war, victory will go to the side with the strongest will."

"But we occupy every city of the old Cornathian Brotherhood, their Holy See is in exile, and nearly two thirds of the old brotherhoods have either accepted our rule or, breaking with the old confederation, have declared their neutrality."

"Declared neutrality until the tide turns, and then they will join all the others."

"Cowan, I sometimes think you are preaching defeat for our cause," Eldric said darkly.

Cowan rose in his chair and placed his hand on the hilt of his scimitar.

"How dare you!" he cried. "I was with the Master long before you and your freebooter scum joined our side. Look to your own men, Eldric. Most of them don't give a good damn about the teachings of Michael; they only joined to be on the winning side and to throw off Cornathian domination. I've heard rumors of trouble in your ranks—we all have. The moment the crisis comes they will fade away like ice in the noonday sun."

Eldric glowered darkly at Cowan. "If you draw that sword, Mathinian dog, I'll cut you in half. I've killed three challengers in the last season, another one is no problem for me."

Daniel stood up, pulled out his ax, and placed it on the table. "Sit down, both of you. It's bad enough as is, without the two of you falling on each other. The first man who pulls a blade will feel the weight of my metal, I swear it in the name of the Prophet."

The two looked at him darkly, but knowing Daniel's fury in a fight, none dared to challenge.

"Enough, from all of you," Seth cried, his own rage barely under control. "I am the counselor, appointed by Michael, and by his command rule in all temporal matters. I've heard all that is worth saying and it is time to pass decision. Eldric, Cowan, both of you are sworn to Michael, and as such are not permitted to draw blades upon each other, so damn it, both of you shut up and sit down."

The other three were silent, and looking to each other, they gradually settled back into their chairs. Eldric leaned over the table, and taking a flask of Yarwinder, he broke the head off the bottle and drained off the contents in a long thirsty pull.

"I think the situation is simple enough to deal with," Seth said softly. "We've faced it before. Zimri is in exile, his followers, though battle-hardened, are few in number. It is our task to make sure they do not regain a foothold in Cornath. Granted, they've established an impregnable stronghold in the Dead Lands, but we'll starve them out in time. As for the rebellions, we've faced others in the past and have always managed to contain them. It will be the same in North Prydain. I shall therefore advise Michael that we are sending ten cohorts, a dozen frigates, and the necessary escort ships to North Prydain. Eldric will command the expedition."

"I wish to go back," Cowan said grimly. "After all, North Prydain was my responsibility."

"No need to," Eldric replied. "I can handle this problem."

"I don't give a damn what you think. I'm going back."

"Then you break my command!" Seth shouted in reply.

Cowan stared defiantly at Seth, but all knew that he could not challenge him without breaking oath to Michael.

Seth extended his hand in a gesture of peace. "Michael might want you here. You've been through enough there already, and I must command you to stay. We'll clear this up within a fortnight."

Daniel started to speak up but decided against it. North Prydain was his home and the Companions were his to command, but something told him that at this juncture it was better to remain in Cornath and not get caught up in what, despite Seth's promises, could prove to be a long and difficult campaign of suppression.

"And will you advise Michael of the seriousness of this situation, Seth?" Cowan demanded.

"But of course I shall report that, Cowan."

Cowan settled into his chair and was silent a moment. "Why can't we report it ourselves?"

"Ah, Cowan, how many times have we been through this? Michael is sick. He has turned over all temporal affairs to me. The strain on him has been too much, and I must insist that he remain alone at the monastery of meditation as he himself has commanded."

Cowan looked suddenly at Daniel, fixing him with his gaze, but said nothing.

"Is there anything else that needs to be brought to my attention?" Seth asked, never taking his gaze from Cowan.

Eldric spoke up and laughed lightly as he told of the summer campaign against Zimri's fortifications on the shores of the Dead Lands. Nothing had been gained and the loss in ships had been nearly even, but he boasted of slaughtering three thousand of Zimri's blue-robe monks and promised that one more year of campaigning would see an end to Zimri's resistance. Five years ago they had discovered the secret refuge. Each year a campaign was launched, and each year the report was nearly the same—the difficult approaches and the stone fortifications were nearly impregnable.

The conference rolled on for some time, and Cowar sat in silence, merely observing. His thoughts drifted away until a demanding voice cut into them.

"Cowan, will you be there?"

"For what?" He looked up at Seth in surprise.

"Didn't you hear me? Michael has requested that we attend the dedication of the new observatory for watching the sky."

"Where?"

"Damn it, man, pay attention. It's located atop the old Cathedral of Dulyn."

"But that will merely trigger yet another riot in Dulyn," Cowan said quietly.

In exasperation Eldric waved his fist at Cowan. "Damn it all, I don't give a pox concerning this foolishness of Michael's about watching the sky, and schools for reading, but he supports my men and if that is the case, the hell with these Cornathian fanatics. If they don't like it, a taste of steel will soon convince them that it is acceptable."

Shaking his head, Cowan stood up and left the table.

"Cowan," Seth said, "let not North Prydain upset thee. Trust my decision on this."

"But of course," Cowan said softly, "don't I always trust the decisions of the one appointed by the Prophet?"

Seth watched him go and then turned to look at the other two.

"Sometimes I wonder whose side he is really on," Eldric said. "Even before the siege of Cornath I felt he was against us."

Seth was quiet, looking off into the distance and not offering comment.

Daniel stood up and started for the trap door that led back down.

"Daniel, what do you think?" Seth asked guardedly.

"I'm not sure, damn me, I'm just not sure. But I do know this: ten years ago me, you, and Michael thought that people everywhere would flock to our cause. And it hasn't happened, damn them stupid bastards, it just hasn't happened. And I wonder what those secret brothers of yours think of all of this."

Daniel went down the stairs and Seth gave no comment to his last words.

Daniel walked down the narrow spiral stairs, and as he emerged from the door concealed behind the altar, he noticed Cowan standing in the shadows of the rectory. Daniel started to turn away, but Cowan hurried up to him and placed his hand on Daniel's shoulder.

"It's gone too far, and you know it."

"So what the hell do you want to do about it?" Daniel growled. His words echoed in the vastness of the great cathedral and he fell into a mumbling curse.

"Let's take a walk," Cowan whispered. "Too many ears and too many eyes here for my taste."

Daniel agreed, surprised with himself for engaging in what he sensed would go against Seth's wishes. Leaving the great cathedral, they cut across the square, ignoring the cries of the Companions who had stood in review less than an hour ago. Some started to come over, but Daniel's scowl warned them off. The two turned into a narrow alleyway that led through a rebuilt section of the city. Some of the people they passed bowed low and mumbled words of praise as they strode by; others turned their faces away as if a great evil was passing. Once Cowan had been acutely aware of this treatment and had tried to talk to such individuals, but that time had long passed and he barely noticed them.

On occasion Cowan looked over his shoulder, checking to see if they were being followed. When satisfied that no one was watching, he doubled back on his tracks and then turned down a stinking alley that was choked with refuse, dirty ice, and snow. The stench was overwhelming, even in the frigid air, but neither of them paid any heed to it. The same smell hung over every city on the ice where water was scarce due to the lack of fuel, and all manner of offal and garbage was cast into the streets. During the brief moment of summer, the residents who stayed in the city would wade nearly knee deep through the slime.

Cowan led Daniel into a small tavern, little more than a basement hovel carved into the side of a cliff. For several seconds Daniel was on guard, wary as always of entering a darkened room after the blinding glare of the snow and ice. Cowan beckoned for him to follow, and Daniel, realizing that the place was known to his companion, walked behind him into the darkness. They passed the innkeeper, who barely acknowledged their presence, and Cowan ushered the old warrior into a back room, bolting the door behind him.

"Why all the secrecy? And why, in the name of the dark one, all this running back and forth through this pox-eaten whore of a city?"

"Because I don't trust them, that's why. Of late I've been followed and watched, I'm sure of it."

Daniel settled wearily into a chair and surveyed his companion.

"*Dit gu pennat slorru,*" Daniel cursed, lapsing into the dialect of North Prydain. "For once will you relax? Anyhow, since we're here, let's call for some good mulled ale and ask this keeper if he's got a fair wench or two. By my aching loins it's been a while, it has."

Cowan surveyed Daniel closely—he knew that was the last thing on the warrior's mind—but Daniel had to play his role even with someone he usually trusted.

"Stop the games, Daniel. This is important, and we've got to decide our response before it's too late."

Daniel stood up and made a great show of scratching his backside. Emitting a loud belch, he walked across the room, unbolted the door, and pulled it open.

"Hey, damn you. Yeah, you, you stinking vomit. Fetch us up some of your best and quick. Me throat's on fire for a good pull of the stout. And don't water it, mind you, or I'll pluck your bloodshot eyes out of their sockets."

The innkeeper waddled into the room bearing a pitcher of brew and two cheap, crudely carved wooden mugs. He eyed Daniel suspiciously and, placing his burden on the table, extended his hand for payment.

Daniel tossed him a silver piece and the innkeeper silently withdrew.

Without offering Cowan a second glance, Daniel picked up the pitcher and drained half, letting a fair portion of the contents spill down his beard and onto his tunic. Belching loudly, he slammed the pitcher down and then flopped back into his chair.

"Ah, that be better now. I already know what you're going to say, but have at it anyway."

"Can't you see what's happening?" Cowan said, trying to calm his voice. "Michael is out of touch with what is really going on. That and his illness have put the control of our movement into the hands of an individual who either refuses to see what is going on or is convinced that everything is all right. We're becoming like the churches that we once swore to replace. Our own people are coming to treat Michael as if he were a God—they worship him and deny that anything could possibly go wrong. Michael is no God, nor is he a religious prophet. He is merely a man who teaches us that religion is not the answer. But he better face up to what's happening and damn quick, otherwise it will all be lost."

Daniel emitted another loud belch and eyed Cowan with cold eyes. "You know what the trouble is with you philosophers? You take too damn many words to say what you think. Get to the damned point, will you."

"We've got to stop this. We've got to see Michael and convince him to come back and take control."

"But he's sick. And anyhow, I doubt if he would listen to you."

"But he might listen to you."

"Do you really expect me to get into the middle of this? I am responsible for the Companions and the bodyguards, not the politics."

Daniel stopped for a moment and looked around the room.

"Anyhow"—and his voice dropped to a whisper—"I've already tried, half a dozen times, and he won't listen. He just tells me that he knows what's going on and to leave him alone, since there's nothing wrong."

"Do you really believe that!?" Cowan shouted.

Daniel smiled softly. "I don't know. I do know 'e's sick at heart for what his cause has become. He taught peace and in teaching that he triggered the most violent war ever seen upon the Ice."

Cowan walked over and grasped Daniel by the shoulder. "Will you talk to him? Just one more time? He used to listen to you, before he became this messiah that the mob worships."

"Damn it all, I remember when he was still a shaven-head bas...Oh, never mind. All right, I'll talk to him. I've been waiting for you to ask me for the last year; I ain't so dumb as some think. I've got eyes and ears and can see what's happening in the streets, and I don't like the smell of it. I think Zimri is planning something big. But the war council and the commanders and, most of all, Seth refuse to see it that way—they tell Michael that everything is just fine, and damn any who disagree."

"Good, then let's leave at once, before Seth tries to interfere."

Daniel stood up, and without offering Cowan any of the stout, he raised the pitcher and drained the rest.

"I've got two horses behind the armory. We can be at the monastery before dawn."

"But damn it, man, you know I can't ride," Daniel wailed. "Let's walk it."

"No time, my friend. You're not afraid of a horse, are you?"

Daniel fixed Cowan with a malevolent gaze. "I'd rather spend another night with my dearest Epana than ride one of those brutes."

"I picked one that won't throw you."

"They all hate me, they do, and by thunder if he kicks or bites I'll knock 'im senseless, I will."

# CHAPTER 4

THERE WAS THE PAIN—THE CONSTANT LOW LEVEL OF AGONY that clouded his senses and cut into his meditation. He rubbed his side and tried to bring the fire under control. Once a moment of thought would drive it away, as all sensation was purged, but that was no longer possible. He gave the meditation up for lost and rose to a kneeling position.

Ah, Niall, he thought sadly, you taught me to ignore the physical, to accept the body merely as the vessel of the spirit. But that is lost to me forever. Niall, my old friend Niall, if only you were alive to help me.

His simple, coarse woollen robes rustled lightly as he walked through the private chamber, past the table where yet another meal sat untouched. The thought of eating caused him a wave of nausea, and he turned away from the tray of broth and bread. Walking to the stove, Michael tossed in another log and settled back to watch the flames as they crackled and consumed the precious wood.

No matter how often approached, the question was still unanswerable. He knew that locked somewhere within the deepest recesses of his mind, there must be an answer to this one, ultimate question. Was he indeed the Messiah? Of late he embraced that image, that he was somehow chosen by an unseen power to guide the destiny of the world in some new, radical direction. Or perhaps to realign the destiny of the world in a path that it had deviated from, when man—or was it God after all?—had brought the world to the edge of destruction in his folly to pierce the sky and touch the stars. The thought both held him and repelled him with its power.

If he was preordained, then none of his actions could be wrong. He was the hand of God, the instrument of some inscrutable source that drove him, and lashed him onward. If so, then any action, any excess, even the massacre of fifty thousand, was merely the acting out of some divine will made manifest in his body. His actions could not be wrong—and that thought was a source of comfort. It gave him the strength to face any test yet to come, for he was beyond mere mortality. If that was true, then his crusade against the organized religions and the power of the churches was the will of some higher power. This made him a God, sent to guide the lives of mortal men.

But another thought hovered always at the edge of his consciousness. Perhaps he was the product of mere circumstance, a chance happening without purpose. If so, then his actions were truly his own, and with that came the responsibility for everything, including the deaths of hundreds of thousands. He turned away from the thought and the enormity of what it suggested to him. The other concept was far more comforting. It gave him the strength to continue the struggle and absolved him of the mistakes of the past, since with such logic they were not mistakes after all.

But in his heart he knew the answer, all the answers, and such an insight guided him as he waited for the slow evolution of events. He let that thought develop even as the echoed shouts drifted up from the courtyard below.

"But I tell you his orders are the strictest. You, my lords, should know that."

In exasperation Cowan turned away. They had ridden through the night and arrived at the high citadel at dawn, frozen and exhausted from the long journey. The citadel had once been a watchtower and shrine that guarded the road to Dulyn. It was rumored that the foundation and one of the walls of the building were from the Before

Time, and as such were held sacred, even by those who fought for Michael. Here, guarded by five hundred men, most of whom had been selected by Seth, Michael Ormson was in refuge, where he had remained aloof from all that transpired beyond the walls.

"And I do not give a good damn for your orders!" Daniel shouted. "Listen, you seal-faced son of a harlot. I am Daniel Bjornson, Commander of the Companions. Do you know me?"

"Yes, my lord," the white-robed clerk said officiously.

Daniel saw him wrinkle his nose at their smell, and he was tempted to slap this so-called Secretary to the Prophet aside. But he held himself in check.

"The Prophet, blessed be his name, is ill again," the clerk whispered in a high, whining voice. "If you wish to see him, you first must go through Seth. My orders are clear, and do not try and force your way in, for there are guards behind me if need be."

"Damn you and your impertinent tone!" Cowan shouted. "I don't recall seeing you in the ranks when the Prophet, as you call him, first stood alone against Cornath. Were you at the Mathinian Gate, or at Vasilinburg, or before the gates of Cornath? No, I doubt it—such as you crawl in after the battle has been won. Now stand aside. Daniel was with him from the beginning, and by all that's sacred I'll cut your throat if you try and stop him."

The clerk backed up, ready to shout for the guards.

"I think they should be allowed to pass" came a quiet voice from the back of the room.

Daniel turned and was stunned into silence by the heavy, almost bloated form in the doorway. It was Michael, or at least he thought it was Michael. He had aged, and Daniel felt his eyes sting at the sight of his leader. Gone was the slender youthful vigor; his hair had broad streaks of gray, and his eyes were puffy and bloodshot, as if he had not slept in days. He leaned on a staff, and it seemed as if the mere act of standing was agony. We've all aged,

Daniel thought, but nothing like this. By all that was sacred, what was wrong with him?

The clerk turned and bowed low.

"My lord, I merely do as you yourself have bid. I think you should retire, my lord, and let these men come at a time when you feel ..."

"Remarth, don't ever dare to tell me what I should do!" Michael shouted, his voice cracking with the effort.

Remarth bowing even lower, backed away.

"Daniel, Cowan, come with me." Michael gestured feebly for them to follow as he turned and walked out of the room.

Looking at each other and trying to conceal their shock at Michael's appearance, Daniel and Cowan followed him up a long flight of stairs and out onto a sunlit veranda that was fully exposed to the frigid wind that howled out of the northwest.

Cowan stepped forward and offered his cape to Michael, who accepted it without comment.

"Michael, it's obvious you aren't well. Let's go inside," Cowan said softly.

Michael smiled and shook his head. "No, I like it here. It reminds me of things, like standing on the deck of a fast-running ship, looking out across the endless Frozen Sea."

Emotions overwhelming him, Daniel rushed forward and embraced Michael, who absently patted him on the shoulder.

"Ah, my old warrior, you want to call me back into battle, is that it?"

"Michael, what's happend to you ... what is happening?"

"The practicer of physic claims it's a cancer ..." His voice trailed off.

Michael looked at Cowan and smiled while wearily settling himself onto a stone bench that provided some small shelter from the wind.

"Michael," Cowan started, trying to keep his voice

steady, "a crisis is coming. A rebellion has broken out in North Prydain, and I believe it will spread throughout our Cornathian holdings. It will touch off a civil war, and Zimri will profit as a result."

"Ah, Zimri," Michael said softly. "Would it have been better to have killed him when I had the chance?"

The two were silent.

"Zimri, where do you figure in all of this, and how do I figure in your plans?"

"Michael, listen to Cowan," Daniel urged. "There's something amiss and I think his words are true. You're not facing the reality of what is happening in our kingdom. Rebellion is coming.

"Besides"—and he laughed with a forced show of bravado—"this pox of yours is nothing. Get out of this damned monk's trap and come out with me on the Ice. Put a blade in your hand and soon you'll feel your old self again."

"I don't think so," Michael replied softly.

"But, Michael..." Daniel's words trailed off as Michael fixed him with his gaze.

"Everything is under control," Michael replied coldly.

"Please, Michael," Cowan started.

"No, Cowan, I don't think you understand what I am saying. All is under control. Every time you come to me, you preach another crisis, another danger. But I tell you, the crisis is not yet here!"

Daniel was shocked at the tone of rebuff and looked away from Michael.

Michael slowly got to his feet and gestured that the audience was at an end.

"Michael, I am loyal to your service," Cowan cried. "If you don't trust my words then send me away and I will accept exile—even death for that matter—but do not believe that just because I speak of a danger that I am the bringer or cause of that danger."

Michael was silent for a moment. He struggled with a wave of nausea and had to hold onto the edge of the parapet to maintain his balance. Somehow he knew that he had to listen to these two for a greater length of time, but at the moment he could not bear the strain.

"Leave me alone," he whispered. "Come back in five days and we'll talk again—perhaps then I will have the patience to listen. I'll leave word with Remarth to admit the two of you without question. Now please leave me, my friends. I'm weary and there is much to think about."

Rising from his chair, Riadent of Inys Gloi beckoned to the hooded form. The figure drifted in from the shadows, walking with a calm, sinuous ease. That was good, very good; he had the mark of a trained man.

"You are Nathan of Cornath?" Riadent asked.

Nathan knelt before him.

"You are, I am told, a former Master of the Knife and monk of Mord Rinn."

"In my former life I was of Mord Rinn, your excellency."

"You may come forward and remove your garments so that I might see you better."

Nathan advanced across the room. Stopping before the Master's desk, he pulled back his cowl and let the heavy wool cassock drop to the ground, revealing his naked body.

Riadent advanced toward him, and Nathan lowered his eyes as custom demanded.

"No, do not lower your eyes. I give you permission to gaze upon me."

Nathan looked up, knowing of course that he would see no features since the Master would be wearing a deep cowl—his face concealed by the shadows, winding headband, and veil. Only the innermost circle knew what the Master looked like, thus giving him freedom to go abroad without being recognized.

"When was the last time you stood naked in such a manner?"

"At the night of my initiation into the Brotherhood of

the Knife. Mord Rinn had me trained by that most secret order."

"And who was the Master?"

"Ulric of Dulyn, blessed be his memory. For he was the best, and died well when the Saints called him."

"And how many missions were you sent out on?"

"Four."

"Your victims?"

"A Mathinian merchant who was once of our order, two followers of Ormson who had discovered a manuscript of the Before Time, and a guild master of North Prydain who was secretly learning to read."

"You have a scar on your shoulder. Where did that come from?" And so saying, Riadent lightly touched the puckered white flesh.

"A crossbow bolt, taken at the battle before the Mathinian Gate. I served secretly with Ormson's fleet, as an observer of his battle tactics."

"So you served Ormson, murdered three of his own, and killed a citizen of your own Church."

"A heretic of my Church, my Master."

"As you now are."

Nathan was silent.

"You've killed four, then."

"You only asked me about my assignments for Mord Rinn; there were others as well. Some for you—shall I elaborate?"

Riadent chuckled softly. "No, I already know. And it really doesn't matter. You see, I know you are a spy, sent to betray Inys Gloi!"

With lightning speed he drew his scimitar toward Nathan's exposed neck, and his two-handed swing cut the air in a deadly humming arc. He stopped the blade at the last possible second, but not until it had already cut into the flesh. A warm trickle of blood started to run down Nathan's chest.

Nathan had not offered any reaction and stood silent, awaiting his fate.

"Defend yourself!" Riadent screamed, still holding the scimitar—the edge of the blade resting inside Nathan's body.

Nathan looked straight at him. "There is no need."

"You are a Master of the Knife. Even naked you could still kill me!"

"No, my lord."

"Why?"

"I am no traitor to Inys Gloi. I left the Knife and Mord Rinn of my own volition. And if I am not mistaken, if you knew that I was a traitor, I would already be dead or on the rack in the cellars below. I am loyal to the cause of the Holy Brotherhood. Therefore, if you wish to kill me for that, then do so."

With a swift, even motion Riadent withdrew his blade, and wiping it clean, he set it back in its scabbard.

"You may dress," Riadent said softly. Turning his back, he walked over to the fireplace and examined the flickering blaze. The Cornathian had passed another test. But there would be other tests. There were always more tests.

"You have been selected." Riadent spoke softly, while settled back into his chair. "Your skills fit a certain task. You were once of Mord Rinn and also of the Knife, and have served under the Prophet as well. I need a bodyguard who can pass on his knowledge to his charge."

Nathan looked straight ahead. The offer still might be a test, but he could feel his heart pounding—the ultimate target was falling within his grasp.

"Do you know of whom I speak?" Riadent asked, looking closely at Nathan.

"He is the son of the Prophet," Nathan replied, deciding that to lie at this point could arouse suspicion.

"How do you know that?" Riadent shouted. "Such knowledge can bring instant death to whomever holds it."

"I have lived here for five years. One hears rumors."

Riadent turned the thought over for a moment. Even a rumor was dangerous. His reports indicated that not even Michael's closest followers knew the truth.

"Be that as it may, I will tell you now that this young man *is* the son of Michael Ormson. You are to serve three purposes. First, as bodyguard. Second, you are to train him in the ways of the Knife, both for defense against it and offense if need be. But most important, you are to give him a sense of the world that you lived in, its customs, dialects, desires, and beliefs. You are to give him insight into what he has never seen."

"And the other?" Nathan asked. "I suspect there is something yet unsaid."

Riadent looked at him closely. He was smart, perhaps too smart, but such men could be used. "Any actions, any words, or even suspicions that you might have about his mother are to be reported, to me and me alone. Are there any questions concerning this?"

Nathan shook his head.

"Then leave me." He did not bother to watch or even wave a blessing as Nathan bowed low and left the room.

He still had his doubts about Nathan of Cornath. But then there would always be doubts about all who served him. Inys Gloi would not survive if it ever trusted anyone completely. But he fits the bill of what I want, Riadent thought. He's aggressive and a trained killer.

If Thomas was to survive, those emotions and skills had to be inculcated in him. He would have to learn to be a killer, and to do it without remorse, unlike his father.

Unlike Michael, he thought quietly.

He clutched his fist at the thought of the opportunities that had been lost in Michael, the first of which started with his sire, Red Orm. Damn him, damn Red Orm forever, and his brother Rifton as well. But not this time—this time we shall train the seed of the Prophet to fit our needs.

"If that is true, then it presents a serious problem."

The messenger looked to the form that was half concealed in the flickering shadows cast by the fire.

"It is true, your excellency. The two arrived, conferred

with the Master for nearly an hour, and then left. The Master left orders that the two were to be admitted again at the end of five days."

"That means we only have four days to act."

"Yes, your excellency."

"Thank your superior for this information and tell him that all will be taken care of."

"But damn me, I still can't understand his refusing to listen. I tell you, Daniel, he is out of touch with his own cause."

Daniel walked by Cowan's side, not responding.

"Can't you see, Daniel, that the responsibility for this endless war rests squarely on his shoulders? He came offering a message of peace and has killed hundreds of thousands as a result. Even if the war ended tomorrow, which it won't, it would take all of us, Cornathians and Southlanders, a generation at least to recover. The burden is simply too much, and he is cracking under the strain."

With a practiced eye Daniel looked up to survey the narrow alleyway they were attempting to traverse. Clogged with filth, refuse, and ice, their path was nearly impossible to cross in the darkness. The half-dozen guards that accompanied them cursed softly as they slipped and staggered in the dark.

"And there is another thing."

"What is that?" Daniel asked absently.

"This illness. Sometimes I wonder if it's all that the healers say it is."

"What do you mean?"

Cowan was about to continue when Daniel stopped and with a muffled curse looked upward.

A window shutter was swinging open, and he started to step back in anticipation of the chamberpot that would be emptied out onto their heads.

A shadow leaned out.

"It's a trap," Daniel cried, and with a lunge he pushed Cowan away from the pointing crossbow.

A weapon fired—its dart slamming into the snow where Cowan had been standing. Another half-dozen shutters swung open on either side of them and the alleyway echoed with the high-pitched whining *crack*s of the discharging weapons. From both ends of the alley came the sounds of fighting and deep guttural screams.

"Death to Mathinians! Death to Mathinians!"

"Quick, the doorway!" Daniel cried. He crashed into the door directly beneath the window that concealed the first assailant. Cowan scrambled after him. The room was dark, and anticipating an attacker, Daniel dived low as he cleared the threshold. He heard another bolt snap.

A shadow ran past him. Pulling out his battle-ax, he sprinted up and dove after the attacker, driving his blade into the man's back.

"Daniel, on the stairs!"

Another bolt was fired—the shot slashing over their heads. Not paying attention to where it landed, Daniel charged up the steps, and before the archer could reload, he brought his blade down in a whistling arc that caught his second attacker on the forehead, splitting him open to the breastbone. A curtain of blood showered the stairs and walls, blinding Daniel in its hot, sticky spray.

Without stopping, Daniel kicked the twitching body aside and sprinted up the remaining steps, bursting into the single room on the second floor. It was empty—the window open. A small lantern cast a feeble light in the stinking hovel that was devoid of any furniture or sign of habitation. Edging up to the window, Daniel looked out. Dark forms struggled below and angry voices echoed in the night.

"Death to the Mathinian heretics!"

A horn, the alarm for the garrison, echoed in the distant square, calling out the nightwatch, but it would be long minutes before they arrived. Daniel watched as the last of the guards fell in the alleyway, swarmed over by at least a dozen dark-robed attackers.

Daniel ran back down the stairs, hoping to find a back

exit, but there was none. Cowan was busy bracing the only door out, which was already starting to crumble under the heavy blows of the assailants. Fumbling with the body on the stairs, Daniel picked up the blood-soaked crossbow and loaded it from the quiver strapped to the dead man's side. The door was going to break at any moment.

"Cowan, back off," Daniel hissed.

Leaping back, Cowan sprinted for the stairs. Before he had even reached the first step the door crashed in.

Daniel fired over Cowan's head, aiming for the doorway—his shot was answered by a scream of anguish. The two comrades scrambled up the stairs and turned into the empty room. Daniel tossed the crossbow and quiver to Cowan, and pulling out his ax, he waited with grim determination.

The first man came around the corner—shield up high. Daniel swung low, driving his ax into the man's groin. With a high-pitched shriek, the shadowy form tumbled backward.

"Ready," Cowan cried.

Daniel stepped back and Cowan drove the bolt into the forehead of the next attacker.

Hoarse cries thundered up from the room below, while from outside the calls of the approaching Companions came ever louder. Another minute or two at most, Daniel thought.

As if his thoughts were read by the attackers, they drove up the stairs, heedless of loss. The first man fell to Daniel's ax—the blade cutting the man's legs off at the knees. Another attacker climbed over the kicking body and drove Daniel back from the stairs with a well-aimed dagger thrust. Cowan caught his attacker in the side and pinned him to the wall.

And then the rush drove them back to the window. Cowan cast aside the bow, and drawing out his scimitar, he traded blows with three attackers. Daniel tried to maneuver to his side. From out in the alleyway he could hear the nightwatch.

"Companions, to me!" Daniel bellowed, and an answering cry echoed up from below as his men poured into the building. The Companions charged up the stairs and the assassins wailed in horror as the Mathinians gave no quarter. Daniel, finishing off the last man in front of him, came around to Cowan's flank and helped him to dispatch the last of the attackers. Panting, they looked at each other and smiled.

"Daniel," Cowan said between gasps, "in a fight I'll always want you by—"

A bolt exploded through his chest and slammed into the far wall—a shower of blood cascading down the front of his tunic. Looking past Cowan, Daniel saw a shape disappear from the window across the alleyway. With a shout of rage Daniel leaned out the window and screamed to his men to take the other house, and then, turning, he looked back at Cowan.

Cowan stood upright, looking quizzically down at the river of scarlet that coursed from his body to puddle at his feet. His eyes locked onto Daniel's anguished face.

"I think they've killed me, Daniel," he said with a strange, distant voice.

Daniel grabbed hold of him, but Cowan pushed him away. "No, don't touch me, don't touch me!"

He started to sway.

"Tell Michael he was wrong to fight for revenge. Tell Michael he must face what has to be done, if he wants to save himself."

"Cowan!"

"I go to see if Michael was right. I . . ."

Daniel stepped back in amazement as Cowan's eyes glazed over. The body trembled slightly and then, ever so gently, collapsed to the floor.

"A good death," one of the guards whispered.

But Daniel did not hear him as he cradled Cowan in his arms and screamed in impotent rage.

# CHAPTER 5

"SO YOU ARE THE NEW BODYGUARD FOR MY SON?"

"Yes, my lady."

"And, of course, I have no control over this decision?" It was not a question and Nathan knew it. Varinna turned away from him and walked back down the torchlit corridor, and Nathan fell in behind her.

"Why were you chosen by Riadent?"

"I am originally from Cornath, I once had training with the Black Brothers, and Riadent thought that my knowledge would be helpful in preparing the boy."

"Not the boy," she said with a note of sharp reproach, "the young master."

"Forgive me the error."

She led him on in silence, her soft robes swirling provocatively. He kept his eyes straight ahead. He knew enough of this woman to understand that she was dangerous. There must never be cause for the slightest suspicion.

She led him into a section of the mountain that he never knew existed. He had tried on many an occasion to calculate the immense internal proportions of this citadel carved out of a single rock, which some claimed had fallen from the heavens. It was nearly five hundred feet in height and three times that in diameter. According to legend, the brotherhood of Inys Gloi had claimed it as its own sometime in the first millennium after the Fall.

They were still carving away at it, painstakingly chipping out room after endless room. Stores were stockpiled to withstand a siege of years and, with the five hundred brothers who were always present, the fortress was impregnable. Even if the outer doors were forced, there were still half a dozen inner lines of defense.

"Has Riadent reviewed your duties?" Varinna asked, looking back over her shoulder to survey the thin dark man behind her.

He nodded in reply.

"And what are they?"

"Riadent commanded that I shall be on duty with him every moment of the day except when the teachers are giving their lessons. I am to test all his food, to teach him all that I know of the outside world, and to train him in the arts of the Black Brothers, both for defense and offense."

"And what else?" she demanded.

"My lady, what else could there possibly be?"

"Damn you, what else? And don't lie, for like his father I can read the aura as well."

"I am to be his companion, his older brother or guide, so to speak."

"You mean a surrogate father. But, Nathan, that you will never be, for he is already beyond that."

He was silent. He could sense her defensiveness for the boy and her anger at Riadent for excluding her from major decisions about Thomas's life, but his orders were clear.

"Was there anything else?"

"Nothing, my lady."

"Such as spying on me as well."

He was silent, and she nodded knowingly.

"My lady, I mean no offense. Please trust me in that, at least."

She looked at him closely and after a moment her features softened a bit.

"No," she mumbled softly, as if to herself. "No, like all the rest, you are only doing what you are told. Just as I am doing only what I am told."

He felt some pity for her—a virtual prisoner to the motherhood of the Prophet's son.

"Here is the room; go on in. I shall leave you with him." And so saying she turned and disappeared back into the shadows.

He stood by the door for a moment. Here was the culmination of all the plans. He was still of the Cornathian brotherhood and about to gain access to Thomas Michaelsson. And if the order ever came, he could kill him with ease.

He opened the door. The room was bare except for a table and a chair, proportioned for a young child. The chair was occupied—its owner sitting with his back to the entrance, his shoulders hunched as if in deep concentration. Nathan entered the room without a sound, but he could sense an alertness in the youth.

Good, he thought, very good. There is no sense in playing the pretext.

"May I enter, young master?"

"Yes. I don't recognize your voice. I thought you were Carl, come to bother me again with my lessons."

The boy had yet to turn around. Nathan advanced and saw the table held a Flyswin board with the blue player in a middle-game attack formation.

"Do you play Flyswin?"

"Yes."

"Good, would you play with me?"

Nathan came around the side of the table and sat down. The boy slowly raised his head to examine the new presence in his life. Only long training prevented Nathan from revealing his shock. So much of Michael was evident in the youth. He was pale and slender, almost delicate of build, with a high forehead and blond, nearly white hair. It was the eyes that were so compelling to look at. They appeared to hold a depth of wisdom, as if they were the eyes of an old man who had seen too much of the world.

Like his father's, they were of two different colors—one pale blue, the other a dark, steel gray.

"Who are you?" Thomas asked, while his small hands started to push the pieces into position.

"My name is Nathan. I am assigned as your bodyguard and trainer."

"Trainer in what?"

"Dueling with weapons and how to defend from attack."

"Will you teach me to kill?" the boy asked softly.

The door had not closed completely and Varinna stood in the hallway listening to Nathan and his easy banter with the boy. She could sense Thomas's fascination with Nathan's words as he wove stories of combat and the thrill of the chase upon the Frozen Sea. And she could sense the increasing deference in Nathan's voice; the man was already falling under the spell of the boy.

After long minutes she slowly closed the door and walked away. Hard as she tried, the images came back; memories of Michael Ormson haunted her. The boy had inherited so much from his father, and foremost was the ability to win support and trust from those around him. She tried to drive the memories away, but they lingered as she entered into her private chamber to spend yet another day alone, weaving her tapestries, contemplating what had been and the future that Inys Gloi had set for her.

"My lord Zimri, I think you should come on deck."

"Is the Bane in sight?"

"Yes, my lord."

"And the rendezvous ship?"

"You'd best see for yourself, my lord."

Setting aside his book of prayer, Zimri donned his outer parka and left behind the incense clouds of the ship's chapel. The enclosed lower gun deck rumbled beneath his feet as he made his way forward. Since all hands were called to battle stations at dawn in anticipation of their approach to St. Judean's Bane, the deck was clear of hammocks. Many crew members slumbered alongside their gun carriages, but those who saw Zimri fell to their knees at his approach, the bolder men reaching out to touch him as if he were a living icon whose mere presence would grant a special blessing. He nodded to the men, knowing most of them by name. Reaching the portside midship gun, he stopped for a moment.

"How stands the crew of the blessed gun St. Jason of Orina?"

"Your blessing, my lord," the gun captain replied.

"Ah, my blessing you'll get, you sons of pirates," Zimri said with a low soft laugh. "Dismasting that Mathinian ram saved this ship."

The gun captain bowed low, his face beaming with pride. Three days ago they had encountered an attack group of Ormson's red fleet. A ram had broken through the outer defense and was less than a hundred yards away when a shot from the St. Jason destroyed the attacker. Zimri touched the gun captain on the forehead, and making the sign of the Arch, he looked to the other four men who knelt by him. Several patches in the hull to either side of the gun marked where a broadside had swept the lower deck in the action, and he remembered the casualties to the crew.

"Tell me, master gunner, how is your young brother?"

The man looked up at him and tried to smile. "He went to the Long Table of the Saints during the dawn watch this morning."

Zimri looked away. "Soon you shall have your revenge, my son."

The gunner was silent.

Grimath came to his side from out of the shadows.

"My lord, you'd better come forward," Grimath whispered with a note of urgency.

"A bottle of Yarwinder for you and your men," Zimri

said to the men as he started away, "and tonight I shall offer a service for your brother."

The master gunner bowed low and mumbled his thanks.

Hurrying forward, Zimri blessed the men as he passed, noting the damage to the ship. Three guns were permanently out, the rough patches to the hull were not airtight, and bone-penetrating chill had invaded the ship.

This cold, this damning cold, will it never end? he thought sadly.

Reaching the gangway to the forecastle, Zimri pulled his parka tight, knotting the drawstrings. He motioned for Grimath to throw up the airtight hatch. A shaft of brilliant sunlight flooded the ladderwell and he pulled down his goggles to gain some protection from the glare. Scrambling up the ladder, Zimri alighted on the armored forecastle and walked over to the forward rail.

"There on the horizon," Grimath shouted above the roar of the wind. "Two points off the starboard bow. Can you see it?"

"Not clearly. Give me the tube."

The sailing master reached into his tunic and pulled out a long brass cylinder. Grabbing hold of one end, he pulled sharply and the cylinder extended out from itself to nearly two feet in length. Taking the instrument, Zimri looked through it.

"Yes, I see it now. Half a hundred ships must be there."

"Those are only the bigger ones, my lord. I daresay the masts of the smaller vessels aren't above the horizon yet."

"Then he's brought out everything he has."

"I think so."

Zimri looked at Grimath and smiled with a wolfish grin. "It could be a trap, you know."

Grimath smiled softly.

"Sail straight for them," Zimri ordered. "Pass the word to all ships, guns are to be double shotted but kept in. If it is a trap, we engage at close quarters then break out to rendezvous off the Bathanian Pass."

At Grimath's command the signal rockets snaked out from the sides of Zimri's command ship. Alone for a moment, Zimri contemplated the cylinder that rested in his hands. Ten years ago ownership of such an object would have been grounds for a heresy or witchcraft trial, for even talk of such a thing violated the First Choice. The Church still remembered that once before the same instrument had helped to shatter a faith. He looked heavenward for a moment. He knew that, in secret, Grimath turned the cylinder to the skies at night.

He should have disciplined Grimath, but he had done so as well, and the revelations had been terrible to behold. He well remembered when he had turned the tube toward a light that appeared to be rectangular. For a moment he wanted to believe that he was gazing at the Long Hall of the Saints, but of course he knew that it was not so, for there above them, hovering in the night sky in defiance of all Holy Writ, was a man-made relic of the past. It was a relic and a lesson as well, for if one thin crack was carved into the structure of a faith then soon the entire edifice would collapse.

He had come close to smashing the evil instrument and to ordering the execution of the brother who had constructed it, but in the end he refrained, for even though such a glass would breed heresy, it also gave advantage in battle, and that above all else was the primary concern. Any heresy could be tolerated if it gave the edge in battle. Ormson had used such things, and so would Zimri, for if he did not he would perish. But would he perish anyhow under the weight of what they were releasing? He prayed that there was still time—that victory would soon be his and with it the power to remake things as they once were. But in his heart he already knew that such a prayer, to Saints that did not even exist, was in vain.

A voice called to him from the distance.

"My lord, your commands."

He turned to see that Grimath was by his shoulder,

awaiting his decision—the responsibilities were pressing in again.

"Signal the ships, Grimath. Tell them to close and form up for a ceremonial approach. I want to show that scum out there what ten years of war has done for Mor."

"As you wish, my lord."

Zimri stepped from behind the protective covering of the armored forecastle and walked forward to the bowsprit. Looking back, he surveyed his vessel as it ran abeam the wind, the dark-blue canvas overhead driving them forward, forcing the ship up onto its downwind runners. Wide sections of the deck were patched and patched again—scars of a hundred actions that had carried them from the Broken Tracks to the far north wastes where the cold was as deep as Hell's. Some of the men had been with him since his rescue off the shore of Caediff and had followed him to the forbidden wastes of the Dead Lands. But most aboard her now were the ones who had followed, recruited from the steady westward stream of volunteers to carry on the fight against the hated Prophet. And as they came, the ships they sailed changed to face the new type of warfare.

Of the masses who had followed him, most long since dead, few of the old sailors would recognize the *Braith du Mor* today. Her masts were tapered to the stern to add more thrust to the sailing rigs. Abandoning the old laws, the Dead Lands were exploited, and in the lost cities of old, strange metals were found. Armor skirtings had been added to the outriggers, and the forecastle was protection against shots and rams. Gone were most of the catapults, to be replaced by dozens of small breech-loading cannons, designed by the brothers of the First Choice. Developed to repel the dreaded ram attacks, which had once made Ormson invincible, the inside of each cannon had curious grooves that gave the gun an incredible degree of accuracy and the punch of a gun four times its weight. Two men could fire such a gun five times for every shot delivered by one of the older guns below. And the shells they fired exploded on impact or ignited. Zimri watched with quiet pride as the men stood by their pieces, ready for action, and then turned his attention back to the approaching fleet.

In response to the signal flares, the half-dozen frigates and a score of light escort ships maneuvered toward the commandship as if drawn by a lodestone, each movement a display of precision born of long practice.

On every ship the blue-robed warriors formed up, their shields and scimitars glinting brightly in the morning sun, their battle chants carrying across the breeze, echoing clear and loud above the rumble of the blades.

Looking forward, Zimri saw the approaching host advancing in ragged formation, their colorful pennants snapping out in the stiff westerly breeze. Zimri's six frigates drew up in line abreast, so close to each other that a man could jump from one outrigger to the other. The frozen sea rumbled and shook with their passing. As the range closed, yet more ships were visible, so that it appeared the ice was carpeted with wood and snapping canvas.

Grimath came forward and stood by his side.

"That must be his," he shouted, pointing to an old ice cruiser running off the portside bow.

"Give the command."

Grimath turned and nodded to the signal crew, and in response, a single red rocket roared aloft.

The frigate farthest to port heeled over violently, towers of spray kicking up from her blades. The next frigate quickly turned and within seconds was followed in her maneuver by the third frigate to port. On the starboard side the innermost frigate dropped back and cut across the *Braith*'s stern, her bowsprit nearly grazing the commandship—the maneuver instantly repeated by the other two ships down the line. Within seconds, the six escort frigates changed direction by ninety degrees, presenting a full broadside to the rapidly approaching ice cruiser. Zimri's vessel cut a broad carving turn and came in behind the cruiser, while the light escort ships of the Morian battle group ranged out to form a protective screen against the rest of the approaching fleet.

Grimath looked to Zimri and smiled.

"With men such as ours," Zimri whispered, "we can never lose."

The gun ports of the ice cruiser swung open.

"Zimri?" Grimath asked.

"They're just frightened by our display, but they wouldn't dare. If they did, they would truly be alone."

Grimath, unable to suppress an old nervous habit, started to stroke his chin.

"Bring her up alongside. I'll board while we're in motion."

"My lord, the protocol. He should come to us."

"They already have. I need to win these people over, and I'm willing for the moment to treat them as equals."

"As you wish, my lord."

Returning to the tiller, Grimath took personal charge of the delicate maneuver, while Zimri walked back to the midship outrigger support arm.

Zimri looked to his honor guard. "Let's go."

Covering up his queasiness at a ship-to-ship transfer, he swung out onto the outrigger catwalk and slid down to the heavy oak beam that carried the support blades of the ship. Several guards leaped across the open space and perched on the ice cruiser's beam. Zimri stepped back as a gangplank was lowered and swung over to the waiting men on the opposite ship who steadied the narrow board. Without looking down, Zimri started across the open space. If the captain of the other vessel wanted to kill him, now would be the time—all he needed to do was pull his craft away, the board would slip free, and Zimri would be hurled to the ice. The two ships held steady. Alighting on the other side, he scrambled up the catwalk and stepped onto the deck of the heavy ice cruiser.

Having fought from the deck of a frigate for so long, he had forgotten just how big an ice cruiser could be. He felt a wave of nostalgia for the old order of things, when such vessels were the ultimate symbol of power—but those days had long passed. The heavy ice cruiser was a beautiful gun platform, but it just could not maneuver against the new sleek frigates that were required to counteract Ormson's battle rams.

He quickly surveyed the crew. They were a motley set. No uniforms in sight, or priests for that matter, just a wild assortment of clothing and weapons. But they looked tough, arrogant, and none bowed at his approach. He stared at them silently, waiting for someone to come forward. The seconds drew out and still no one approached. They knew who he was by his robes. Well, he had made the first gesture by coming over; he would not beg for an audience.

Zimri looked to his guards and beckoned. "This is a waste of our time." Turning, he started back to the catwalk.

All these games of face must be played, he thought. But if they don't stop me, I've lost an ally and might have to fight my way out.

"Wait!"

Zimri stopped and looked back. A short stocky figure, dressed in bear skins, was advancing toward him.

"Are you Zimri, the Holy See?"

Wordlessly he nodded in reply.

"I did not expect you to come. I assumed one of your lieutenants would do your bidding."

"That is not my way," Zimri said coldly, as if he had been insulted.

The man came forward and stopped before Zimri. He threw back the hood of his parka and removed his goggles, and in a gesture of openness Zimri did the same.

"Yes, you are Zimri. My man told me what you looked like. He said your scar was an ugly sight to behold."

Yes, the scarred face. That is what they always remember—but any sensitivity Zimri had to that had disappeared long ago.

"Funny, if you were not a priest you could have grown

a beard to cover it, the way I did." The man grinned a gapped-tooth smile, his misshapen nose wrinkling with laughter that was joined by those around him.

"I am Norn."

"Yes, I know," Zimri replied. "My man told me that even a beard could not cover what you really looked like."

Norn stepped back. Reacting quickly, Zimri stepped forward and smiled as best he could while extending his hand.

Norn looked to his henchmen, but they laughed at their leader's discomfort.

"Yes, you must be Zimri; only he would insult me so and know that I would suffer him to live."

"We two are alike," Zimri said quickly, deciding to ignore the implied challenge. "How we look matters not; it is how we lead and fight our common foe that matters."

As the warriors who crowded around nodded their approval, Norn looked up at Zimri and gave him a wolfish grin. "Let us go below and talk."

The cabin was garishly appointed with the spoils typical of freebooters' loot and so crowded that Zimri had some difficulty wading through the clutter to the high-backed chair offered by Norn. Interlocking demons pursued one another in a spiral winding around the legs and across the back of the chair, to culminate in warriors cast in silver, who were locked in mortal combat with the dark forces from below. Settling into the chair, Zimri examined the tapestries that covered the walls of the cabin. Portraying the Fall of man from Grace, they were in the rich, flowing style typical of the master weavers of Cadez, full of deep, vibrant blues and reds. One in particular held Zimri's attention, since it showed a group of monks dressed in Morian blue falling into the icy pit of eternal torment. Norn followed Zimri's gaze, and walking up to the tapestry, he examined it with mock gravity for several seonds, then with a mumbled curse against all priests he turned away and went over to a silver box set into one wall.

Opening it, he pulled out a bottle of Yarwinder and poured two full measures for Zimri and himself. Without toast or ceremony he drained his goblet then refilled it before collapsing into his place opposite the waiting See.

"You are prepared to join my crusade, then?" Zimri asked softly.

Norn leaned back in his chair and started to laugh with a loud, hoarse bellow. However, after several seconds the laughter changed to a choked, rasping cough that filled the cabin. Norn doubled over, gasping for breath and, with a long shuttering wheeze, coughed up a thin trickle of blood.

Zimri looked away, a tingle of fear running down his spine. Norn had the burning lung. It was all too common with ice runners, and he feared it even more than the shock of combat. Norn panted weakly, and as the spasm passed he picked up the bottle, knocked the stopper off, and drained most of its contents. "Ah, my friend, death comes to us all." He laughed softly at Zimri's obvious fear.

He offered the bottle to Zimri. "Care for some more?"

Repelled, Zimri shook his head.

"Now let me make this clear," Norn wheezed. "I'm not joining your crusade, and your religious quarrel with Ormson is none of my concern."

"Then why do you wish to join...excuse me, fight alongside me?"

"'Tis simple enough," Norn whispered, his voice hoarse with passion and lust. "I want Eldric. I want to personally see that scum pinned down to the ice and staked out for the sport of my men. When they are finished it'll be my pleasure to castrate him and take his head to mount on the bow of this ship."

With that Norn started to cackle softly and rubbed his hands together. Zimri tried to appear impassive, but Norn could sense his revulsion.

"I've heard enough about you, I have. My men fought you for ten years—you are a good 'un, you are. A proper warrior to help my revenge. But you can't understand that, can you? You're a sterile priest without emotion, just a cold burning logic without emotion or hate."

"And who are you to lecture about revenge and hate?"

"Who else than I? Today I've brought you a hundred ships and nearly eight thousand battle veterans from my guild and clan. Who else but I to lecture since indeed my men might shift the balance? I don't give a damn about you and your pox-eaten church. My desire is simply to kill Eldric and restore my name, which he took away with the death of my son."

"I understand it was a fair challenge fight."

"My son was provoked by Eldric's followers, and besides, he was right—we've become the servants of a religious madman."

"Your actions could destroy Michael Ormson, you know that?"

"I care not one bit for him."

"And your men, many of them will die in the months to come."

"It doesn't matter. They go where the greatest prizes are. They've agreed to serve me—Cornathian, Ezrian, Sol, or freethinker from Mathin. My men have sworn no religious quarrels amongst themselves, and they sell their sword to the highest bidder. In that I have the tool for my personal revenge. All they'll ask is payment for services rendered."

Zimri looked at Norn for a moment and then from the folds of his robe he produced a simple document and handed it across the table.

"Have one of your readers review this."

"There is no need, I can read it myself."

Zimri smiled. How much it has all changed, he thought. Fifteen years ago I would have had this man assassinated for knowing how to read. He shook his head at the thought that Michael's revolution had become so all-pervasive.

"The terms are simple enough," Zimri stated. "All booty taken by you in battle is yours, except for ten percent which goes to the Church. That's better than Michael's, to be sure, since he has eliminated all prize money."

"So he has, the fool. I tried to tell him that men fight for booty before all else, but he would not hear of it, claiming that it hurt discipline."

"I agree with Michael on that," Zimri said softly. "But I need you and your men, so prize money it shall be. I also give you charter to raid all shipping south of the Broken Tracks, and at the completion of the campaign you shall be military governor of Bathan, with all rank and privilege."

Norn nodded slowly and smiled. "It is as your representative promised. I agree to serve with you. What are your orders for the present?"

Zimri smiled softly. After all the long years, the crisis at last was past. One major defeat would have destroyed him forever, but now he had a reserve. With that reserve he could at last risk an offensive.

"We sail to my base in the north. There your men shall have their fill of drink and women, and there I shall reveal my action for the winter. I know it will please you."

Zimri stood up, signaling that the meeting was ended. Norn did not bow or offer his hand, but knowing he was aboard Norn's ship, Zimri didn't press the issue. There would be time enough for that later.


"It went well then, my lord?"

Zimri took the goblet from Grimath's hand and settled back into his chair. The deck vibrated beneath his feet and then tilted as the *Braith du Mor* hiked up on its starboard runners to run close-hauled into the northwesterly breeze.

"He agreed to everything, the filthy scum."

Grimath was silent at the vindictive tone in Zimri's voice.

"The pig knew I needed him, and damn me, I *do* need him. But he is a traitor nevertheless. I need traitors now, but there is no telling when he will betray me as well."

"His men are good, some of the best freebooters in the south. I can't believe that Ormson would be so stupid as to let them go over to our side."

"Ormson is out of touch with his own cause. He's never quite managed to grasp the baser nature of man, and in that is our salvation, for we can use that baseness and the superstition of man to stop Michael's cause."

"And you think it is time?"

"Yes, my dear Grimath, I think at last it is time that we take on Michael Ormson in a full action. We have the ships and the men. North Prydain is in revolt. People have had their taste of freedom under Ormson, and as always they have finally turned from it. They look for someone to protect them, to promise to them, and to rule them. Ormson was never quite capable of that. I am. Now the question is, can we act before Inys Gloi completes its plot, or before Michael is foolish enough to give the victory to them?"

Grimath was silent, as the ship heeled even higher against the freshening wind that soon promised to blow at nearly full gale.

# CHAPTER 6

"YOU MAY ENTER."

Damn them. At this point he wanted nothing more than to be alone, but there was always someone, something to be attended to. He did not even bother to turn as the door opened behind him.

"I'll come back later if you like; it's nothing important."

Wearily Michael stood up and walked toward the door, his face wrinkling with a careworn smile.

"No, Seth, no. Perhaps I do need someone to talk to. Maybe you read my thoughts and came—please sit down."

The old advisor settled into a high-backed leather chair across from Michael's, his creased face and graying hair shining softly in the firelight. Absently he rubbed the stump of his arm and looked into the fire.

"Your wound, does it pain you?"

"No, 'tis nothing. You know, Michael, it's funny; there are times when it feels like I still have my hand. I can feel every finger itching, calling, almost like a ghost following me through life, as if it waits to be reunited again."

"Perchance a lost limb waits in limbo, ready to be reunited again in the next world."

Seth laughed softly. "Don't tell me that the Prophet who never speaks or preaches of the afterlife now speaks at last of the Beyond."

Michael looked away for a moment and then turned back to face his old advisor and friend.

"Before you came I was thinking that tens of thousands

say I am the Messiah. Yet others claim I am the false messenger of death. What do you and those behind you really think? I'm asking not what they preach but what they believe."

Seth looked straight at Michael and smiled softly. "It was Inys Gloi who first preached of your coming."

Michael lowered his gaze. "Yes, I see."

He was quiet for a moment and then looked at Seth again. "I've lost count of the numbers—of how many have died for me. Cowan was just one amongst thousands. Janis, Andrew—two more of the thousands. And what to come?..."

Seth leaned back in his chair, silent, waiting.

"We buried Cowan last week, you know that?"

"Don't you remember, Michael; I was there."

"Oh yes, so you were," he said absently. "Today I went out onto the Ice, concealed in ordinary robes."

"Why?"

"To visit Cowan at the Place of the Dead, the *Aiten du am Aog*. Daniel was with me, and for the first time in years I saw Daniel cry, but for me the tears would not come. I was alone and afraid, Seth. I was truly afraid. The blood of all of them, Cowan and all the others, is on my hands, and I cannot wash that away."

Seth did not reply but sat quietly, watching Michael with hawklike eyes.

"I wanted to tell Cowan what I thought of him, to reassure him at the end, and I said the words out loud while Daniel stood by my side. But the words fell into the frozen silence and disappeared."

"What did you say?"

Michael leaned back in his chair and looked vacantly into the fire. "You know, it's funny, Seth, nearly twenty years ago when I first met you, I was an unknown. From your words and the preachings of Inys Gloi I became the Messiah."

"For you are the Promised One."

"From the beginning Cowan never accepted that. He

followed me as a revolutionary, believing in a new age, free of the fear of religion. A new age where reason alone would dictate man's actions. That dream killed him."

"We'll catch the Cornathian scum that did it," Seth replied, his voice carrying a soft, distant chill.

Michael looked at Seth and smiled sadly. "Of course you will. But as I was saying, Cowan never accepted me as you or the others wanted me. And he could never accept what I was becoming. With Daniel, however, it has always been different—his trust, which is almost blind, was carried through him to the Companions, and I found that I needed that."

"It is only what you deserve as our leader."

"Am I really?" Michael's tone was cold, almost accusing, but before Seth could protest, Michael raised his hand and waved off the comment.

"Never mind that for now. I was talking of Cowan. He alone of my advisors never worshipped me. He followed me for some other ideal. In the beginning that is what drew me to him; he reminded me so much of his beloved uncle Zardok, who I still miss after all these years. For that reason I drew him into my councils. But after the murder of Janis, we grew apart. I knew from the beginning that Cowan did not approve of my actions. On the one side I hated him for it. The day we took Cornath, I even wished for his death in the final assault—that is why I sent his men back into action, for that reason alone, and thousands died needlessly because of that order."

"But, Michael, by sending them forward you pinned down Zimri's defenses."

"Don't argue the battle with me, Seth," Michael said quietly. "I know the truth and so did Cowan. Yet he stayed with me, and his presence was a constant reminder of my guilt. You know, the morning before he died, he came to me?"

Michael fell silent for a moment and looked at Seth, but Seth did not reply.

Michael suddenly leaned forward, covering his eyes,

and gave out a convulsive sob. "Damn *me*! This afternoon I tried to tell him that from the beginning of our estrangement I understood, and he would now understand as well. That some perverse destiny drove his advice and friendship from me, yet all along I agreed with everything he said, even to his advice on the day he died. But it's too late, far too late for that."

The fire crackled, filling the room with its soft glow and pungent, thick smell. Long the two sat in silence, until finally the fire drifted down into a bed of glowing ashes, and then, as if from some deep meditation, Michael finally stirred.

He looked at Seth with hollow, distant eyes.

"It can't go on like this. I thought that I could, but not now. Cowan in his death made it clear that I am not dealing with some obscure destiny but with the lives of men. We've failed in the north, my friend. I once thought that the people of the Cornathian brotherhood would greet me as a liberator. Well, they might have, if we had let things follow their natural course. But we tried to force them and thereby fell into Zimri's hands. I did not listen to Cowan in life, but I think now that I might listen to him in death."

"What do you mean?" Seth asked softly.

"The leech master claims I am dying of cancer. My stomach burns constantly with a fire, I can feel my limbs grow weaker with every passing day. Death has come a step closer and I wish this to end before my passing. I am considering that we might just simply withdraw from Cornath, give it back to Zimri. This will end the reason for the wars, and in the haven of the Southward Ice we can live in peace as we once did."

"But that is impossible," Seth cried. "Such a show of weakness would destroy us. Perceiving that you had grown weak, our allies would fall away and join Zimri. And what of the tens of thousands that live in the northward cities and follow you as the Messiah?"

"I would tell them to come with me. But most, I believe, will merely cheer Zimri and fall back into the other side."

"The war must go on," Seth cried, coming to his feet. "Michael, it's just a matter of time before Zimri and his followers collapse."

"That is not what Cowan came to me to say. Why did he therefore die, my friend?"

Seth was silent for just a moment. "He was murdered by Cornathian assassins. It was a random act, Michael. It could have happened to anyone. They were murderers out to kill a couple of Mathinians."

Michael smiled softly. "I think not, Seth. I think someone or something feared that I might listen to Cowan. You know, Seth, even Daniel half agreed with him. And for that old berserker to agree on a peaceful path is indeed indicative of something. I've thought long on this. Cowan's death was no accident, as it is now made out to be. Someone, or something, wanted him silenced before his words could gain sway."

Seth looked at Michael. "Are you accusing me?"

Michael, his features frozen, looked straight at Seth. "I wonder what Inys Gloi thinks of this."

"Inys Gloi, as always, will support you."

"Why?"

"Did not their prophecies create you?"

Michael leaned back in his chair and smiled at Seth as if slightly amused at his comments, but there was a deeper underlying emotion which sent a cold chill through Seth's body. Since the murder of Janis, Michael had not mentioned Inys Gloi. It was as if he assumed their support and did not want to know anything further, sensing that from them came his power as the Messiah and to question that contact might set the seeds for its destruction.

A deathly silence hung over them. The only sound filling the room was the soft hissing and popping of the fire as it gently subsided.

Seth finally broke the silence, shifting forward in a vain attempt to meet Michael's penetrating gaze.

"What is it that you want to know?"

"You are an agent of Inys Gloi, are you not?"

"You know the answer to that. It was we of the Secret Brotherhood who nurtured you, guided you, and gave into your hands the power to destroy the old order of things."

"And what do you—the brothers of Inys Gloi—gain?"

"We are everywhere, guiding the events, setting the world in shape for the new renaissance and the ending of the dark age. Our forefathers, three thousand years ago, did the same thing. Protecting knowledge, gradually preparing the way. We could have given the world an age of peace, if only the world had listened to our counsel. We took the teachings of the One from Before, but others twisted his words and destroyed us. Now you are the new Messiah, descendant of a sacred line, and from you shall come a New Age."

"*Damn* you, you did not answer me. What does your order gain from this?" Michael stood up, wavered for a moment, then strode over to Seth. Reaching into his tunic, he pulled out a stained, sharply creased parchment and flung it at Seth.

"Now, before you read that, I want an answer. What does Inys Gloi want, and what does it gain?"

Seth looked into Michael's eyes, his heart pounding. A mad fire raced in the gaze that met him, and as if against his will, the response came out. "Power. We shall be the brokers of power in your New World."

"Ultimately what we all desire, I daresay," Michael said softly, as he returned to his chair and poured another goblet of Yarwinder. "The ultimate power?"

Seth was silent.

"Answer me!"

"Yes, the ultimate power." He could not believe what he was saying, but it was as if Michael had overwhelmed him and was dragging out the answer. "Through you Inys Gloi will achieve what it has always desired. Originally all three churches were one, climbing out of the ashes of despair and night when the world went into the frozen darkness. The various brotherhoods were formed and in the beginning it was acknowledged that we were the first—the father of all. But the children betrayed the father, breaking away over questions of doctrine and the First Choice. It was the same the last time man crawled out of the dark age. We realized the path that had to be taken. We could fight them openly, but we all hung on the edge of disaster, and to do such a thing would destroy us forever. Therefore we decided to withdraw to the Holy Island of Inys Gloi and await our time."

"And my power, the Messiahhood that is mine?"

"There are some who say that the action of the soothsayer is a circle unto itself. He reads the signs and sees. But when he sees, he must also act to insure that what he has seen, indeed does come to pass. And so it was with us. We saw the signs in our meditations and waited a thousand years until the signs were ready."

"What signs?"

"The readers of the stars claim that there are twelve seasons to the year—but each season is also part of a grand cycle of twenty-four thousand years. Each age shall last for two thousand. So it was two thousand years ago when the world passed into the Ice, and so it was two thousand years before that, and so it was as well, when you were born—for two thousand years had passed and a new age was born with you. The Age of Water and Ice was coming to an end, and you were the sign. So we waited for that moment, saw the signs, and insured that it would be so. Thus we fulfilled the destiny of the soothsayer, that he sees and then prepares. And, Michael Ormson, it was we who prepared you."

"And in guiding me, your order will come again to power?"

"Yes..." His voice trailed off into silence.

"But perhaps I merely use you for some higher destiny, beyond your ability to see."

Shocked by the implication, Seth did not reply.

"Now read the letter," Michael commanded.

Obeying, Seth unfolded the parchment, and before he even started, his hand began to tremble, for he knew whom it was from.

To the one who is called the Prophet, Greetings from His Holiness Zimri, Holy See and Protectorate of the Faithful, Master of the brotherhoods of Cornath, and Defender of the One True Faith.

Michael Ormson, commonly called the Heretic, I write this with my own hand, for I will not trust its contents to others. This shall be delivered to you by a servant of your inner guard, who for the last ten years you have judged to be faithful. He was faithful to me, however, before all else. I ask that you spare his life and allow him free passage, for he is a man of honor.

Seth looked up at Michael for a moment.

"Yes, I spared him. It was one of the Companion Guards; he fought by my side and never did I suspect."

Seth nodded slowly, then returned to the document.

We are divided, you and I, by a barrier that shall never be crossed with compromise. I for killing your family, you for destroying my kingdom. And through those actions we have become linked in a struggle that has sustained us and will carry us to our graves. We shall both win, Michael, and we shall both lose. But I am confident that in the end it will be I that shall see you dead. Do not take offense at these words, for if you were writing them, so would you say to me.

I write to you now not to threaten, or to disarm through guile. I write to you for my own benefit. My power is linked to yours in war, and how often has it been that a leader in war is destroyed by peace. Michael, a net is drawing about you which could destroy both of us and grant neither the victories we desire. This day I have received documents, written orders out of the cursed island of Inys Gloi. The letters say that you have a son.

Seth again stopped for a moment and looked at Michael. "Of course, you knew that, didn't you?"

"But of course, Seth, and you knew as well."

Seth nodded slowly and returned to the letter.

Inys Gloi has decided that whatever their reasons for supporting you, the support is coming to an end. The war between you and me has played the part required. We have crippled the civilization we both pledged to defend, and have destroyed the established order of things. Sol is gone, Cornath is crippled, and only Ezra is left. However, the hatred of our two sides for each other is now too deep to be bridged. The reconciliation you might have had was destroyed in the fires of Cornath, as I knew it would be.

No cause can survive without an example. No religion can be born without a martyr. It is time that you become the martyr. You are more valuable dead than alive, Michael Ormson. Inys Gloi has decided that you shall die and that your son shall be brought forth to replace you.

Now, you might ask why I am telling you this. Simple enough, Michael Ormson. When you are safely dead, Inys Gloi will not need me either, and I shall fall to their assassins. Upon my death your son shall declare that he embraces many of the doctrines of Cornath. Therefore both sides will have what they want. A semblance of the old Church shall be preserved, and there will be a martyr to pay with his blood for the sins of the war—out of that shall come the reconciliation. A seven-year-old boy shall rule in his father's name, and Inys Gloi shall guide his hand. The final victory will be theirs.

I warn you of this so that you shall live, Michael
Ormson. I want you to live so that at last I can meet
and destroy you in battle. For if I do, Inys Gloi will
lose as well. Heed my warning, Michael Ormson,
for in your heart you know it to be true.

We shall meet again, Michael Ormson. And at
that time one of us shall pass from this frozen world
forever.

Seth let the parchment slip from his hand and it flut-
tered to the floor.

"You know it to be true, don't you, Seth Facinn?"

Seth was silent.

"Damn it, answer me!" he shouted. "Inys Gloi plans
to kill me!"

"It's a maneuver on Zimri's part, an attempt to drive
a wedge between you and the secret order that supports
you."

"So I reasoned at first," Michael said coldly. "But not
now. Not after Cowan's death. His death was worth
something after all. It made it clear to me at last."

"What?"

"I had slipped too far from Inys Gloi. You never really
had me, even in the beginning, despite your prophecies.
Oh, you might have, but then Janis lured me away, and
we both know what happened to Janis. But they got something else, a son to raise, something my uncle had prevented your order from doing to me. And now I shall ask
you what I have always wondered since the beginning.
Will you stand by me? You don't know the path I intend
to follow; no one suspects what I truly intend to do. I
would like you with me, my friend. Will you come over
to me once and for all?"

Seth looked into Michael's eyes and could sense an
infinite sadness and weariness—the illness was taking its
toll, even this brief conversation had drained him. "Of
course I will stand by you, Michael."

Michael held Seth with his gaze for what seemed to be

an eternity. Seth felt as if his very soul was being stripped away. With a sigh, Michael smiled in a sad, distant way, his eyes filled with tears.

"And, of course, you must go to Inys Gloi and find out the truth of this issue."

"I would like to if it is your wish."

"But is it your wish?"

Seth slowly nodded his head. "I think I should."

"I am doing something else as well," Michael said coldly. "I know where the base of my power is located—in the Prophecies created by Inys Gloi. The First Choice is part of that power, the mystery of what occurred."

"Of course."

"Then you know that it was an accident that created the Ice. Man was testing some engine to take him to the stars and it destroyed another world, creating the Arch above us. And you know that the churches decided in their wisdom to suppress all knowledge of this and other technologies as well. I've never publicly stated what I know, since I must confess that my power in some cases is derived from the mystery.

"You, Inys Gloi, Cornath, all of them have weaved their web, and I've become part of it. Now I shall cut it free. I shall tell my followers, all of them, of the First Choice. And the power of Inys Gloi shall be undermined in this. At the same time, I shall tell my followers of Inys Gloi and all that is behind it."

"Madness!" Seth shouted. "You'll destroy yourself!"

"And there is one other thing as well. Cowan was right; we are defeated here in the north. We cannot win followers at the point of a sword. No one has ever converted or changed his beliefs because of the blade. Therefore I shall give Cornath back to Zimri and withdraw before the next season of light."

"Your allies will fall away at such a sign of weakness. You're insane!"

"I will not need them then, for the cause of the war will be at an end. I cannot be taken in the south, Zimri will have rewon his homeland, and the war will end. Then shall come the final step to the New Age. Now, Seth, do you still intend to go to Inys Gloi?"

Seth looked at Michael for several minutes, waiting for him to speak again, but the illness and the excitement had so weakened Michael that he seemed to sink into himself, unable to continue.

Picking up his cloak, Seth walked out of the room.

"I knew you would, old friend," Michael whispered sadly. "I knew you would."

"And so, my friends, I have decided on our course of action."

Michael looked down the length of the table to his fleet and legion commanders. Several of the men whispered to each other about the vacant chair next to Michael, but no one dared to venture a question. The room, located beneath the towering cathedral, was simply appointed and overly warm due to the roaring fire.

He studied each closely, looking for some clue, some sign, and he could already sense the tension and anxiety. They knew what was coming, already the rumors had swept through the barracks and ships.

"Do not say anything premature," Eldric replied. "Granted there is rebellion, but it is a minor detail. We can control it."

"A minor detail," Michael said, his voice rising. A wave of nausea swept over him and the men before him wavered in his vision. He bent over, burying his head in his lap, and the men in the room murmured.

Either kill me or let it pass, Michael thought. Do not have me linger like this.

The trickle of cold sweat on his back chilled Michael; he started to shake. I need my control now. They're watching and think I grow weak. And they will believe that weakness causes this action. A weak man taking a coward's course. He struggled with his body and slowly regained control.

He looked up at the men and wiped the sweat from his face. He tried to steady his voice. "We withdraw."

A swelling of voices echoed through the room. It slowly grew in intensity. In brief snatches he could hear what was being said.

"No, it is not the illness," Michael said softly. "We've fought for seven years and have gained nothing but another hundred thousand dead. How much longer can we stand it?"

"Till Zimri and his band are dead!" shouted Valdimar, commander of the green fleet.

"No, Valdimar, I think not. That was never the intent to start with. I thought that in time the people of Cornath would abandon their church and come over to us, but it is not so. The rift between us grows deeper with every day. That is not the way to victory, over a pyramid of corpses. We shall withdraw and give the Northern Ice back to Zimri."

"And what in return?" Eldric asked coldly.

"Nothing, 'tis that simple—nothing. In doing that we can still succeed."

"Nothing! And what of the dead, those who gave their lives for you?" Aldmark of the white fleet shouted. "What of them?"

Michael looked at him sadly. "Are we to sacrifice more on the altar of the dead, more living to honor the dead? Can't you see that we've fallen into the trap that the churches have created?—Each generation dying to avenge the generation before, so that their deaths, as it is said, 'can have some meaning.' The dead are dead, Aldmark. Let us not destroy yet another generation."

"Zimri will destroy us."

"I think not. The Broken Tracks are defense enough. Rather he should worry about us still destroying him. Ignorance created by religion will in the end be destroyed by the knowledge we can create by free thinking."

"'Tis madness, it is—we can still win," Aldmark shouted, and the others raised their voices in agreement.

"There are some other issues as well that we must now discuss," Michael shouted, trying to be heard. "Of what really stands behind me, and where we as a people really came from."

But his voice did not carry, so loud was the shouting around him.

Michael came to his feet, slamming the table before him with clenched fist. The room suddenly grew quiet. He tried to speak but the words would not come, and as if in a dream he saw a ghostlike image at the end of the room. With a strange, twisted smile he tried to reach out, but the world collapsed on him in swirling confusion. His thoughts fled away into the darkness and silently he crumpled to the floor.

The passage was always a brief one; he had taken it innumerable times, often slipping away at night and returning the night after so that few if any ever knew of his absence. But tonight, as he stood alone upon the prow of the ship, letting the wind tear through him, numbing him with its icy grip, he knew that this was somehow different—a journey from one age into another. The struggle within was tearing his soul apart, so that he half wished he could stand upon the prow until the wind sucked the life from his body, leaving him frozen, dead, removed forever from care.

The hours passed quietly, the sailing master and crew leaving him alone in silence. Half a dozen times he started to mouth the words of command to order the ship back, but the words would not come, as if the wind had drawn them out of his soul and frozen them into a black eternity.

And finally, at dawn, he could see the high tower, illuminated by the first scarlet light of dawn. And he knew that the Grand Master of Inys Gloi stood atop the battlement awaiting his arrival.

Seth Facinn bowed his head in acknowledgment to the fate that awaited him, and stood silent as the ship passed through the gates to the harbor hidden within.

# CHAPTER 7

"Now tell *them* what you have told me." Zimri pointed to the assembled warriors who, turning from him, looked to the heavyset figure at the other end of the room.

He stood before them dressed in a heavy white parka and wearing the signet and helmet of a commander. In his nervousness he absently rubbed the dull scar that creased his jaw. He looked around the room in what some read as open hostility, but others could see the coldly professional stare of a seasoned battle commander.

"You are Grimath, are you not?" the warrior asked, pointing down the length of the table to the aging warrior who sat next to Zimri.

Grimath nodded in recognition.

"I've fought you twice, first before Cornath, again at Vasilinburg two seasons ago. You're good, your men well disciplined. My compliments on your retreat from Cornath; it was masterful."

Grimath smiled slightly and nodded in acknowledgment.

"Your reputation precedes you, Aldmark," Grimath replied. "I remember you well. But before you tell us what you know, answer me this. Why did you sail so close to our base in a single light corsair—you knew you would be captured, did you not?"

Aldmark looked around the room and saw hostile stares. He knew they were thinking that he was a traitor, and even if he had betrayed the Heretic, he was a traitor nevertheless. The hell with them, they did not understand. Anyhow it didn't matter.

"Yes, I knew that; I knew it full well."

"Then why betray your master?" shouted a thin young monk, dressed in the burgundy robes of the Archbishop of Mord Rinn.

"Now, now, dear brother Demarn, I am not interested in his motivation at this point," Zimri said softly. "Besides, I've already talked to him in private. If I thought he was lying, he would be dead, not talking with you, my assembled commanders and warrior leaders. Go on, Aldmark, tell them."

"I was from Cornath once," Aldmark said, looking defiantly around the room. "I was an acolyte of Mord Rinn, the brotherhood of the Inquisition. I was defrocked, my family and name disgraced. I fled to Mathin and there became a follower of the Heretic, back in the beginning, back when I was young and could still believe. For fifteen years I've fought beside him, led his men, won his battles. But now he has decided to throw it away. Two weeks ago I attended a council meeting and there he announced that before the season is out he shall take his fleets and abandon the north."

A flicker of excitement ran through the room. Several of the men called upon the Saints and cried aloud in joy.

"Silence!" Zimri shouted.

The cries died away.

"Continue, Commander."

"Before the meeting ended the Prophet collapsed in convulsions and was taken from the room. Rumor has spoken of his illness; this confirmed it. The illness has destroyed his will."

Again there was a murmur of excitement. The enemy, the hated enemy, was suffering at the hands of the Saints, who at last were striking him down for his blasphemy.

Zimri did not command silence this time, and let the men talk excitedly among themselves. After several minutes they were aware at last of his silence and turned their attention back to Aldmark, who gazed at them with barely concealed contempt.

"And now, Aldmark, why do you tell us this?"

"He is mad and will throw away the victory earned by the blood of tens of thousands. My men, all of them, died for nothing, and I have been following the vain hope of a fool. I see the folly of my actions. After Michael was removed, wild consternation broke out, with some shouting that the Prophet was mad and dying. Fighting broke out, Daniel drew his blade and injured a ram commander who shouted that the Prophet would soon be dead. At last Daniel had the doors barred and order was restored. Daniel took control of the group and stated that Michael was indeed ill, that his words might have come from the illness. Then Daniel made all swear that not a word of what was said would be repeated."

"Daniel took command?" Grimath asked softly. "But I thought Seth Facinn was his second in command."

Aldmark hesitated for a second. Zimri leaned forward, his features set in an impenetrable mask.

"Yes, that's true," Aldmark replied. "But Facinn was not there, he was nowhere to be found, and it is rumored that he has fled from Michael's side."

"It is of no consequence," Zimri said quickly. "Let's not worry about that now. Most likely he returned when word of Michael's illness reached him."

"Of course," Aldmark replied.

"And the result of the meeting?" Zimri asked.

"The men swore their oaths to follow Daniel's words. But I know the seeds have been sown. Each man is now afraid. We all somehow dreamed that the Messiah was immortal."

"Blasphemy," Demarn shouted. "Even the Saints die to sit at the Long Table and await the return of the Father for the Final Judgment. No one is immortal on this cursed world."

"Enough, brother Demarn, this is not an Inquisition

by Mord Rinn. Time enough for that when we have retaken what is rightfully ours."

Aldmark looked nervously to Demarn, who glowered at him from beneath his cowl.

"With exceptions, of course," Zimri added with a soft chuckle. "And now, Aldmark, your desire from us."

"I came to you for I knew that in spite of Daniel's words the damage was done. The Prophet will die, our cause will disintegrate. I wish to survive and be on the winning side, and to be immune from Mord Rinn's wrath."

As he finished, he stared coldly at Demarn, who returned the killing gaze.

"Reasonable enough. I pledge to you the following for this service—my personal protection from Mord Rinn, a financial reward of one thousand lomans, and a place aboard my ship as we go into action."

Aldmark shifted uneasily. "I've had enough of war and wish not to strike my former comrades."

"But you already have struck your former comrades. Remember, you were once of Cornath. I advise you to take this offer, for there shall be no other."

Aldmark nodded.

"My chart makers will consult you this evening. We wish detailed plans of Cornath's fortifications, troop dispositions, and a full report on fleet locations."

Aldmark hesitated.

"You are in too far already, my dear friend. I think you will agree to serve me in this."

Aldmark looked around the room, took in the cold stares of contempt. He knew he could be dead within seconds. He nodded.

"Good, now leave us." Two guards came out of the shadows, and taking Aldmark by the shoulders, they guided him out of the room.

As he walked down the corridor Aldmark smiled inwardly. They had taken his offer. He had expected the further demands and he would agree in full, but in so doing they would serve him as well. Michael might not die after all. And if Zimri attacked first, thinking Michael weak, the retreat would be out of the question. Let the cursed Zimri attack, for if he did, Ormson would fight in what could only be a pitched battle with full stakes. Ormson would fight, and when he fought again and defeated Zimri he would see the folly of his ways. But most importantly Aldmark's men would not have died in vain, and even in death he would be justified for bringing about the final encounter that would destroy Zimri forever.

"So, my brothers, what say you?"

Demarn stood up and bowed low. Zimri acknowledged the leader of the Inquisition brotherhood.

"It could be a trap. He could be a plant sent by the Heretic to deceive us. Remember, even with the help of Norn"—and so saying he bowed in the direction of the freebooter commander—"we are still outnumbered in ships and warriors. Perhaps this is a trick to lure us into a full confrontation."

Several of the other men nodded in agreement. The wild enthusiasm was replaced by a look of concern on the faces of many, as if they had awakened from a beautiful dream to face the harsh reality of their world.

Zimri nodded knowingly, as if in agreement, and the room fell silent. "And if it is a lie and we attack, what will happen, Grimath?"

"Another battle like Cornath—like the last one—we hurt him but again he comes out on top. But this time I think not."

"Yes?"

"He's spread out. We know of the rebellion in North Prydain. Eldric's fleet has been detached there for service. Elements of the main fleet are stationed at the other ports and serve on convoy duty to the south. He suffers from the classic problem of defense. He has to anticipate action from any quarter and cannot choose the moment of attack. Our roles are reversed. Seven years ago it was we who were divided both physically and in spirit. We know he is divided in arms—if this traitor is telling the truth, he is now divided in spirit as well."

Zimri leaned back for a moment and closed his eyes. Even before the meeting he knew what his action would be. Before he would have given the orders and expected immediate obedience, but he had learned in his years of war that it was best to have the men believe that an action was their will as well. But he had concealed something from the debate—the question of Seth and Inys Gloi. If Michael had truly been foolish enough to announce such a move, the hand of Inys Gloi would be forced. They would quickly kill the Prophet, and then everything would be lost. He had to get to Michael first and strike him down. Trap or not, he would attack, but first the game had to be played out.

He opened his eyes and looked to his battle commanders and the representatives of the half-dozen religious orders that still fought by his side.

"My brothers, I know what I wish, but first I desire your words. Tell me what you want."

Grimath knew his part and what was expected in the charade. He stood up and surveyed his men. A thin smile crossed his face, he grasped his dagger by its silver hilt, held it aloft, then slammed it into the table. "Death to the Heretic!"

After a moment of silence, the men rose to their feet calling Zimri's name as they pulled out daggers and slammed the blades into the table. Zimri listened to their voices and smiled. They were the instruments of his will—the force that shaped his growing power.

"So it shall be—death to the Heretic!" he shouted. "We sail at dawn."

The cold wind of night cut through his robes—its icy fingers probing for any opening that would allow entry. He shivered silently, cursing the chill, and like all of his race lapsed for a moment into quiet, seductive fantasies of heat, of a time when the stories of the Garden were true, a time of warmth, when a man could feel the heat of the sun bake into his bones. He wandered for a moment in the reverie until the calls for a blessing penetrated his consciousness, drawing him back to the responsibility of command.

"The crew of the *Saint Bruce*, they lost half their men last month off North Prydain running weapons in to the rebels," Grimath whispered, prompting Zimri for the appropriate response.

Zimri walked over to the assembled men, who knelt at his approach. He made the Sign of the Arch, and as he did so he looked to the heavens. Directly overhead the silvery band of light cut its line across the midnight sky, while to the north the aurora flickered and snapped in deep indigo and green.

"My special blessing to you, my brothers. For tonight we sail to our final destiny. You served me well before Prydain; I know I can trust you for this next encounter."

The men came to their feet and called his name as he pressed through them extending his hands in blessing. He could feel the surge of power being generated by the enthusiastic warriors. He pushed on through the crowd, his guards clearing the way. The harbor was ablaze with light as a hundred heavy ships of the fleet and the dozens of support craft and heavy battle rams prepared for action. Large rafts scurried across the harbor carrying last-minute supplies. Columns of troops, laden with weapons and gear, marched from the barracks and filed into the dozen heavy transports that would carry them across the frozen sea to battle. Torches lined the decks of many of the ships, and aboard them he saw men lashing down equipment, hoisting supplies aloft, storing away the myriad items necessary to an ice ship going into battle.

As he finally approached his flagship, *Braith du Mor*, a wild chanting filled the air from the ranks of blue-clad monks who made up his elite striking force. He never ceased to marvel over them. Seven years ago most had said that the days of the Cornathian Church were over.

But in this hour of adversity an unending stream of recruits fled from the dominion of the Prophet to the holy vow of the warrior brotherhood of Mor. At times he thought that only in adversity could enthusiasm be generated, for his warriors were consumed by a desire to strike down the Heretic and bring back the rule of Holy Church.

He approached the ship and ascended the ornate ice ladder that had been carved for him. Stepping onto the fighting forecastle, he picked up a flaming torch and held it aloft, signing for silence. From the other ships amassed in the harbor the men broke ranks and crowded forward to hear his words. For long minutes he stood there alone, holding the torch, waiting for them, his followers, until he could see only a sea of upturned faces awaiting his command.

A wild delirium of excitement swept through him. At one time his power had been one of quiet intrigues, played out in darkened cloisters and abbeys. But now . . . now he could sense a different power that intoxicated him with its grandeur. Nearly twenty thousand men gathered around him, all sworn to serve him, and to die, if need be, at his command.

It is almost worth dying for to experience this moment, he thought. To feel the joining of wills into one iron hand. These are *my* men. My moment of supreme confidence. He could almost thank Michael Ormson for the experience, for without Michael it never would have happened. Nothing in this world of Ice—no title, no office, no other human emotion—could compare to this moment, as the thousands waited his command. He half believed that if the battle was a failure, if all was lost and the men died, it would still have been worth it to have felt this moment of supreme control.

"My brothers," he began, "for we are brothers tonight. The world has come full circle at last."

He held his torch high, casting a crackling, shimmering

light that illuminated his features, revealing the scarred face and the blazing light of his eyes.

"It has come full circle. I can imagine, I can *see* that there was a time when the Heretic held such a gathering; some here might have been with him at that moment, and they can remember it. There was a time when *they* were few in number, yet somehow knew that in their hands was the power to take the world as their own. But those days are passed. For here, tonight, a new force has been reborn. The Heretic is in disarray. His men bicker one with another, and our cities, smoldering under his bloody fist, are bursting into flame. And even he, the false one called by some the Prophet, has been stricken by the will of the Saints, so that he languishes from a dreadful pestilence."

A murmur swept through the assembled men, and he allowed it to continue. He felt it was time they should know for it would strike down the superstitious fear of the Prophet that many had.

"Yes, Michael Ormson is merely a man as ourselves, and God does not speak to him as many now claim. He is a man, nothing more, and the Saints have willed him to die.

"My brothers, most likely you have already guessed our mission. We sail tonight for Cornath. We sail to meet the Prophet's home fleet. We sail to retake that Holy City which was the birthplace of our sacred brotherhoods. And most important, we sail tonight to deliver the deathblow to the Prophet and to bring a rebirth of our Blessed Church."

A wild cheer went up from the men as they called out Zimri's name.

The roar of their voices washed over him in waves, and he gloried in the moment, letting it sweep him along in its wild enthusiasm. After several minutes he held his hands aloft, then gestured for all to kneel.

Grimath brought up another torch and, holding one in each hand, Zimri extended his arms to bless the men.

"For as it is written in the Holy of Holies, 'The Saints shall prepare a place for thee, and know ye that in the hour of thy sacrifice they shall watch over thee and guide thee to the Long Table of the Blessed. Know ye that life is but an illusion, that the Ice is our punishment, and all who keep faith shall sit at the Table of Feasting until the Return of the Father.'"

"Amen."

"The hour of our trial has come at last, for there is no turning back. All shall be decided or lost forever in the days to come. Go forth with belief in the One True Faith, in the communion of the Saints, and in the supremacy of the Sacred Confederation of Cornath. Go, my children, to war with a light heart, for in this hour shall come the redemption of our Church from the darkness, and with it our Salvation.

"I bless you in the name of the Saints and, as Holy See, I absolve you of all sins, so that at the moment of battle ye shall be pure. Go ye to battle assured of Salvation and the Feast Everlasting. Amen."

The men looked up at him, awaiting his command.

The wind whipped his robes, causing the torches to flare and shift with wild fluctuations of light. He looked again to the sacred Arch, and for the moment he again believed—in spite of all that he knew—for one brief moment he believed. And his heart was filled with a wild, religious ecstasy.

"Prepare your ships!" he cried. "We sail within the hour, for the Saints are with us!"

"The Saints are with us!" the men cried. And some of them called out that Zimri, who stood before them, was already a Saint incarnate, walking in the form of mortal man.

From the shadows a distant shimmering form emerged. Slowly it came into focus. Yes, he could see her, dressed in her favorite robe of burgundy—her dark, flowing hair tied back with a light-blue ribbon.

"Janis?"

She nodded gravely and then a soft, gentle smile flickered across her face. A smile that had greeted him so many times when he had returned after a voyage, to be met first by a stern look of admonishment over his lengthy absence until her angry resolve finally broke and she ran into his arms.

"Janis?"

She walked from the shadows and he rushed to embrace her. The delirium tumbled into confusion—he could imagine the wild embrace, the playful talk, and then the mounting passion as they took delight in each other's bodies. He stopped, his hands extended, fingertips almost brushing her face.

"But no—you're dead, Janis. Dead and lost forever."

She shook her head, and by her side another form appeared. Andrew looked up at him and smiled, his five-year-old eyes alight with joy. He was still five, forever five, frozen in eternal childhood.

Crying out with joy, he advanced to them, but they floated back and away, tantalizingly out of reach, and yet so real.

"Michael, my love," she whispered softly, "don't. Don't rush to me, not yet."

He stopped, looking at them, trying to fill his mind with their image and they started to fade back into the shadows.

"Janis!"

A rough hand was on his shoulders, shaking him, calling from another world.

"Michael, please!—Michael, don't!"

An old familiar, rancid smell came to him. He opened his eyes to a large, bulky shadow leaning over him. The gnarled, heavy features came into focus.

"I had a dream," Michael whispered, "it was only a dream."

The old warrior was silent for a moment. "Yes, I know. I heard you talking to her."

Michael was silent. The dream faded from his consciousness—the momentary joy slipped away.

"Why are you here, Daniel?"

"Do you know how long it's been, Michael?"

"No, what do you mean?"

"You've been in bed for nearly two weeks this time. We thought for a couple of days that we would lose you."

He climbed out of the bed and his legs buckled beneath him. Daniel put him back on the bed. Wrapping the blankets around Michael's shivering form, Daniel picked him up like a child and carried him to a chair by the huge stove. Opening the stove door, Daniel tossed in an armful of logs and let the fire brighten the room.

"Two weeks?" Michael whispered.

"Aye, Master. Since the night of the meeting."

Two weeks. So much could have happened. He could remember the wild chaos, the shadowy presence, and then the room spinning away into darkness. "What has happened? Do the men know?"

Daniel shook his head sadly. "Rumors have spread. In the streets some claim you are dead. There has been rioting in nearly every city, triggered the moment your illness was made known. The sparks of North Prydain have flared across the north. And there is more to deal with as well. I've detailed over half our men and ships to try and hold things in check, but we're hard pressed and there's yet worse news."

"Go on," Michael said wearily, "what is it?"

"Michael, there's plague," Daniel whispered with superstitious fear, as if the mere mention of the word could cause him to succumb.

The plague. The memories of childhood flooded back for a moment—the death carts in the street, the anguished cries of the dying, and then the worst nightmare of all. His mother and father, dead, and his clinging to their frozen, bloated forms until his uncle came to take him away.

"The first cases were reported in the city this morning,"

Daniel said haltingly, "but it's been reported in Dulyn, Caediff, and North Prydain as well. It's spreading like fire. The preachers of Cornath are claiming that it is the punishment of the Saints."

"They would," Michael said, his voice hard and cold. "Everything is the punishment of the Saints, and the mob believes them."

"They claim it shows the anger of the Saints. If someone dies against us, he will not suffer plague death, and any who come back to the Church will be saved."

"The damn fools, can't they see Cornathians dying from this as well?"

"It doesn't matter. If you die it's because you really did not believe, that's what they are saying."

"Damn them and their religion. I thought people would see the charade once it was shown to them."

"They think you are losing command, Michael, and they want to be on the winning side. Besides, your wild talk about abandoning the Cornathian cities has shaken the morale of our commanders."

"It wasn't wild talk," Michael said weakly.

Daniel looked at him carefully and Michael could sense the disapproval.

"Go on," he said wearily, "tell me what you are thinking."

"After you collapsed and were carried out, I barred the doors. Michael, I took command. If you find fault in that then tell me, but I know I did the right thing."

"And what did you do with this power?" Michael asked.

"I told them you were sick, Michael. That the illness had weakened you. I told them that we would fight and hold on and that you would agree to that."

Michael could feel his anger rising. How dare he? He started to stand up, a torrent of rage building up inside of him, but his body would not follow his commands and he collapsed back into his chair. He raged at himself feebly, beating his fist against the arm of the chair until the flesh was bruised and purple.

"How dare you countermand me!"

"I dare not do otherwise," Daniel said evenly. "If I had not, you would have awoken to an empty palace, your allies gone and only the Companions left to serve you. Eldric would have gone over for sure. As it is, there is more than enough bad news. Norn deserted Eldric— we got the word last week. He's gone over to Zimri, taking his men and ships. Eldric is wild with rage and demands revenge. If you show any weakness now, Eldric will declare himself neutral and pull out. That is why I dare to go against you."

Michael looked at Daniel, his rage flickering out. So often in the past it was sufficient. So often had Daniel bowed to his wishes and served without question.

With a shocking swiftness Daniel leaned over and grabbed Michael by the shoulders.

"Damn it, Michael, listen to me. You are in trouble. You might be dying from this illness. Even if you survive, your cause is in deathly peril. This rebellion is taxing us to the limits; we can barely hold our own against it. We must be strong. Now is no time to talk of retreat. Thousands are dying out there right now because of you. Remember that."

"Never do I forget it," Michael whispered.

"You must show yourself to your men," Daniel said coldly. "Bring back to them the confidence you could once give. Remember when we set out, a mere handful to defy the entire church, and we won. We can do it again."

Michael looked at Daniel and smiled sadly.

"If only you truly understood."

"What do you mean?"

"Nothing," he said, his voice sounding lost and distant.

"And Seth, tell me of Seth," Michael asked, changing the direction of the conversation.

"Gone."

Then he had left after all.

Daniel looked at Michael, wanting to ask, but after

long seconds he decided against it, not wanting to know the truth.

"Michael," Daniel whispered, "you have to go out to your men and speak to them. If this retreat is in your heart, and is your plan, please say nothing of it at the moment. In the spring there will be time enough to consider it. But not now. If we try to pull out now, we'll be overrun. As it stands now, the entire fleet, except for Eldric's, is returning to Cornath early next week to pick up more supplies and men. We need to show a strong face at that time, to set our enemies off guard and to encourage our men and allies. Please trust me in this, Michael. I'm begging you."

"In a world without trust, you ask me to trust you," Michael said softly.

He looked into Daniel's eyes and could see the pain that his words had created. "Forgive me."

A faint smile flickered across Daniel's face. "Between us there is nothing to forgive."

For the first time in years Michael felt as if there were no defenses left, and leaning out of the chair, he embraced his friend.

# CHAPTER 8

A STRANGE, SURREAL SENSE OF URGENCY HAD BROKEN HIM free of his meditation—a growing fear that took him from the high chamber out onto the battlement that towered five hundred feet above the frozen sea. And he saw in the light dawning in the east a solitary craft running close-hauled into the wind.

A single figure stood upon the bow of the ship, his white robes whipping in the wind, and at that moment Riadent knew that the final moment of decision and crisis had arrived. Seth had returned for orders to kill Michael.

Two weeks had since passed, and some inner voice was telling Riadent it had been two weeks too long. He should have acted alone at once, but faced with the final monumental decision he hesitated. It had to be meditated upon for one last time. It had to be reviewed in the collective mind of all the brothers locked in the meditation, in the joining of wills wherein the path was made clear to the hidden priests of Inys Gloi.

It was time to see Seth and to tell him—but the telling was mere ritual, for Seth had joined them in meditation as well and knew what the decision would be. Even now, he was making his final preparation, as Riadent had demanded.

Seth drifted through the darkened corridor, guided by a single flickering torch that shone at the end of the long, secret hallway. Nearly two-score years ago this section had been prepared for the Prophet who had slipped from their grasp. Here the brothers were to have kept Michael, to train him for his task, and to perform the final indoctrinations that would make him the true Prophet of Inys Gloi. But that was gone now—the moment lost through circumstance. He thought about that for a moment—was it truly circumstance that had let Michael slip away from them to reach another destiny? But his training forced the thoughts away; there was no logic in pondering such things now.

But the rooms at the end of the corridor were not empty. Another vessel was being prepared in them, and he would at last come face to face with the new force of destiny that Inys Gloi was weaving.

As he reached the single door at the end of the corridor, the hooded guards stepped aside and opened the door for Seth Facinn, and without a word of acknowledgment he entered the room.

Turing from the fireplace, she pulled back her hooded cloak and bowed curtly. "Ah, Seth, if you have come to see me, then I must assume that the time has come at last."

"You, if any, should know, Varinna. You were always quite capable of getting the information you wanted."

Shaking her head, she laughed sadly. "Not I, Seth. I am nothing more than a mother now. They no longer need my body or my mind for more exciting details."

He walked over to the fire, such a rare sight, and an honor that surprised him. Only the Grand Master had such a luxury in his chamber. Extending his one hand, he warmed it in the glowing heat.

"Have you been sent here to tell me something?" she asked softly.

"No, just to see Thomas, that's all. The Grand Master requested I do so before meeting again with him."

"And why should you see Thomas now? You've been here a hundred times, no doubt, since his birth, and not once did I see you. Remember, Seth, one could say that you were influential in his conception." She laughed coldly, taunting him with her eyes.

"I need not be reminded. I did what had to be done and so did you."

"I felt at times that you truly loved Michael. Tell me, Seth, throughout the time I was with him, did you ever think of Michael and what would happen to him?"

"And who are you to ask?" Seth replied, his voice edged with anger.

"Just curious. You see, Seth, I believe that the reason you are here is because you will be the final traitor—it has been decided that you will kill him."

He tried to stare her down but it was useless—her cold, penetrating eyes cut into his soul—and he turned away.

"Get the child," he whispered, his voice cold and husky.

She came up to his side and touched his hand. "You do love him," she whispered.

"And who are you to judge love?" he shouted. "You're nothing but a harlot recruited from the gutter to serve Inys Gloi. You've sold your body to the highest bidder." He backed away from her and even as he did so he braced himself for an explosive response, but none came.

She looked at him sadly. "If only you understood, Seth Facinn. I sold myself to the highest bidder, and so have you. We are alike, my friend."

"Get the child."

She turned away and left him alone in the room. After several minutes he heard their approach, and turning, he looked into the eyes of Thomas Michaelson.

Yes, the same light is there, he thought. The same light I saw over twenty years ago. He closely examined the boy, who gazed back at him with a quiet, confident stare. Michael's paternity was written on the boy, but the child bore a coldness as well, unlike Andrew, the first son, who had inherited the vivacious charm of his mother. Thomas was different, far different, and in his eyes Seth could make out a wary glint of calculation, born perhaps of a life in the dark cloister of Inys Gloi.

Finally he turned to examine the bodyguard, and his attention was suddenly riveted.

"Yes, Seth," the priest said quietly, "we've met before. I am Nathan of Cornath. I served briefly in the Companions and was assigned for a while to Daniel's command."

"And all along you were of Inys Gloi. Why did I not know?"

"Ah, that came later. I was yet to be recruited." Nathan watched his reaction closely, but Seth turned his attention away.

He looked back to Thomas, who was examining him with patient, adultlike eyes.

"Thomas, do you know who your father is?"

"Yes."

"And where is he?"

"Out there." Thomas pointed vaguely. "He is the Prophet."

"And you, Thomas, what are you?"

"I shall be a Prophet as well."

"Who's told you this?"

"The Grand Master. He has told me many things."

"Your time is coming, Thomas. My name is Seth the Far Seeing, and soon I shall stand at your side."

"But what about Nathan? Will he come, too?"

Seth looked at Nathan and could see the faint tracing of a smile on his lips.

"Yes, no doubt he will."

Seth looked back at Varinna. "I must leave. The Grand Master awaits me."

Varinna nodded to Nathan, who, taking the boy's hand, guided him out of the room.

She looked at Seth and smiled softly as the door closed behind her son.

"And what of you in all of this, Seth? I've often wondered. For a thousand years Inys Gloi has planned and waited for the moment when it will take control. But after you have it, what then?"

Seth was silent.

"I know that you hated me, Seth. I know that you hated what we did to Michael, but your hand was in it as well. You knew Janis was the key problem between Inys Gloi and Michael. And I know, Seth, that you were somehow aware of her coming assassination but did nothing to stop it."

Seth looked away from her.

"It had to be an agent of Inys Gloi that blocked the escape door—one of your own men."

Seth started to walk from the room.

"And you say that I sold myself for the highest bidder. What about you? Michael trusted you, Seth. Can you ever tell him that Janis's blood is on your hands? When I first came to Michael, he was nothing to me, nothing but a task set by my masters."

"At first?" Seth said softly, turning to look back at Varinna.

She nodded slowly, looking into his eyes.

"But there has been no one since, has there, Varinna? Every time you look at Thomas, you see someone else, don't you?"

She smiled softly. "Ah, we wound each other in this little encounter, don't we?"

"Go to hell, bitch. You did what had to be done, and now I must do the same. From the beginning I have served but one cause—Inys Gloi. Michael fulfilled the Prophecies that we had made and spread. I am the servant of those Prophecies. Now, at last, it is my duty to fulfill the Final Prophecy."

"And that life which He has spared will in the end guide Him to the end."

Seth looked at her in surprise.

"Yes, I have seen the Book of Prophecies, thirty-seven pennod, verse three. Michael saved your life once, so that in the end you would have the power to take it."

"And I shall."

"And tell me, Seth, after you have killed him, what then for you?"

Without answering, he started for the door. He stepped into the corridor and then, at the last moment, looked back at her.

"And the same for you as well. After he is dead and the power has been transferred, your life is meaningless."

"Of that I am sure," she said softly.

"Stand, Seth Facinn, and hear my command."

Rising from the kneel, Seth looked at the veiled form of the Grand Master.

"I sent you first to the child before coming to me; do you understand why?"

"To see if he has the power of the father."

"And your judgment on this."

"He is not his father, at least, not now. There was an innocence to Michael when I found him. Thomas has already lost that."

"It's his mother, of course. Michael was the one we wanted from the beginning, all the Prophecies said so, but fate intervened three times with things we did not foresee. First his father's not bringing the child to us as was promised. Then the kidnapping by Rifton. And finally the woman Janis. At three crucial points we lost the one that destiny set into our hands. Those moments have passed, and the plans of a thousand years now hang in the balance. But through the son we can yet regain our goal and bring our One True Catholic Order into the power that it has awaited across the endless millennia. The son will serve, even if the matching of the mother was not completely to our wishes. That is what I wanted you to see. I ask you now, can the boy take the place of his father?"

"He will have to."

Riadent looked closely at Seth; the strain upon Facinn was obvious. Riadent was tempted to forbid his ever leaving the fortress again, but Seth was the only one who could reach Michael and perform the task in the manner required. He would have to do.

"I await your command," Seth whispered.

"You already know it, Seth the Farseeing."

"Michael must die."

"And it will be by your hand."

Seth wavered for a second and Riadent watched him closely.

Seth looked back into Riadent's eyes. "It is the command of the Brotherhood, therefore I must obey. Only I can kill him, since it was I who helped to create him and all that he has become. It must be I, for I alone have prepared him."

"So it must be," Riadent replied. "Sail within the hour. You must strike quickly; I fear our good friend Zimri might be acting as well. I suspect he will try to take Michael first."

Seth hesitated for a moment.

"Is there something else?" Riadent asked.

Seth looked straight through Riadent as if he was not there. "No, there is nothing else. When I return, Michael Ormson will be dead. The way will have been prepared. Our hour will have come."

Riadent nodded slowly, allowing a smile to crease his face.

"There is one last thing," Seth continued coldly.

"And that is?"

"We have prepared a thousand years for this moment when we retake control. It has been the reason for our existence for fifty generations. But after the goal has been taken, what then?"

Riadent looked away for a moment. He could not confide what he thought. "We will rule, of course. As has always been our destiny."

"But of course," Seth replied.

\* \* \*

"Heave away, there. Haul in that jib sheet. Lively now, lively."

Zimri stepped aside as the crew responded to the commands of the foremast sailing master and set to tightening in the sails. All across the deck and in the riggings above, the sail crews strained to their task, as the crew pressed for every bit of power that could be squeezed from the brisk northwesterly breeze. As the sails were tightened down, the *Braith du Mor* gradually hiked up on its downwind runners, so that the deck was steeply canted, and even the seasoned hands had to grasp a railing or rope for support. Belowdecks the gun crews labored at their practice. One of the starboard twenty-four pounders recoiled with a thunderous roar—a quick puff of smoke eddied clear of the hull and was snapped away by the wind. Two hundred yards away the target raft exploded in a brilliant flash of light and, snapping free of its towrope, tumbled out of control. The small corsair that had been dragging the target quickly came about and started to run up the wind to recover the wreckage.

Zimri looked at Grimath and smiled softly.

"I still do not understand it," Grimath whispered in awe.

"Brother Andersson called it a fulminate of mercury. Our armorments people consulted Balor, leader of the First Choice, and it was decided that the information had to be released. Andersson explained it to me and said that when this substance strikes a hard surface, it explodes, and can ignite the new type of powder that is packed into a hollowed cannonshot. It's deadly at close range—why, these new shells will blow out a whole section of deck. One hit against a ram and the ram is destroyed. If it strikes a heavier ship at any point near the magazine, the ship will explode. Think of that, Grimath, one shot destroying an entire ship. It's one of the keys to our winning."

"But how did the leader of the First Choice know of such things?"

"That is not your concern, my dear Grimath."

Bowing low to the Holy See, Grimath returned to his duties.

Zimri looked astern to where the target raft was now nothing more than distant smoldering embers. As defender of the First Choice it had been his sworn duty to make sure that no knowledge of the past arts, and the cursed sciences, should ever be revealed. But his was a time of crisis, and in defiance of the very laws he was sworn to defend, he decided to use whatever means necessary to bring about victory. Ormson would do it, and now so must he. The glass for seeing far was one; the special powder and exploding shells yet another. If other things were required, then so it must be.

The sails having been secured, Zimri again had the foredeck to himself and he paced the slanting deck in solitude. The final attack orders had been given in the morning council—evening was approaching but they would sail through the night. By morning Cornath would be in sight and, if the Saints were with them, battle would be joined in a surprise attack. The few picket ships of the Prophet had been swept up before they could spread the warning. The report from the spy ships appeared to be correct. Michael was spread too thin—his fleet scattered to suppress the rebellion in the northern cities. Only the home fleet was in Cornath—a fleet that still outnumbered him two to one, but with surprise and luck, victory could be his.

The sun was already setting, and as darkness spread across the ice, the ships closed up their formation. Zimri watched in quiet fascination. His entire fleet, everything, was to be gambled on this one roll. If the information he had received was part of an elaborate trap, then this time tomorrow he would be dead—along with the final remnants of the Cornathian Church.

Something else as well remained to be concerned with. Their approach to Cornath would take them within sight of Inys Gloi. He had planned it as a show of defiance toward the Grand Master. But if the Grand Master merely laughed, knowing that Zimri's efforts were already too late? . . .

# CHAPTER 9

HE FOLLOWED DANIEL'S ADVICE AFTER ALL, AND THE THOUGHT troubled him. No further mention was made of withdrawal, even though the fleet commanders knew what was in his heart. They gathered their shipping together, drew up outside the harbor wall in preparation for the morning sail, ready to carry reinforcements to the beleaguered garrisons throughout the northward holdings.

The dream still haunted Michael—Janis had come again in the night, Andrew by her side. Her ghostly presence was so real that he cried out her name in a loud, piercing voice, but only Daniel had responded to his call.

And something else came in the dream—a clear sense of foresight, but he kept its counsel to himself.

As evening passed across the frozen sea, they had seen the ship coming to harbor. Overhead the Arch was already casting its pale, shimmering light, and in spite of the golden band of luminescence to the west, the pale greens and reds of the aurora could already be made out in the northern sky. Many of the ice runners of his fleet looked to the lights and talked one to the other, for such intensity of light so early in the evening was taken by many to be a Sign. But Michael Ormson made no comment. Commanding Daniel to see to the final preparations of the fleet, he retired to his chamber, which had once been the office of his uncle. And there, alone, he awaited the arrival of his old, trusted friend.

And a hundred leagues away, in a high tower, Riadent of Inys Gloi knelt before the altar, bowing low. In preparation for the long night of waiting he filled the censer with incense brought from beyond the Flowing Sea. Soon the high chapel was cloaked in wavery clouds of impenetrable smoke.

"Come in, my friend. I have been expecting you."

The door opened slowly and a tall slender form, concealed beneath dark billowing robes still covered in ice, drifted slowly into the room. Pulling back his high peaked hood, the ice runner removed his goggles and face mask. His face was creased and weary; the normally smooth face was now stubbled with flecks of gray, which covered his deep hollow cheeks. Using his one hand, Seth Facinn unclasped the heavy parka, tossed it over a high-backed chair, and came to sit by Michael's side.

Without even looking at Seth, Michael continued to poke at the fire with a long stick whose end was slowly charring.

"'Tis already a cold night out," Seth said wearily, as he eased into his chair. "You should bank that up if you wish to be warm tonight."

Michael looked absently at Seth and smiled softly. "I can remember the first time I saw an open fire burning like this. It was in Mathin, and I was amazed at the waste of precious wood. I wonder what Rifton would say to this indulgence—a place to burn wood installed in his old office. What would he say?" His voice trailed off into a whisper.

"Does it really matter?"

"Perhaps it does, but that is not the question for now. You went to Inys Gloi, didn't you?"

Seth nodded.

"You left when you thought I was dying."

"You don't really believe that," Seth replied coldly.

Leaning back, Michael looked at the ceiling. The images of the Saints and the Long Table looked down at him, painted centuries ago by a forgotten hand, and he contemplated them carefully. How many times had he seen Rifton do the same when considering some serious question.

"No, I don't think so. You went because of what I said, that I wanted to reach some accommodation with Zimri. You went for orders regarding me."

Seth did not answer this time.

"In your silence I read that what I say is true."

"You've always known that Inys Gloi was behind you and that I was the necessary link."

"But something is changed between Inys Gloi and me, is it not?"

"How so?"

"I've known from the beginning that my actions were never my own. It is the age-old question—is all this preordained, or do we merely stumble blindly through an existence without purpose or meaning? I've felt that much of mine has been charted, but not, perhaps, as some have foreseen. I now contemplate the final direction, and it defies what has been planned."

Seth looked into Michael's eyes. The old look was back again for the moment—deep, powerful, and all-penetrating, as if he could tear into one's soul and rip out the truth that was hidden. There was still a power in Michael that was beyond fathoming, and it held sway over Seth even now.

What indeed was real? Was Michael the dream of Inys Gloi, or was Inys Gloi merely the tool of Michael? Seth experienced a growing fear in Michael's presence. He was part of Michael, but Inys Gloi had held him long before.

"What is it that you are thinking, Seth?" Michael asked softly.

He felt he was drifting in a nightmare, and Michael's words snapped him back. It had to be now, he had sworn on the altar of his forefathers that this must be done.

"Many things," Seth replied, his voice cracking.

"Would you care for a drink first?" Michael said, still looking into Seth's eyes.

"Yes, yes, that would be good. Let me fetch one for you as well."

Standing up, Seth went to the side cabinet in the rear of the room where the Yarwinder was kept. Looking back, he saw Michael staring vacantly into the fire. With trembling hand he pulled out Michael's favorite goblet—a simple cup of gold, given to him long ago by Zardok. The days, the years of contemplating the moment were finished; the dreaded moment had arrived. The packet was emptied; the drink poured. Silently he returned to Michael's side and offered the chalice.

Again Michael looked at Seth while he took the goblet from his hand.

"Do you remember, Seth, a night we spent out on the Ice when first I sailed in Halvin's fleet? On that night you revealed to me that I would one day be the Prophet, that from my hand would come the great change, the new renaissance that would awaken man from his slumber."

Seth nodded slowly, remembering a scared young acolyte who had yet to face his destiny.

"And I remember what I felt that night. Let this bitter cup pass from my lips. Let me not drink of the power that could be. For I knew in my heart what would come of it. Hundreds of thousands dead, a way of life—an entire world—destroyed, all because of me. Any that I loved or would ever love would be destroyed by my hand. And that vision was true, Seth, all of it true. Oh yes, the changing of the age has come, to be sure, but for me and all who followed my words and dreams, nothing has been but destruction and despair.

"Nothing but destruction and despair," he whispered. "I've set the wheel in motion and it has crushed all in its path, including me. I am called the *Messiah*, the *Prophet*, but it gives nothing save ashes, bitter ashes. That is the cup you brought me long ago, my friend. But tonight is different. I take this cup, I call you my friend, and now I shall drink deeply of it."

So saying, Michael Ormson brought the goblet to his lips, and Seth's eyes grew wide with terror.

The smoky clouds swirled around the altar. Dimly perceived through the high, paned window, the explosive kaleidoscope filled the northern sky, illuminating the room with scarlet shades.

All was silent except for the deep, distant chanting of the brothers in the chapel below. Not told, they nevertheless sensed what the night would bring. The threads of destiny are like a web, each strand supporting the whole. Each strand weaving in and out in patterns of such complexity to be beyond mere mortal comprehension. Yet in the moments of oneness he could dimly comprehend. For tonight the weavings of centuries came together as one. A single thread could now bind the whole, and its parting would release the future to them.

He could see it. Yes, he could see it swirling in the smoke. The face he had never seen shimmered before him with the cup to his lips.

"Drink and forget, Michael Ormson. But we shall call you the Messiah, as we once did for another. Your words shall be Sacred, your actions Holy, and we your priesthood shall again be the center of power, as it was planned for in the beginning, and now, forever shall be.

"Drink and live forever."

The power of the moment was upon him, and as it swept him up in its intensity, he willed his energy to Seth, pushing him over the edge. And in that moment, his power strained to the utmost, the room was suddenly flooded in blinding light, so that he swooned and fell away into darkness.

"No!!!"

With a crashing blow Seth smashed the cup out of Michael's hand, spraying its contents across the room.

In quiet amazement Michael looked up at Seth. Their gazes held for a moment—the two wills locked together. With a strangled cry Seth turned away, slamming his fist into the lintel over the fireplace. In blind, furious rage he struck again and again, so that flecks of blood ran down the wall to explode in metallic steam as they met the hot coals. Michael, as if lost in a dream, watched in silence. From a great distance he suddenly perceived that the doorway was framed with guards, Daniel at the lead, looking in at the strange drama being enacted.

"Michael?"

Silently he shook his head, signaling them to leave.

"Michael, there was a light—a light crossed the heavens."

"I know," Michael whispered.

They withdrew.

"I should have left with the light, shouldn't I?" Michael said sadly.

Wild-eyed, Seth looked back at him. "You knew."

"But of course, in fact, I almost welcomed it. It was release, an end to it all, the coming of the long sleep."

"You knew," Seth whispered, backing away, a trace of fear crossing his features.

Michael nodded his head slowly. "I was too dangerous for Inys Gloi; it was the only way for them to respond."

Stunned, Seth wavered. He was now the traitor to both sides.

"It is finished then, this unwritten covenant between my creators and me."

"You know the rest as well?"

"I suspected after a while, but what could I do? If I confronted you, then you would only know, and besides, at times I no longer cared."

"Then you knew that your illness was not a cancer, that for the last five years I have been slowly poisoning you?"

Wearily Michael looked away—all the pain, the slow

wasting, the clouding of the senses. "I suspected, but I wanted to believe it was not *you*, Seth."

Numbly Seth looked at his bleeding, shattered hand.

Standing up, Michael started to walk toward Seth, extending his arms in a sad, weary gesture of compassion. But Seth backed away.

"I helped to create you," Seth whispered. "And I came to believe. Now I *know* you truly are the One, that you shall destroy the Brotherhood that created you."

"And you could have stopped me, but you can't now. If Zimri defeats me, then Inys Gloi shall lose, and if I live, they shall lose. And it is your fault, Seth Facinn. But then, you always knew it would be."

Michael's words tore into his soul. And in his heart Seth understood that he had always known he would fail in his mission to kill the Prophet.

"You will have to leave me forever, Seth. You can return to your brothers. Tell them that you were discovered, that I outguessed you. To spare your life, out of respect for what we once were to each other, I shall say no different."

"They will send others—as many as necessary."

"I have Daniel and some of the Companions. I know that Daniel was once a brother as well, but he is with me now. I know that our first meeting was arranged—that Daniel was assigned by Inys Gloi as my protector and trainer, but I know as well that Daniel renounced them long ago, after Janis, for he suspected, and rightfully so, that your brotherhood had a hand in the act to bring me back under their control."

Seth stood rigid, almost catatonic—the shock of what was happening washing over him.

Michael walked up to Seth and touched him lightly on the shoulder.

"I've loved you, Seth. I always will. Without you I would have been lost. As I prepared to drink, I decided that I should let destiny decide. I let it act through you. All these years you've spoken of destiny, and now I shall let it lead me to whatever end. I asked death to take me tonight, to end it, and it would not. I shall take that as a sign and shall continue."

Numbly Seth nodded.

"Before you go, I want to know something."

"What?"

"Who is Inys Gloi?"

"A light! It is a sign, a sign!"

Rushing up on deck, Zimri could see the blazing tail of fire disappearing over the eastern horizon. Many of the crew were on their knees, calling on the Saints, and in their fear they looked to him for its interpretation.

A dim flash lit the far horizon. A Saint had fallen from the Arch, but why? He felt a moment of dread. Perhaps the act had been completed, perhaps this was indeed a Sign. In doubt, he turned away for a moment until a soft whisper drew his attention back.

"My lord, quickly, the men look to you."

He turned to see the hooded form of Demarn the Inquisitioner.

"Something has happened," Zimri whispered.

"I don't care what it is," Demarn hissed, "but the men."

"Tell them something, anything," Zimri replied, his thoughts paralyzed with fear, and turning, he went back below.

In the distance he could hear Demarn calling that it was an omen of good—the light traveled from west to east, showing that their fleet was carrying the fire of victory. A ragged cheer swept the deck, but to Zimri it was nothing. He feared that Michael was already dead, or worse.

"They are the first brotherhood," Seth said softly.

"Go on, tell me all, Seth, as your final act to me."

Seth nodded wearily, and slumping into the chair, he stared into the fire.

"The Accident. First the Accident, as we of the brotherhood know it. Man was reaching to the stars. He had machines of immense power and strength that took him to the heavens. In the heavens, on a world that sailed in the night, they tested a machine of strength unimagined—a machine to take them to the lights of the stars. And something went wrong, what it was we'll never know. But the machine destroyed itself, and so potent was its power that it shattered the very world it was placed upon—thus destroying the world that lit our night sky. From that destruction was the Arch created.

"Man then turned his weapons upon his neighbors in blind panic as remnants of that lost world rained down upon the Earth, forever changing the face of the land. And the sun disappeared from the sky, so dark was the smoke. We should have been destroyed but somehow we were not. Throughout all of this there was one entity, one institution that survived—the Church."

"The Church?"

"Their power goes back long before the Accident. At one time their dream was almost complete, for they nearly controlled all in the name of a Prophet. In the retelling of his story he has become associated with the Sun of the Night, the Chosen of the Father. We destroyed him with our folly and our machines, and for that it is taught that the Father has abandoned this world.

"A thousand years it took man to come out of the darkness, and our Sacred Brotherhood, now living on the island of Inys Gloi, relived its role from times past, keeping the knowledge and guiding mankind back from the edge of extinction. But as the numbers of men increased, so did those in the brotherhood, so that soon new orders were founded and dissension arose over doctrine and methods. So it has always been. Finally came the Council of Cornath, a thousand years ago. There was decided the First Choice.

"To suppress all knowledge until man had evolved enough to safely hold the power.

"Yes, but there came the split as well. The various

leaders broke one with another, and of the original followers of our Brotherhood, few were left. We were the Father, but we gave all our strength to our sons, who would not listen any longer to our counsel or accept our leadership. So we retreated unto ourselves, abandoned by those we had nurtured, and have lived alone for the last thousand years, awaiting our return to supreme power.

"We held some knowledge of the Before Time, which we suppressed. But we had learned new arts as well. We learned of the collective meditation. The joining of wills, so that dimly we could see the future. We learned the art of reading the stars and the patterns they reveal concerning the destiny not only of men but of entire races. And we learned the Great Secret—that the year of man is divided into twelve signs. Twelve signs equal the passage of a year, but they reveal that there are twelve Great Ages, as well—each equal to two thousand years. Four thousand years ago there had been the Change, and from it our brotherhood was formed. Two thousand years ago was yet another change in the sign of water which is frozen, and now your sign and this New Age which started the night you were born."

"And I?"

"We knew a thousand years ago that at the ending of the cycle a great change would come. Through hundreds of years, we, the Hidden Brotherhood, came to perceive that a teacher would be born. Remember, Michael, the seers and prophets can see the future, but to insure the future we act to bring it about as well, and so we acted. We created the Book of Prophecies, we established the hidden cults which the other brotherhoods could not wipe out, and we knew at last that through your family would the Prophet be born."

"My father, then."

"Red Orm was one of us and so was your mother, and so for a while, before he betrayed us, was your uncle."

"Rifton was of Inys Gloi?"

"I shall come to that. For the Prophecies to be fulfilled,

you needed to be of Cornath, and so you were born there. I stood guard upon your house that night, I heard your first cry, and I wept with joy at your coming. For Inys Gloi knew that if we could create you, if we could guide you, then through you we would take the power of the Earth that was ours, and one day hold the reins of man's destiny. Then the Garden would return.

"But fate hides all its cards from us. In your fifth year came the plague, and in one week your entire family was dead, the guards of Inys Gloi, dead. I was sent to find you, to bring you back to Inys Gloi, but your uncle betrayed us. He feared you and the power we would seize. He took you from your dead father's arms and hid you in the monastery. There you lived until one of ours tricked Zimri into having you released. Rifton's guard was down; he had let it be known that you were dead and thought that we had forgotten. But Rifton did not know our power. Rifton did not know that I was still alive and would be waiting. The rest, you know."

"My father as well," Michael replied sadly.

"You are beyond us now. We did not see—fate hid the final moves—that you would not be ours. Why did fate hide all from us?"

"Perhaps because it was willed."

Seth looked up at Michael. "Do you believe that?"

Michael only smiled softly.

Slowly Seth regained his feet. "I've often thought, we have dreamed this dream for a thousand years, it has been the one desire of our Brotherhood. I have often wondered, did we ever truly think what would happen to us after the long dream had ended? For sixty years I've lived the dream of Inys Gloi, but now it is gone for me. Gone forever."

With his crippled hand he tried to drape his parka over his shoulders. Michael came forward to help but Seth beckoned him away. Grimacing with pain, he drew on the heavy sealskin.

"I have your leave to go then?"

"I shall not harm you."

"I shall go back then to the only thing I have left, my Holy Brotherhood."

Turning away from Michael, he started for the door. "You know the rest then—Zimri, Varinna and Thomas, and of Janis?"

Michael looked away from Seth.

"And Janis too, you knew what was going to happen?" he whispered.

But there was no answer, only the gentle closing of the door as Seth Facinn, called the Far Seeing, disappeared into the darkness.

# CHAPTER 10

"SETH TRIED TO KILL ME."

In the early light of dawn Daniel stopped to look at Michael; he had suspected something terrible had occurred when Michael woke him so early and asked him to come alone out onto the Ice.

"Not Seth," he moaned softly, "not him, not now."

"You have to face it," Michael said softly. "All that was is over, over for all of us. All is changed now forever."

Daniel turned away from Michael and together they continued their shuffling stroll across the inner harbor. They walked wordlessly across the ice for several minutes until Michael finally broke the silence.

"You're to take command of everything, answering only to me. If"—he hesitated for a moment and then continued—"if anything should happen to me, then you are to rule in my stead."

Daniel stopped again and looked closely at Michael.

"Do you know why Seth tried to kill you?" he asked, his voice almost carried away by the gale-force wind that was sweeping in from the frozen north.

"Inys Gloi, they could no longer control me. In their estimate, it was time for me to die."

"And yet you ask me to be your second."

"Come now, Daniel. I knew long ago that you were of the Secret Brotherhood. But I know as well that with the death of Janis, any loyalty they had was passed to me."

Daniel nodded his head slowly. "I always suspected they had a hand in it. I told Seth that if that was true I didn't want to know, so he never told me. Was Seth involved?"

"He was."

Daniel nodded in response. "As I thought, as I thought. We all knew that Janis turned you away from the path they had intended. But on that issue is where I broke with them. My loyalty to her and you came before that damned brotherhood."

"Do you know who Seth's men were?"

"I think so."

"Have them arrested at once. Do not kill them—I shall let them live. Find them a ship and give them a day to leave. If they are seen again, however, it's death. And the practicer of physic and my cook are to be deported as well. You see, I was not dying of a cancer: Seth was slowly poisoning me to cloud my senses in preparation for the final blow, so that it would look a natural death."

"You know, Michael, most likely there are brothers of the Holy Island here that neither Seth nor I were ever aware of. One of them can still get to you."

"I realize that. My guard will have to be strengthened. The final crisis is coming, the one that shall decide the game, and Inys Gloi will try whatever necessary to stop me."

"What do you mean by that?"

"After this I truly realize how far I have drifted. I had the cup of poison in my hand and at that moment I truly wanted to drink it, I felt I would let destiny decide. I have to trust in that now. It has decided, and I shall act, as I planned to long ago. Despite your protest, within the week, I shall withdraw from the north. I shall go back to Mathin, where my strength will be intact. Those who desert me were never truly with me from the start. Those who stay shall be sufficient to fend off any advances, and then in time, my teachers, our beliefs, will spread peacefully and will infiltrate the others and end them forever."

Daniel started to speak but Michael stared at him, his radiant power commanding acceptance.

"I shall not argue with you," Daniel said softly.

They passed through the inner harbor and out beyond the barrier defense lines. Half the fleet was drawn up beyond the gate, ready to sail with the dawn. They had been ready to leave the previous evening, but Michael had delayed their departure when word came to him of Seth's arrival. The relief forces for North Prydain and Caediff stood ready, along with the fifty patrol craft that were to relieve the picket line established a hundred leagues out from Cornath. At the sight of the Prophet many of the crews stopped in their labors and called his name.

"So that is why you delayed the fleets sailing this morning?" Daniel asked.

"Precisely. The reinforcements are to sail to their destinations and deliver my new orders. They are then to provide support for the pullout and escort all who leave back to Cornath. Reunited, our fleet shall withdraw to Mathin; before Zimri can react, we'll be gone. As for Eldric's freebooters, they can stay if they wish or pull back with us, it does not matter."

"If that is your wish," Daniel said softly, "I pray that you're right."

A slashing roar cut across the ice. Startled, they both looked up.

Three red rockets rose from the deck of a heavy frigate parked in the middle of a mass of shipping.

Michael looked at Daniel. "It's the alarm signal. It must be a mistake."

After a pause another set of rockets arched into the scarlet light of dawn.

"It's an alarm, no mistake!" Daniel shouted. Michael scanned the dark horizon to the west. Nothing, there was nothing.

"Come on! To the frigate, maybe we can see something," Daniel cried.

Together they ran across the ice. Michael was soon winded, and Daniel pulled him along until they reached the massive outrigger blade. The deck captain, recognizing Michael, ran over to the railing and helped him aboard.

"Locke, deck captain of the *Ishmael*," the commander shouted. "My lookout here was standing watch in the foretop, claims he's seen ships in attack formation."

"I have, Master, I have," the young boy shouted. "They're coming out of the darkness to the west."

Locke looked back up at the foretop where several men had scurried aloft, replacing the lookout who had come down.

"Do you see anything?"

They were silent for a moment. Suddenly all three pointed to the west.

"Sails, 'undreds of 'em," one of them screamed, "'undreds of 'em coming abeam the wind."

Locke looked at Michael, who stood transfixed.

From another ship on the other side of the bay alarm rockets soared aloft, and within seconds dozens of rockets were dancing across the sky.

"It's an attack!" Locke shouted. "Damn it, Michael, it's an attack. What shall we do?"

Amazed, Michael looked at Daniel.

Daniel stepped forward and seized Locke by the shoulders. "Where's your ship's captain?"

"Back in the city."

"You're in command of the fleet then."

"Do we have time to get the rest of our fleet out from behind the walls?" Michael shouted.

Locke called up to the lookouts. "How fast are they closing?"

Even as he cried out, men standing on the prow of the ship started to shout that they could see the enemy as well.

Wild confusion started to break out on the deck. Daniel turned to Michael. "There isn't enough time," he whispered, coming up close to Michael's side. "Most of them here are dead; they'll never make sail in time."

Daniel turned back to Locke. "Take command of the

fleet. Fight them. If there are too many, break out, and circle back tomorrow at dawn. The rest of the fleet will rally then and we'll link up. Send messages to Prydain and Caediff and all the other cities—tell them to withdraw. Do you have that, man?"

"I think so."

"You better, or it's your head."

Rockets soared across the ice from the assembled ships. Alarm horns sounded.

Looking past Daniel, Michael could see the enemy ships approaching, a host of rams before.

"We've got to get back to the city," Daniel said. "We can't fight 'em here; this fleet's as good as dead. But the Companions and our heaviest ships are still safe behind the walls."

Michael looked at Locke and nodded briefly.

"Your blessing, Master," Locke whispered, his eyes wide with terror.

Michael touched him on the forehead. Turning, he left the deck of the ship. Men were already swarming into the riggings, gun-ports were being pulled open, anchor lines cut. Sliding down to the outrigger, Michael looked to the west and the approaching doom.

"Zimri! He must have known and wanted to strike first. Zimri."

"There's not time," Daniel shouted. "Let's go!"

"In the end, it is always Zimri," Michael whispered.

"Alarm rockets, Master. They've seen us."

"I had hoped we could close in farther," Zimri shouted, trying to be heard above the high-pitched shriek of the wind.

Turning to the Holy See, Grimath handed him the glass. Zimri adjusted the tube and the enemy fleet came into focus.

"We've caught them!" he shouted. "By all that's holy, we've caught them napping."

He turned back to Grimath; despite the mask and goggles, Grimath could sense the grin of delight.

"They know we're here now," Grimath shouted. "Signalman, battle formation."

The fiery green rockets *shwoosh*ed off the deck of the flagship, slashing across the rapidly lightening sky.

Zimri looked back over his shoulder to the fleet that was following the line-astern formation. Within seconds after the first rocket exploded, the hundred fifty ships of the attack fleet started to shift into line-abreast formation. Zimri, carried away by the thrill of battle, climbed into the lower ratlines to watch the maneuver unfold. Grimath ordered the sheets of the flagship loosened, and before a minute had passed the first wave of rams passed on either side, their crews cheering wildly. On the deck of the *Braith du Mor* the monks stood ready, calling their chants to the counterpoint of battle horns and drums. Zimri extended his hand in blessing as the fleet forged ahead into the attack. The wind roared through the rigging, setting it to humming and shrieking as the gale mounted in its fury, driving the fleet forward at ever increasing speeds.

Next came the light corsairs, armed merchantman, and the assorted craft of Norn. Behind the freebooters came the rest of the fleet, led by a mixed force of twenty heavy and light frigates that made up the striking core of Zimri's fleet. And in the rear the transports, wall rams, siegecraft ships, and their escorts pulled back into reserve formation, awaiting the results of the opening attack.

Returning to the deck, Zimri noticed that Grimath was pointing forward. Looking toward Michael's fleet, he saw that the first sails were going up. He looked back to his admiral.

"Never make it in time. I can't believe they would leave their ships out beyond the wall overnight. A madness must hold their leader to do such a thing. We've got them, damn their pox-eaten souls, we've got the bastards for sure."

\* \* \*

"Cut those anchor lines free, Meehlsson. Run up the foremain, lively, damn you, lively."

Locke looked back to the west; he didn't want to but an irresistible urge drove him to it. The rams were almost upon them, the heavier ships not far behind.

"By all that's holy, step to it, you bastards." Hysterical with rage, Locke slammed his fist on the railing, cursing wildly as each second brought doom closer upon them.

Across his bow a light schooner started to make way, dragging anchor lines, some of her crew running to hop aboard, while others, looking to the enemy fleet, turned in panic and ran back toward the city.

"You there, halt, halt!"

Locke looked over his shoulder. One of his own crew members had begun to slip over the side, but a Companion lowered his crossbow and pinned the man to the railing with a single shot.

"We're dead men," a voice alongside him shouted.

Locke turned to his ensign, Hansson, whose face mask was off, revealing features white with fear.

"Shut up, you sniveling scum. Set your back to the mainsheet."

Sails started to run up behind them, the canvas cracking in the wind.

He could feel a rumble below his feet; the gun crews were running their cannons out. Catapult crews rushed past him and struggled with the tarps that covered their weapons.

Inexorably, the Cornathians drew closer.

The first scattered shots echoed across the ice as several motionless Mathinian frigates opened up with ragged broadsides. Half a dozen ships were now underway, running on a broad reach out onto the frozen sea.

But it was too late.

The first formation of church rams closed in. In grim fascination Locke watched as the enemy ships zeroed in on targets that could not be missed. A Mathinian light frigate cut across the *Ishmael*'s bow, momentarily obscuring Locke's view. As the wind filled its sails, it started to pull away. A ragged volley thundered from her side. Suddenly, through the smoke, Locke could see a double-hull ram closing in, her crew abandoning the vessel. With deadly accuracy the oaken ram slammed into the Mathinian frigate, driving clear through the vessel. With a blinding flash the frigate disintegrated, soaring high into the air in a swirling nightmare of fire and smoke. Even above the roaring explosion Locke could hear the screams of her dying crew.

A torrent of debris rained down around him. All along the deck of his ship men were cut down by the showering wreckage, and fires quickly spread across the deck. To Locke's horror, a human form, its legs gone, crashed down on the foredeck. The body still twitched feebly and screamed with a horrible sound. Locke rushed forward and, with a single sweep of his scimitar, slashed the poor wretch's neck, ending his agony. Suddenly the deck lurched beneath his feet. They had caught the wind— maybe there was still hope!

"Hansson, steer us west by south."

As no answer came from the helm, he turned. The pilothouse was empty.

"Hansson!" Looking over the railing, he saw Hansson with dozens of others sliding off the outrigger, deserting the ship.

"Hansson, you bastard!"

Hansson never looked back, joining the panic-stricken exodus running toward the city gate.

Locke took the wheel. Another frigate exploded to port and then another. Every ram hit produced an explosion. He started to ponder that—not every ram could be hitting a magazine. What were the Cornathians using? But his thoughts were interrupted.

"Rams dead ahead!" came a hysterical cry from the foretop.

Two rams, emerging from the smoke of battle, were closing in on him not a quarter mile away. As soon as he saw them Locke knew he was a dead man. Only seconds were left. His orders, his orders—only he knew of Daniel's command. What would happen now? But for this one final moment he was captain. Grimly he held the wheel, shouting his defiance and his rage. The rams hit.

"They got him, Michael."

"I know. I can see it as well as you."

They stood on the outer wall. The concussion from the exploding ship washed over them, drowning out all other sound. One after another the pride of his fleet went up in thunderclap roars. From horizon to horizon his fleet was in flames, as ram after ram slammed into helpless targets. And above the roar came the screams, the screams of thousands dying upon the ice.

Daniel turned to his guards.

"Listen to me. We've got to get a message out. Go, all of you. Get out there on the ice and try to board a ship, any ship. When you do, take command in my name. Get a message to our fleets in Caediff or North Prydain. Tell them to rendezvous off here and attempt to raze the siege."

"No," Michael said calmly, "it's hopeless now; no one out there will get out alive."

Prepare to jibe!"

An enemy shot screamed through the rigging, tearing a hole in the foremain, but Zimri paid it no heed. His attention was riveted to the approaching line of Mathinian frigates, desperately trying to cut their way out of the flaming nightmare before Cornath.

Wild cheering filled the air as his fleet closed for action, ready to complete the slaughter started by the rams. Looking back to the west, Zimri saw his transport ships, which had slowed to a near-walking pace, disgorging the assault crews. Hundreds of blue-robed men were tumbling through the open sternhatches, and within seconds the men were on their feet. Forming up into assault teams, they hoisted one-man skatesails and charged into the attack.

"Jib ho, watch it now, watch it!"

Instinctively Zimri ducked low, even though the head clearance to the boom was sufficient. With thundering cracks the booms swung across the deck as the wind caught the sails on the opposite side.

"Cleat in, there," Grimath roared. "You there, on top-main sheet, cleat in!"

The *Braith du Mor* suddenly accelerated away as the wind filled its sails, driving the ship forward with such speed that Zimri had to hold onto the railings for support.

Off to port another frigate of the Prophet exploded with a thundering report as the last rams closed in. From horizon to horizon the frozen sea was awash in flame, wreckage, clouds of billowing black smoke, and struggling forms. Never had he seen a battle joined with such swiftness, or with such devastating effect.

"We've got them for sure this time, my lord."

Zimri turned to face the hooded form of Demarn, who smiled fiendishly at the sight of such slaughter. Zimri merely nodded in response.

Explosions washed over them as they ran down the length of the enemy's wall, only a quarter mile away.

"There, my lord," Grimath cried. "Quarter league ahead, light frigate breaking out."

"Go ahead, then," Zimri shouted, "finish the bastard."

The vessel was already crippled. Its sails were flaming torches lit by the burning destruction of its neighbor. Alongside the ship a small corsair was attempting to break out as well, and seeing the approach of the *Braith du Mor*, its captain cut to windward, attempting to use its comrade as a shield from the broadside.

Speaking trumpet in hand, Grimath called out the command to the gunnery captains who passed the word below.

"Full broadside. Fire when she bears. Ready now, stand ready."

With terrifying speed the range closed. As the frigate

saw the approaching ship, her captain started to turn into
the wind in a desperate attempt to present a broadside,
but there wasn't enough time. At less than fifty yards'
range the *Braith du Mor* crossed the enemy's T astern.

"Fire!"

With almost a single report the twenty-gun broadside
was discharged, slamming a quarter-ton of iron into the
cornered ship. Explosion after explosion marked their
success as the shells slammed into the target and detonated with thunderous reports.

The enemy's foremast disappeared in a blinding flash
—the full weight of its rigging crashing down on the
screaming men below.

With a sudden, stunning intensity the ship simply
disappeared, its magazine detonated by an exploding
shell. The force of the explosion washed over the light
corsair, which was still using the frigate as a shield.
Her sails flashed into flames and the light craft spun out
of control, easy prey now for the assault teams following.

"Back her out to sea," Zimri ordered. "Call off the
remaining rams; we'll hold 'em in reserve. Order in the
cruisers."

The *Braith du Mor* turned away from the slaughter,
and signal rockets called off the last section of rams from
the assault.

All along the base of the harbor wall, the fighting raged
as the stunned survivors of the action fled the burning
wrecks and sought what sanctuary could be found in the
city. From atop the ice battlements, guns started to open
up, but it was too late to save the ships.

"We've taken them," Demarn said, his voice alight
with fervor. "Saints damn them, we've taken them."

"It's not as easy as that, my dear Demarn," Zimri said
wearily. "That was not all their fleet, and besides, where
is Michael? He is the key to this after all—where is
Michael?"

\* \* \*

"Have any broken out?" Michael cried.

The men around him were silent, grimly watching the destruction unfolding around them. The near passage of enemy shot was barely noticed above the roar of battle.

"It's complete. Not since the Mathinian Pass have I seen such total annihilation," Daniel said softly, his voice betraying the stunning impact of what was happening.

Smoke now obscured their view, as the fleet in front of the wall burned wildly. Choking, Michael turned away from the madness.

"Master, three cruisers, there—can you see them?"

Michael turned back to look. Columns of black smoke eddied past him, blinding him.

Suddenly it parted for a second.

"There," a young Companion cried, "straight ahead."

He looked closer. Yes, he could see them bearing straight for the wall.

"What in the name..." Daniel whispered.

Zimri had learned more than one lesson from him—he had taken the ship rams and, with some new knowledge, had made them explode with devastating effect on impact. He had taken something else as well.

"Battering rams!" Michael shouted. "Old cruisers converted into rams. Clear the wall!"

His words spread an infectious panic. Those men who still fought grimly along the battlements wavered and then gave back, running for the stairs off the wall.

"Quickly, quickly, Daniel."

Together they ran from the wall, away from the point of impact.

"Here it comes!" a Companion screamed. Looking over his shoulder, Michael could see the towering mast of the first ship bearing down on the wall.

With a cracking explosion the ship plowed through the wall, tossing blocks of ice a hundred feet into the air. The heavy logs strapped to the bow snapped clear, skidding across the ice, crushing any unfortunate in their way.

The wreckage of the ram passed clear through the thin

barrier of ice and finally skidded to a halt nearly a hundred yards beyond the breached line, smashing several ships parked in the inner harbor. Within seconds the first assault teams of blue were swarming through the broken wall, scimitars glinting coldly in the morning sun, calling on the Saints to bear witness to their cause. A light regiment of Companions formed a protective arc to contain the break-through into the city.

But there was little time to prepare. From the boiling clouds of smoke the second ram appeared. In quiet fas-cination Michael watched as it darted at a section of the wall north of the gate. At the helm a cluster of blue-robed Morians stood chanting their death songs. Along the wall artillery opened up, firing on the ram and heedless of the damage caused by errant shots to their retreating com-rades still trapped outside the wall. But the vessel could not be swayed from its course. With a thundering impact it smashed into the icy battlements. A blinding flash erupted the ice into a towering column of wood, wreckage, and bodies, as the ship disappeared in a flaming column of smoke. The concussion rumbled across the ice, drowning out all other sounds of struggle.

All was wild confusion as panic seized the men. In desperation Daniel left the wall, calling for his men to rally and hold.

The third ram was closing for the attack when a scath-ing volley from the city's high battlements finally found the mark. A well-placed shot dismounted the starboard steering blades and with a slow, almost graceful action the cruiser collapsed onto its side. Spinning out of control, the ship plowed into the ranks of a Morian assault team, scattering bodies in every direction. And then it was gone as well, exploding with a sharp report that seemed to shake the ice for miles around. Where an entire regiment had been advancing now were only scorched and burning bodies, and bloodied, tortured forms that shrieked hor-ribly—their high voices reaching even to the city wall.

Encouraged by this first favorable turn, a wild shout

of angry triumph swept the wall, but Morians still poured into the two breaches gouged by the other ships. Trembling with exhaustion, Michael left the wall and started toward the fierce combat raging around the city gate. All around him streamed the shocked, dazed survivors of the first attack.

Michael called for a scimitar, and a guard stepped forward to hand over his weapon, but Michael hesitated. He knew he was weak, both from the shock and the poison, and to enter the wild madness below could be deadly. Daniel, having organized the defense, came back up the stairs to join Michael.

"'Tis grim, Michael, but we can hold for now," he shouted above the roar of battle.

Michael looked at Daniel and shook his head sadly. "I should have known. Zimri had to attack. He had to. If I had offered peace first or if Inys Gloi had killed me, then his cause would have been lost. I should have expected this."

Sadly he turned away from the scene of destruction. "I forgot what it was like to be desperate. In desperation you're forced to do the unlikely, thereby taking your enemy off guard. This attack was brilliant."

"We can still almost match him with our home fleet," Daniel shouted. "If that third ram had hit the gate and blown it, we'd be in trouble, but they'll not get through the wall now. He can attack the walls but it will take more than what he's got to get 'em. Michael, we still have *our* men here. These aren't freebooters; it's the Companions we've got here."

"But that's it," Michael replied. "The only ones we can truly count on are in here. Do you really think Eldric will come to our relief? For that matter, we haven't even gotten a message out to him."

A growling howl filled the air and they ducked low as a cannonshot hummed past. It arched into the harbor, and striking the ice, the shot exploded, smashing down a section of men who were advancing to the city's defense.

"So that's it," Daniel said softly. "He's made a way for the shot to explode. That explains the rams, and our magazines going up. It's devilry, it is, devilry."

Within minutes the shelling increased as Zimri's ships ran at extreme gunshot range, hurling shot over their own men to crash into the city. All attention was in that direction until a young shield-bearer by Michael's side suddenly looked back to the city.

"Look, it's in flames. The warehouses are in flames."

Turning, Michael cried out in alarm. The storehouses of foodstuffs and supplies were on fire, raising a dark pall of smoke against a blood-red sun.

He could make out hundreds of antlike figures struggling on the wharfs.

"The city is in revolt," Daniel announced quietly. "We can never hold it now."

"My lord, do you see it?"

"Yes, Demarn, I see. I'm going below. Send the prisoner to me." Smiling softly, Zimri left the bridge of the ship and returned to his cabin. The belowdecks thundered as a twenty-four-pounder recoiled with an explosive roar. All was murky, sulfurous smoke cloaking the ship in darkness. Advancing down the length of the vessel, Zimri paused for a moment to offer encouragement. Bowing low, a grimy gunner offered him a lanyard. Blessing the weapon, Zimri pulled on the heavy cord and the gun slammed back on its mount.

"'Ats for 'em, it is," a gunner cried. "Smash the filthy heretics."

Smiling, Zimri blessed the warrior and continued on to the sanctuary of his cabin.

It was still cleared for action—all his personal belongings stowed away, the center of the room dominated by the cannon, whose gun crew was standing easy since they had no target to bear on.

"You're dismissed for now," Zimri said. "Stand by in the corridor."

Bowing, the men left.

So the city was burning, and not just near the center of fighting but far up on the hillside as well. It could only be from one thing—the people of Cornath had rebelled, attacking the warehouses.

If so, then more could come out of the attack than he had hoped for.

A knock came from the door.

"Enter."

Two guards dragged in a shaking, slender form.

"You can leave him. Stand outside."

The man looked up at him still trembling, his voice near to breaking.

A volley thundered in the distance, followed by another farther away.

"Why have you summoned me, my lord?"

"Simple enough. A man of your intelligence should know the answer to that."

Aldmark looked away from Zimri. His gaze turned toward the view of the burning city, which was framed by the ornately carved windows of Zimri's cabin.

"But you said that if my information was true, you would spare me."

"Ah, my dear Aldmark, a lawyer you will never be. I said I would consider sparing you."

"But my information was true," Aldmark cried, his voice revealing a note of panic. "You have him—I heard the prisoners being brought in. They claimed that Michael lives. Didn't I give him to you?"

"Not yet!" Zimri shouted, standing up to face the traitor. "We only caught half his fleet, the other half is still in the city. He's no fool, that one. I haven't fought him for twelve years to think that Michael Ormson is a fool. So don't try to flatter me by saying I have him."

Zimri turned away from the trembling warrior. "Demarn!"

The door behind Aldmark slowly slid open. The dark-burgundy robes of the Archbishop of Mord Rinn shimmered softly in the smoke-filled doorway.

"He's yours," Zimri whispered softly.

"But why?" Aldmark screamed, all self-control disappearing. "I did as you asked."

"Oh yes, you did as I asked. You did everything that I asked. But what use are you now? I cannot trust you, Aldmark. You betrayed someone who trusted you, you would do it again. You are already dead to me, but, of course, no one will ever know, since I need yet more traitors if I am to win. But just because I need traitors is no reason for me to trust the scum once their usefulness is finished."

Before Aldmark had time to react, two Inquisitioners stepped from behind Demarn and grabbed Aldmark by the arms. Screaming incoherently, the man was dragged from the room.

"Let no one see it," Zimri said softly. "I condemn him to death, but make it swift; a knife to the throat, and then dump his body over the side as soon as it's night."

"As you wish," Demarn replied, grinning with anticipation.

"Damn it, get out of here. There are times when you make me sick."

Bowing low, the high priest of Mord Rinn disappeared beyond the closed door.

Another volley of gunfire rocked the ship, while in the distance Zimri could hear Grimath's shouted commands.

"Prepare to come about. Port battery, roll 'em out."

As the ship turned to run into the wind, the stern windows revealed the panorama of Cornath in flames. The memories were too haunting, still too close to what had once happened there. Pulling up his cowl, Zimri lowered his head. It was up to Michael. How would Michael react?

Their faces showed the shock strain of combat.

"Where is Dubarth?"

"Dead, Master. Ship took a ram."

"And what of Kevin and Livollen?"

"Both dead as well, Michael. Kevin was killed by the second battering ram, Livollen when the mob stormed the powder warehouse."

Yes, the warehouse. He had stood upon the Place of Watching, observing the battle for the gate when the warehouse disappeared in a thunderclap of flame. Nearly two hundred men lost in a single, blinding moment. He looked up at his captains. Silently they watched him, while echoing from the distance came the muffled sound of battle. It was already night but still the fight for the wall continued. But that was no longer the main concern.

Twenty thousand people in Cornath, and nearly half of them had risen up, almost as if on command. Michael's forces were now divided yet again. Half were at North Prydain or Caediff, thousands of others scattered as garrison troops, and the remainder, those who had survived the morning's assault, were fighting on two fronts.

Wearily he surveyed his men. "Suggestions?"

Gregorson, second in command of the battle fleet, spoke first. "We can hold them on the wall, Master. Send out word to Eldric at North Prydain. Within two weeks he will be at our gate and then we can sally and raze the siege."

"But what if he doesn't?" Dalgrin of Mathin asked coldly. "He's a freebooter; he follows the direction of the wind. Granted he might appear at the gate, but on who's side in these circumstances?

"We know Norn has gone over to Zimri. Eldric could go over as well, with demand of Norn's head as payment. Then what? Eldric again commands all the freebooters. All our holdings in the south will be open while we are bottled up here. Think of that, Michael. Mathin could fall and then we are truly finished. Wait not for that bastard, Michael. He'll betray us, I'm sure."

"And what do you suggest instead?"

"I don't know," Dalgrin said softly. "We've lost half our powder reserves, a quarter of our food, and nearly half our fleet. We can try and withstand a siege, but I remember what we did to Zimri, who thought he could hold out, behind fortifications far more elaborate than ours."

Michael looked around the room. The men stood quietly, waiting for him, and he knew their thoughts. "You know what I said at our last council meeting. I wanted to end this war. I wanted to leave the north, give it back to Zimri, and return to the south. But events have rushed in upon us, jumping ahead of what I desired.

"Something else must be considered as well. Last night Seth betrayed me."

There were quiet gasps and murmured comments.

"You have all heard of Inys Gloi. Most of you have suspected from the beginning their connection to me. Seth was their agent, and this morning he tried to poison me. I was not sick; I was never sick. I was slowly being poisoned and Seth was to deliver the final dose. It is obvious therefore that we now face not only Zimri as our open enemy but the Secret Brotherhood as well."

The men looked one to another, and he could sense their fear.

"We are alone, my friends. Inys Gloi has also turned against us. Zimri, I daresay, knows this, thus prompting this attack. Many of you have been with me since the beginning. We have fought many hard battles together; now we must face the hardest of all.

"We have failed in the north. The people did not come to us. A vision was offered to them but their feet were rooted in clay and their thoughts could not soar into the sky."

The men were silent. A volley of explosions echoed from the distance and several turned anxiously to the door, but the crescendo of sound drifted back to the low, constant rumble of battle.

"We can hold against a siege, if we are lucky, but in the end what will we have won? Look around you, my friends. We started our crusade a decade ago with the dream of one day ending the wars of religion. Instead we have created the most devastating religious war since the forming of the Ice, and there is yet no end in sight. Perhaps I am weary, perhaps I have grown tired of the bloodshed that is caused in my name. I have had enough of this madness. It's strange to think that if things had been but slightly different, those people who are attacking us would instead be fighting by our sides."

He looked away from them, as if gazing off into a distant land that only he could travel.

"For is it not true," Michael whispered, "that the prophet is never recognized by those whom he once called his own? That is, at least, until they have killed him."

His men stirred, uneasy with his words. He looked back to them and smiled.

"I've said enough. You know my heart. Tomorrow at dawn we shall open the gates. I shall break out of Cornath. Anyone who wishes to follow me may do so. Once clear of the city, any that desire to become neutral, or go over to Zimri, have my leave to do so. I would suggest that you first join Eldric. Under his protection you can strike a deal with Zimri. If Eldric stays loyal to me—and I doubt it—then go to the Ezrians. I promise you, any that leave will not be fired upon."

The men looked one to another; Michael sensed that some in the room had long since made up their minds.

"Once in Mathin we shall seal off the barriers. I can promise you this, my friends. Zimri can retake Cornath, but in that he will find the same trap that I have fallen into. We have planted the seed here. It will be impossible to root out. Someday, no matter what his wish, it will blossom. For in the end Zimri must still deal with Inys Gloi, and Ezra as well."

Michael looked away from the men and with a weary gesture beckoned for them to leave.

"Pass the word," Daniel commanded. "We will leave no one behind who wishes to sail with us. Strip the warehouses, prepare the ships to sail at first light. The Prophet and I will board the *Hope*. Have your signalers meet with my secretary to prepare the recognition and command signals. You are dismissed."

Michael heard them leave, but knew after several minutes that one remained. Looking up, he saw Daniel standing by the door.

"Do you believe what you just said?" Daniel asked.

"Do you?"

Daniel shook his head.

Michael smiled softly. Rising from his chair, he walked out the door and Daniel followed.

Weaving down the corridor, they passed frenzied warriors who had just received the commands. All was confusion as men hurried past, carrying their possessions and loot. Wild cries echoed in the distance. Ascending the long stairs, Michael and Daniel finally came out onto the Place of Watching. Below them the battle still raged, the smoke of a hundred fires filled the air, while in the distance Zimri's fleet was marked by the flash of guns that lobbed shells into the city.

Daniel finally nerved himself to ask the question again. "Do you believe what you said?"

Michael turned to Daniel and smiled sadly, his face illuminated by the fires below.

"Do you know that it was here that my uncle once said farewell? It was here that I also came to realize that Janis was lost forever, and I said my farewell. And it is here as well that I must face what has happened to my dream. In my name have come war, destruction, and agony undreamed of. In my name, Daniel. Once all I asked for was to be left alone. Then all I asked for was for my beliefs to be left in peace. But now, at last, I must face that what is happening out there was caused by me and me alone. For I believed that ignorance will quietly go away and die. But that is not so, and there are times when ignorance might, in fact, win. But I know what will happen in the end, I have always known that, in spite of my trying to escape it. But some things yet remain to be done."

He looked at Daniel and smiled softly. "Go prepare the ship," he whispered. "I will be with you shortly."

"But you haven't answered me!" Daniel shouted, his voice edged with anger.

"Nor will I."

Sensing the futility of his questions, Daniel turned away, leaving Michael alone.

Long was the night, and as the hours passed among the bright flashes and flares of battle, he watched the exodus. Thousands passed through the narrow winding streets of Cornath—the sailors returning to their vessels, mingling with the white-clad hosts of the Companions, who for one brief moment had held the Ice in their power. Following them came the ragtag collection of ten thousand lives—the women who had followed them, the children born of their passions, and the meager possessions of a starving race that clung to survival in a godforsaken world. And as each section of the city was finally abandoned by the Prophet's men, the wild orgy of destruction began as those loyal to the old order poured into the streets in search of loot and vengeance.

Long he watched, until with the coming of dawn the messenger came from Daniel—telling him that all was ready. For one last time he looked out upon the city of his youth, the city of his aging. He would not step foot in Rifton's old office again. Too many ghosts lived there to greet him. With a vague, distant smile he turned away from Cornath. The guards fanned out in every direction, and as if in a dream, Michael Ormson prepared to take ship. He knew at last what had to be done.

# CHAPTER 11

"MICHAEL, WE'RE READY."

He looked to the young captain who stood behind Daniel and nodded slowly. "Just another minute, that's all."

The fires of the city filled the eastern sky, muting the growing light of dawn. The decks of the ships were packed with men. All guns and catapults were run out and loaded, ready for the fight. He looked across the ships and sensed the quiet desperation of the move. He had to be decisive—there could be no sign of wavering or doubt.

"Pass the signal. Open the gate."

The captain nodded and, turning to the signalman, he gave the command.

A single flag broke from its casing and was run up the line. It snapped into the fresh northerly breeze, revealing the battle-scarred standard of Michael, not carried in action since the taking of Cornath years before. A ragged cheer swept across the deck of the fast corsair *Mathinian Hope*, as the men set to the sails, running the canvas into position. Every second was precious. Nearly a hundred vessels would have to clear the single gate, and within minutes they could expect the Morian barrage to cover that route. If a single vessel was disabled in the narrow channel, the rest of the fleet would be trapped.

Michael called Daniel to his side as the *Mathinian Hope* slowly gained headway. For the first time in years Michael had the urge to pray.

"Hoist the sails there. Step lively to it, men."

Within seconds thousands of square feet of canvas was

151

snapping out sharply in the morning breeze. Standing on the fighting foredeck, Michael watched in silence as the harbor of Cornath drifted past. Along its shore the last of the rear guard stood in formation, guarding the final approaches from the raging mob that swarmed through the back alleyways of the town. His gaze lingered on Rifton's old monastic fortress until the ship suddenly lurched beneath his feet, as it turned into the approach to the gate. With lightninglike speed they accelerated away as the ship pointed into a broad reach.

Suddenly they were past the stone watchtowers and into the outer harbor.

"We'll know any second now," Daniel shouted above the roaring of the wind.

They looked to each other hoping against hope that surprise was theirs.

Turning, Michael saw the next ship, a heavy corsair, already clearing the harbor entrance. One after another the ships were following, but it would still take half an hour to bring out the entire fleet.

A rocket flare rose up on the western horizon.

"Their first alarm!" Daniel shouted.

"No volley fire yet," Michael called, trying to conceal the anxiety in his heart.

A wall of ships was now visible, and a sea of canvas sprouted across hundreds of masts as the Cornathian brotherhoods pressed on canvas for the engagement. Michael looked back over his shoulder; they were committed. Already a dozen ships had made sail, to turn back now would be a total disaster. The next minute would tell. Then, from horizon to horizon, half a hundred broadsides thundered out, sweeping the ice in a blinding storm of fire.


"Sound the alarm!"

Rockets slashed out of the launch tubes but Zimri paid them no heed as he raced to the fighting forecastle.

"It looks like a breakout, my lord," Grimath shouted, racing up to his master's side.

"What madness. What absolute madness." Grabbing the telescope from Grimath's hand, Zimri swept the approaching line of ships with his gaze. He should have surmised such an action. Ormson must be more desperate than he thought . . . or insane.

"My lord, that lead ship, do you think Ormson is aboard it?"

The gunfire started to swell around him. Suddenly entire broadsides cut loose as Zimri's ships, already prepared to support the morning assault, now turned their fire on the approaching ships.

"He must be. He has to lead in this attack, otherwise the rest might be reluctant to take such desperate action."

"We've hit one!" Grimath shouted.

A rolling cloud of smoke from the blinding broadsides mushroomed out of the besieging fleet. A heavy frigate was cutting across the ice under full sail, then disappeared under a hail of shot and explosive shells that tore the ice around it, sending up towering plumes of spray. All three masts went over, and as the ship pulled to the side of the channel, it exploded with a thunderclap roar.

"Close in on Ormson's ship!" Zimri shouted. "Perhaps we can end this war today!"

"By all that's holy, Michael," Daniel whispered in stunned awe. "Two hundred men were on that frigate."

Michael turned away. "Follow the plan for breakout."

The riggings above shrieking in the wind, they aimed straight between two Cornathian frigates. The full volley against the frigate gave them a chance. It would be a minute before the guns could be reloaded, and in the interim they would cover the distance to Zimri's fleet and be in the middle of it. The seconds dragged by in agonizing slowness as they ran straight down on their tormentors. With less than a quarter mile to run, a few ragged shots from the enemy ships rang out. A gap of at least a hundred yards separated the two Cornathian frigates.

"Steer for it!" Michael shouted. "Steer for it."

With lightning speed the corsair shot through the gap, and they were into and among Zimri's fleet.

Another thundering volley erupted behind them and Michael did not bother to turn—the cries of those around him told him that another ship had been destroyed. The guns below his feet thundered a defiant but futile reply.

"Master, look at that ship off to the north."

Michael turned and gazed in the direction that the sailing master pointed.

"That's Zimri's flagship, I'd know it anywhere. Fought it, I did, last year." Daniel looked at Michael with an expectant gaze, but Michael was silent.

Another volley thundered behind them. The battle around them was breaking up into a swarming confusion as Michael's ships struggled to break out. All about him were wild cries of confusion, as shot thundered past, wounded screamed, and battle madness seized the crew.

"Shall we take him on?" Daniel shouted.

Michael looked back at the engagement and the madness revealed by the morning light.

"No," Michael said quietly, "sail on, sail on. It's a long way back to Mathin."

The city was open to him at last. From the distance came the echoes of battle as half his fleet pursued the remnants of the battle group that escaped. Around him the ice was a scene of unbelievable carnage. Nearly eighty ships had made it out before a heavy frigate exploded at the gate, blocking escape for the last twenty vessels. Even now their crews were casting down their arms, surrendering to him rather than face the wrath of those in the city.

Michael had escaped in the confusion of battle. But for the moment that was not important, pursuit could be left to Grimath and his flagship. Zimri was returning to his city in triumph. Tonight he would celebrate Holy Offering in the Cathedral, and then there would be tomorrow and the plans for the final destruction of Michael Ormson.

The pursuers were in check for the moment, holding back to the horizon as darkness fell. Nearly half his crew was dead or wounded, a third of the guns out of action. Only twenty ships had shown so far at the rendezvous point. All ships commanded and crewed by the Companions. Undoubtedly some that had broken out were already heading for neutral ports to sit out the conflict.

"It's been a hard day, Daniel. Signal all ships to sail to Mathin. We don't stop tonight, or any night, till we reach the Southward Shelf."

"Master, this is the beginning of the end, isn't it?"

Michael looked sadly at Daniel. "What do you mean?"

Daniel turned away for a moment. "It's just that from the very beginning, I always feared that it would come to this."

"Not yet, Daniel, not yet. There is still too much to be done."

Without another word Daniel went to the signaler and passed on Michael's orders.

The rockets flared across the evening sky, illuminating the heavens for a moment, then gently settled and disappeared on the darkening ice. Onward they sailed through the night, ever southward. And Michael stood alone on the sterncastle watching the occasional flickers of light as enemy ships crossed each other in the darkness, while the aurora overhead seemed to reflect the actions of men and filled the northern sky with a blood-red fire.

# BOOK VI

**Frigate**

# CHAPTER 12

HE FELT WITHDRAWN, DISTANT, AS IF WHATEVER EMOTIONS he had once carried had been carved from his heart, leaving an empty shell. The encounter to come could end his life, but that was of no concern.

"For Judas was complete at the moment of his betrayal, and only death was left to take him," a voice whispered in the darkness.

Startled, Seth rose from his knees and looked toward the blackness of the alter.

"Yes, Seth Facinn, a Judas who has failed both the master apparent and the master within."

"Riadent."

"Yes, your other master, asking now why Michael Ormson still lives."

"You know already, so why torment me with yet another recitation?"

Seth drew closer to the altar and a shadowy apparition approached him. Raising his hand in a gesture of command, Riadent left the chapel and strode into his office. Following, Seth lingered for a moment and saw the aurora, which even at that moment Michael was watching not twenty leagues away.

"Now tell me, damn you, why did you fail?"

"I warned you often enough in years past," Seth said quietly. "I told you of my fears. That somehow Michael Ormson was beyond our ability to control. Throughout this time you have sat here, comfortable and safe, not seeing what others can see, removed from the center of the struggle. It was I who stood by the Prophet's shoulder, day after day. First I directed, then I listened, and finally, like so many others, I lost my soul to his power—as you would have if you had come too close."

"I don't give a damn for your analysis. I want the answer to a simple question—why did you fail to kill him?"

"By all the bloody Saints, I'm telling you. His power finally was beyond my ability to control. I brought him the poisoned cup and stood with trembling hand as he brought it to his lips. And in that final moment, when he brought it to his lips, his eyes looked into mine and pierced my soul. He knew, Riadent, I could sense his thoughts as if they were somehow being projected into me. He knows everything—you, our plans, our entire cause, and to him they are nothing more than pawns in his own game!"

Seth turned away from Riadent and staggered to the window. "Kill me and end this," Seth cried. "I can't bear this life anymore. When I fled from his presence I tried to kill myself, but I was a coward and failed, even in that. That is why I returned: I look to you for release. End my life and be done with it."

"You have yet to answer my question."

"Can't you see what I'm saying?" Seth shouted. "He looked into my eyes and it was as if every thought, every desire, and even my very will were ripped out of my heart and consumed by his gaze. He knew it was poison, he told me that even before he brought the cup to his lips. And by all that is Holy I swear before you that he knew beforehand that I would strike the cup away, as if the act between us had been ordained a million years before the seas ever froze."

Seth stopped for a moment and drew closer to Riadent.

"Listen to me. Listen to this even if you forget everything else that I say. We've thought all along that it was we who controlled Michael. We're fools to even imagine it. Riadent, it's the other way around. Michael controls us. He let us create him; he let us do all that we have done. Riadent, he is a power beyond our imagining. And we, the Hidden Order, are merely his puppets, acting out his plans yet revealed.

"We're nothing," Seth screamed, "nothing at all! And I have betrayed both him and you."

With a strangled cry Seth fell to the ground, the cold chamber echoing with his shrieks of anguish.

Riadent knelt by Seth's side and touched him lightly on the shoulder.

"It is not yet lost," Riadent whispered. "Listen to me, it is not yet lost. Even now Michael is in retreat, driven by Zimri. Zimri, who somehow second-guessed what was about to come.

"You have failed us, Seth Facinn, but I foresee that there is something yet for you to do. And it shall be my decision and mine alone that will end your life, but I still need you if this crisis is to be resolved in our favor."

Without another word Riadent left the room and gave orders that Seth was to be taken to a place of rest and there given a potion of sleep. He wasn't quite sure why he had spared him, but, of late, many things were happening that he was not sure of. He went to his private chamber to rest and to pray, and to struggle with the temptation that had increased to unbearable proportions.

Varinna slipped through the corridor and without a sound passed the final door. The room was dark, but she knew he was there and was in fact aware of her presence. The final moment of testing had come. For years she had contemplated the act, but fear had always held her back. Now, at last, a greater fear drove her—a fear and a plan, as another desire continued to grow in her heart.

She knew full well that Thomas's days in the monastery were numbered and that when he left she would disappear forever, her part in the game complete. She had noted a subtle change in the routine of the citadel in the last day, and whispered rumors that Michael had been killed, or that his fleet had met with disaster. Riadent's time to strike had come, but she must act first.

She listened to the rhythmic breathing and knew it was a sham. He was fully awake and had been awake the moment she slipped into the room. He was only feigning sleep to throw her off guard. She had to act, or death would be the response.

Walking lightly, Varinna slipped to the side of the bed and knelt down.

"It is you, isn't it?"

She did not answer but let her fingers gently touch his shoulder and neck, still covered in long robes and cowl.

"I should kill you for this—how *dare* you?" He started to stir.

Reaching into the darkness, she took his hand. He struggled for a moment and she could feel the ripples of tension and fear running through his body. Ever so gently she took the hand and guided it to the folds of her loosened gown. Gently she parted the gown and placed his hand over the warm, full swell of her breast.

"You've wanted this for years," she whispered softly.

"No, don't."

"If you don't want me, then simply withdraw your hand."

She could feel a tremor wash over him, as if he were struggling with a demon of the night. The hand started to pull away, and then, with an unexpected ferocity, he grasped her breast with such strength that she gasped from the pain.

"Yes, that's what you've wanted," she choked out. "Shall I guide your other hand as well?"

Forcefully he pulled her onto the bed, and she could sense the wild confusion ripping his soul apart. But she knew that finally, after endless years of suppression, the will of the flesh would win at last.

"Yes, my lord Riadent, take what was last known only by the Prophet."

\*   \*   \*

Before the first light of dawn and the call to prayers she slipped from his chamber, knowing that the door would be unlocked again that night as it had been for weeks, in anticipation of her coming. He had confessed that, along with other things in the wild confusion of their love-making. There was still a cold fear in her heart, for she knew that in a moment of remorse over his falling he might slay her to ease his guilt.

Slipping down the corridor that was empty of guards— yet another action on his part to allow his seduction— she gained the confines of her private quarters. Opening the door, Varinna started into the rooms and then stepped back in surprise. Thomas was already awake, sitting by the stove, wearing the simple black robes of an initiate. Someone was with him.

The form turned and drew back its cowl with trembling hand.

"Seth."

"And where were you, my lady?" he asked with cold sarcasm.

Trying to gain control, she quickly entered the room and closed the door.

"You are the one in my chambers; I think I should ask that first. Just what are you doing here?"

"Ah, lady Varinna, should we go back to Riadent and discuss this together?"

She was silent and looked away.

Seth laughed sadly and turned back to Thomas.

"You're such a remarkable young man, my good Thomas. So like your father. So like your father in some ways, but that is a story long in the telling."

"Please tell me of him," Thomas asked eagerly.

Seth looked into the eyes of the boy, and again he saw the dream floating before him. He wanted to cry out and flee, but he felt another desire—a dream to live it yet again, and somehow not to fail. Not to fail. All their plots were now centering on this boy—hers, Riadent's, and now his own as well. Riadent might yet order his death in the days to come, but he knew that Riadent would approve of his telling Thomas of Michael's greatness. To school him in the history and lore of the Mathinian movement, so that when the time came, Thomas could take control. Yes, there was a purpose here.

He looked back at Varinna and smiled again. "Have you now found your final purpose as well, Varinna?"

# CHAPTER 13

"WHAT DO YOU WANT OF ME THIS TIME, PETER OF MOR?"

In the distance could be heard the monastery's mid-morning service, with the soft tenors counterpointing the deep, rich basses as the Holy Ritual of the Mass was offered for the five hundred brothers who served in the monastery of St. Ezra.

Bowing low, Peter waited for the command to rise. No anxiety troubled his heart, no fear that he would again be played off for a higher game on another court of action. He knew, at last, that the moment had come to press for the final conclusion.

"As I said, Peter, I know what you want, but go ahead and explain this plot of yours anyway."

With a smile Peter stood up and gazed at the aging prelate of Ezra, his Holiness Palao III. To Palao's side stood the Archbishop of the Holy Order of St. Ezra, Ortaz of Lismar, whose oppostion to Peter's rise in the Ezrian court was well known. Peter half wondered why Palao had brought him along and could only conclude that for such a major decision Palao wanted a foil for Peter's argument.

"I must take it that your agents have already told you what has occurred in the wider world, my friend Peter," Palao stated softly.

"Though not as good as yours, I think I know some of what has happened."

"And that is?"

"In an unexpected victory that borders on the miraculous, Zimri defeated Michael before Cornath and drove him southward to the Mathinian Pass. Within a matter of days rebellion exploded across the Cornathian holdings and Ormson's remaining garrisons were driven out."

"Are you pleased with your old master's victory?"

"My lord, I am still of the Cornathian Brotherhood. Zimri is my Holy See, and, of course, I rejoice with his triumph."

Ortaz laughed softly and I looked with mock sincerity at Peter. "You've answered that one neatly enough," Palao replied gently.

"What else would you expect me to say?" A disarming smile lighted Peter's features.

"But of course, Peter, what else could I expect from you?"

"My lord," Peter continued, choosing to ignore the slight, "are you also aware of the fact that the freebooter Eldric is considering allegiance to Zimri?"

Palao hesitated for a moment; that was indeed news to him, but he dare not show his intelligence network to be inferior.

"And what if he does?" Ortaz's voice was edged with contempt. "Eldric is nothing but a filthy pirate, a leader of scum who tremble at the sight of our imperial fleet. One more pirate on Zimri's side is nothing."

"Don't let your arrogance get in the way of reality," Peter replied coldly. "Eldric represented nearly a third of Ormson's fleet. Our estimates run that Michael lost nearly half his men and ships in the debacle before Cornath and the subsequent withdrawal. This, coupled with Eldric's possible defection, could tip the scale back to an even position."

"So let them continue to fight," Ortaz replied. "It is to our everlasting benefit that they do so. We sell food to Ormson, who in turn allows our trading post to flourish. He fights against your Cornath, which keeps their power in check, and we profit without risk. After all, you're nothing more than heretic scum anyhow, so why should we interfere?"

Peter bristled at the insult. For twelve years he had lived in the Ezrian court, accepting such insults as his daily lot in life, waiting for his opportunity.

"Such words might come more from an agent of Inys Gloi, rather than a high archbishop of the Ezrian Church." A year ago Peter would have remained silent, but not now. They needed him and he would take something back from them in return.

Ortaz stepped forward, pulling back his robes to reveal the hilt of his dagger.

"*Despada demontia*," Ortaz spat.

A deep rumbling laugh filled the room and Ortaz hesitantly looked back to Palao, who sat upon his high-backed throne chortling.

"And what do you know of Inys Gloi to accuse my beloved Ortaz of being such an agent?"

"Enough to realize that their machinations have crippled any effective response to Ormson, and they can still turn this temporary setback into a victory for him."

"So let them," Ortaz said coldly. "Let the scum of the north fight until there is no one left to draw a sword, and then it shall all be ours, united under the one true brotherhood of the Ezrian Orders."

Peter turned away from Ortaz, as if ignoring his presence, and looked straight at Palao.

"So, what do you wish to say, Peter of Mor? I want to hear this dream from your own lips."

"Your Holiness, for twelve years I have served this court, first as an ambassador and then as a brother in exile after the collapse of my Church. I came here first to serve Zimri, but in the years that have passed, it is you who I've come to serve. And with that in mind, I offer you this plan."

"Spare me the flatteries, Peter, I know you. We are cut from the same cloth and serve only one thing—and that is our own quest for power. I shall hear what you say, but do not cover it in such lies. If I think your plan can serve me as well, then I shall agree. If not, I shall refuse."

Peter nodded, looking at the floor like a child who had suddenly been caught in a lie. Ortaz chuckled softly in the background.

With a defiant air Peter looked up and continued.

"The war between Ormson and Zimri has come to yet another balance. For the moment, Zimri has gained an upper hand, but in fact the situation is no different than it was seven years ago, before the assassination of Ormson's family. Even if he loses Eldric, Ormson's hold on the Southward Islands is strong enough to ward off whatever attacks Zimri can throw at him. Zimri shall of course attack next season; he has to keep the initiative. And Michael need only wait in his stronghold. The pendulum has returned to the center, except for one important detail. Ezra is now the kingmaker."

"How so?"

"With my help you can break the deadlock."

"And for what reason?"

"If Ezra remains uncommitted in this next action, both sides will hold back. Neither Michael nor Zimri are stupid enough to throw every last man and resource into the fight, knowing that Ezra, who is still unscathed, sits on the side waiting for the pieces to be delivered. They are not that stupid, but you do have an advantage at this moment. Palao, it is time you used this advantage."

"That's easy for you to say," Ortaz replied.

"It most certainly is easy for me to say. But it will be my life that is placed on the line, not yours."

"How so?" Palao asked, his voice edged with curiosity.

"As I said before, you are the kingmaker, and also the maker of the next Holy See of Cornath."

Palao leaned forward and smiled. "You, of course."

"Yes, I."

"Enlighten me."

"Appoint me as your special ambassador to the

Cornathian Holy See. Place in my hands the full power of negotiation for war or peace. When I approach Zimri, my offer shall be quite simple."

"And that is?"

"Ezra will commit its full fleet to the Cornathian side at a time and place of Zimri's choosing."

"And what do we get in return?" Ortaz asked softly, a gentle curiosity edging his voice.

"In exchange, Zimri must appoint me Archbishop of Mor and First Secretary to the Holy See of Cornath. In addition, my good brother and assistant, Kerwin, shall take the position as master of the Mord Rinn."

"But what of Demarn, who now holds that office?"

"What of him?" Peter replied with a smile.

Palao laughed quietly in response. "You ask a lot, both of Zimri and of me. First, why should I offer to set you up into this position of power?"

"It is simple, my lord. Besides Mor, only five brotherhoods remain in the Cornathian Order. The others are dead, disbanded, or in exile. Mor and Mord Rinn are the two most powerful—they will control the Church for a generation to come, and from their offices shall come the next Holy See."

"I think I see what you are driving at," Palao replied, his brow knitted in thought. "But surely Zimri will see through that in a moment and know that you are maneuvering to take his power and position. So why should he arrange his own destruction?"

"For he is already on the horns of a dilemma, and knows it. He has defeated Ormson in the short run, but the war is far from over, and Ezra has been untouched by the action. I shall make it clear to Zimri that if he fails to agree to this, Ezra shall put its full support, both in supplies and arms, to the side of Michael Ormson. If he does not agree, within a year Ormson, with Ezra at his side, shall sweep Cornath off the Ice forever."

Palao threw back his head and laughed, and even Ortaz smiled briefly at the thought.

"Masterful. And of course that will never come to pass, since Zimri will agree to our demands," Palao replied, but his features suddenly grew cold and threatening. "But why should we bother, what do I gain from this?"

Peter stepped forward until he was almost within arm's length of Palao.

"It is quite simple, my master. We ally with Zimri. Once the war is ended, your fleet shall stay on in the south while I return north. With the fleet in the Southward Isles, we have the stranglehold on trade. Within a year it will be quite easy to arrange an accident for Zimri—a bad meal that will upset his stomach, a wreck while sailing, an accidental fall, or some such thing."

Peter looked straight into Palao's eyes and smiled. "And then, of course, I shall become the new Holy See. With myself in the supreme position, a firm alliance between Cornath and you will be offered, and I shall cede to you all control over the Southward Isles. You're order has always coveted them and in fact will already occupy them. The Church of Sol is already dead, Cornath shall be your ally, and Ezra shall hold supreme power. At that point Inys Gloi will have to make an accommodation with you, and all power shall be yours.

"Zimri gone, Michael gone, and the kingmaker, in fact, will himself be king. That is the plan, and only I can carry it out. For above all else, I am a Cornathian and a Morian brother, but I am also aware that my power base rests with you, and if you withdraw it, I'm dead."

Palao looked to Ortaz and gave a knowing smile. "It is what we said it would be."

Looking back to Peter, Palao slowly stood up, his short, withered frame barely reaching to Peter's shoulders. Leaning on the shepherd's staff, the mark of his high office, he stepped closer to Peter and locked him with his gaze.

"There is one thing that you do not control."

"Inys Gloi," Ortaz said softly. "How does Inys Gloi

fit into your plan? There is a rumor that Ormson has a son. What will be their part in your grand design?"

"That is why we must act at once," Peter replied, while looking straight into Palao's eyes.

"How so?" Ortaz asked, his voice edged with cynicism.

"Ortaz, certainly you must realize that Inys Gloi lays a thousand false trails to confuse its real intent. One that has always been most effective is to have one of their people preach caution at a time of crisis."

"You dare to accuse me of being their agent!" Ortaz cried.

"Enough!" Palao commanded. "Peter, you are to speak only to me. Ortaz, you are to remain silent."

"As you wish, your Holiness," Ortaz replied, bowing low.

"As I was saying, there are several reasons why we must act at once. I think we can assume that Inys Gloi misjudged the situation with Michael. How grievous their miscalculation, we know not. But if we give them time to regroup, only Inys Gloi will profit in the end. For the moment the situation between Michael and Zimri holds a curious balance. I daresay, Inys Gloi will take advantage of that unless we do so first. There is also another factor. I've had reports that Zimri and Balor have for some time attempted to infiltrate agents into Inys Gloi. Of course I must assume that you have tried the same as well."

Palao look briefly at Ortaz, and Peter could read all that he needed to know in that glance.

"And you have yet to be successful?"

"That is not your concern," Ortaz hissed.

"Enough, Ortaz!" Palao shouted. "Try my patience no longer.

"And tell me, Peter, what if your plan is successful and you eliminate both Michael and Zimri? Will not Inys Gloi come hunting for you as well?"

Peter looked at Palao and smiled, giving no answer.

"Ah, I understand, perhaps it is best that you discuss not your plans for such a situation."

Peter nodded in acknowledgment.

"Yes, there will be a reckoning with Inys Gloi when the time comes, and I daresay it will be so. United under the banner of Ezra, perhaps the Ice can turn on them and in one swoop take the power that is theirs and smash it forever."

"Perhaps," Peter replied, "perhaps."

Palao looked searchingly into Peter's eyes but read nothing. For a moment Palao felt a deep stirring of suspicion, and he hung on the edge of doubt. Often he had let a momentary feeling decide a major policy, and in almost every case his instincts had revealed the correct answer. But these were treacherous times, and he knew that a risk must be taken with this ambitious man. The world of the Ice was changing far too rapidly, and if Ezra did not seize the power, someone else would. The decision must be made.

"Hear my words, Peter of Mor, and obey my command."

Peter knelt before the Primate.

"I knew already, before we met, what you would request, and on most points my heart was decided. I shall therefore agree to what you have said."

Peter lowered his gaze, so that Palao would not see the look of triumph on his face.

"You shall leave as soon as possible in greatest secrecy to appear before Zimri. You shall make him the offer that you have outlined to me. I shall pledge on your behalf the fleets of DellaCroce, Vitalae, and my regiments of heavy siege troops. Only the home fleet shall I keep in reserve. All bases to the south shall be open to Zimri, and come the campaign in the fall, I shall guarantee the opening of the pass to Gormath, so that Zimri shall have access to the Southern Ice. Tell him as well that if he does not agree, all my strength shall be turned against him and my shipyards will rebuild the losses suffered by

Ormson. And that in exchange, you must be appointed Secretary and Archbishop of Mor."

"Thank you, your Holiness, and I swear my oath of fealty to thee."

"But of course, Peter, but of course. I am not yet finished though. Ortaz shall accompany you and shall be my personal ambassador to you. If any harm befalls him, if he should suffer any illness, or even the slightest injury, then know you that my wrath will be upon thee and that I shall reveal to Zimri the full extent of our conversation here today."

Peter did not look up. He could feel the triumph radiating from Ortaz. If Peter deviated one step, Ortaz would gain the power.

"And Ortaz, rather than Kerwin, shall be appointed Archbishop of Mord Rinn."

Peter could not contain his astonishment, and he looked up at Palao. "But he is merely a deacon, a low ambassador between the old order of St. Awstin and your court. He will not be accepted."

"If not, then Zimri shall not have my fleets, it is that simple."

"He has not stepped foot in Cornathian territory in twenty years. All know that he sold out to your court long ago."

"A fair number know the same of you, Peter," Ortaz said coldly, with a glint of sadistic pleasure in his eyes.

"Scum of St. Awstin, what qualifies you to be of Mord Rinn?"

"The protection of my Primate, what else?"

Peter looked to Palao and knew that part of his plan had been checked. Palao was placing a rival in another position of power, who would block him if he deviated from what Palao desired.

For the moment, he was defeated.

And Palao, sensing his mood, cackled softly.

"So be it, my lord, I shall follow your command."

"Good, you will sail at once. Take the usual precautions and let no one see you. Absolutely no one must be aware of this action. If Ormson should find out, he will attack our southward holdings before next year's campaign. Surprise must be complete. Now leave me, and the Blessings of St. Ezra be with thee."

Peter bowed low to Palao, kissing his ring. Turning, he left the audience room, Ortaz at his side.

As the doors closed behind them, Ortaz came closer to Peter. "Thought you could have it completely your way, didn't you?"

"No, I expected Palao would attach a rival like you to the deal. He's no fool."

"And neither are you, Peter. But I'll always be watching. By the way, Peter, what of Inys Gloi?"

Peter looked at him and smiled. "Freeze in Hell, you misbegotten son of a slut."

"And, of course, I know you'll be waiting there for me, since I fully intend to spit on the Ice that covers you," Ortaz replied. Bowing low, he turned down a side corridor, leaving Peter alone in the dark, winding corridors of the Holy Abbey of St. Ezra.

"Inys Gloi." Peter laughed softly to himself. He would present them with an accomplished fact. Ruler of Cornath and Ormson's holdings. All he needed to do then was to go to them and offer his cooperation in their power bid, and he, Peter of Mor, would control all the Ice, including Ezra's.

Then both Ortaz and Palao would see what they were dealing with.

# CHAPTER 14

"It's late, Daniel. Can't it wait till morning?"

"I'm afraid not," Daniel replied quietly. "A dispatch boat just came in. They've had a hard run, and their information is urgent."

Michael got up from behind the pile of documents that littered his desk and walked over to the fireplace, beckoning for Daniel to take a chair next to him. Picking up a slender stick of birch, he started to poke absently at the coals, which flickered with a bright, shimmering flame.

"So what is this urgent dispatch that you trouble me with?"

"It's our agent out of Lismar. He reports that a light corsair with half a dozen escort vessels sailed from there last week, bound northward."

"So?" Michael leaned back in his chair, realizing that this news could only be bad; Daniel was never very good at hiding his anxiety or disappointment.

"Our agent recognized Peter of Mor as he boarded the corsair. The escorts were all Ezrian, and very heavily armed."

Yes, Peter. Of course he would now enter the drama. Michael still remembered their conversation after the victory at the Mathinian Gate. He remembered Peter's promise as well.

"The carrion pickers are starting to circle," Michael said softly, as if musing to himself.

Daniel was silent.

"Peter was serving as Morian ambassador to the Primate of Ezra, wasn't he?"

"Yes, as far as we know, and out of favor with Zimri for some reason."

"We must assume he is going back to Zimri on a mission, but for what?"

Daniel looked at Michael and for long moments they sat in silence.

"We'll have to extend the range of our patrols," Michael suddenly concluded aloud, rousing himself from his lethargic pose, "and we must prepare to seize the two eastern passes owned by the Ezrians. But first we must send an envoy to Palao. We need a guarantee of neutrality, and also a reading of Ezra's possible stand. If it appears that they are going to betray us, then we have only two choices—either turn on Ezra first and block up the passes, or concede the eastern passes to Zimri and retreat here for a final defense."

"Either one could be dangerous, Michael. We have to count on Ezrian neutrality at least for the next year."

"Yes, yes, I know," Michael replied distantly. "Send the envoy back out at once; we must know as to our situation, before the summer season comes so that the appropriate strategy can be planned."

"As you wish, Michael."

"Fine, Daniel, fine, could you leave me alone now? I need to rest for a while."

Quietly Daniel stood up, stopped by the fire for a moment to add an extra log, then wordlessly retreated from Michael's presence.

Michael leaned back into his chair and closed his eyes, wishing to float into the realm of meditation. But he knew in his heart that it would never come again, now that Seth was gone. The nightmare of the retreat came back to him instead. The harsh, agonizing images of a two-week running battle that stretched across the endless Frozen Sea. He could not destroy the memory of defeat and the sight of shattered bodies being dumped over the sides of the ships as they ran ever southward to the sanctuary of Mathin. Back to Mathin, the home he had not seen in seven years, and even there the war had worked its changes.

It was not the city of his memories. The wealth of conquest had poured back into the city, enriching it beyond the wildest imaginings of the old freebooters who had once called it home. The forests beyond the wall were long since gone; only the Sacred Grove remained, maintained out of respect to the Prophet, and even that was edged by sheds, hovels, warehouses, and woodcutters' yards. The woodcutters now went nearly to the far end of the island in search of their trade.

It was a city in mourning as well, as the fleet returned with the news of the disaster. Within hours every home had learned of its loss and bereavement, as the exhausted, battered survivors left the ships with the news of the tragedy before Cornath.

Barely a family was spared the anguish of death, and the cries of pain echoed in the city to haunt his days and weeks to come. For the next month scattered remnants of once-proud fleets fought their way back to the south, and each brought more stories of the madness in the north. As word spread of Zimri's stunning victory, an explosive flame seemed to ripple across the Ice, triggering near-suicidal rebellions against the remaining occupation troops. The flood of survivors soon slackened to a trickle, as Zimri's forces strengthened their blockade.

And suddenly Eldric had appeared. His fleet, still relatively intact, had cut its way through a thin curtain of opposition and crossed through the Bathanian Pass to their capital. Eldric had assured him of his loyalty, but somehow Michael was not sure.

He would encounter Eldric soon enough.

"Enough of this," Michael mumbled.

Standing up, he walked to the window and looked out over the lights of the square. Even in the middle of the night Mathin was not quiet. Down by the ice occasional showers of sparks ascended into the midnight sky as the ironworks pressed on with the casting of blades, ship fittings, and guns. Two years ago a renegade Morian had come over to their side, revealing the secrets of turning out cannon, so now, at last, Mathin had its own gunworks where Michael's master craftsmen were experimenting with new weapons. Only the week before, the master gunsmith had presented him with a breechloader that could triple the rate of fire, matching the new guns of Zimri. He chuckled softly to himself. Now he was matching the technological gains of Holy Church.

On the surface it appears as if we have been checked, he mused, yet few can see the trend we have unleashed. But still there is the war, the war that must press to its final encounter, which holds yet more suffering and death—all because of me.

Turning away from the window, Michael returned to his desk, knowing that the first light of dawn would show before his labors for the night were complete. It would work in the end; he knew that in the end it would work.

"My lord, Zimri, a monk outside wishes to see you at once."

"Not now!" Zimri shouted. Haven't I told you that I am not to be disturbed?"

Zimri flung his quill to the floor and looked up in exasperation at the trembling deacon who stood by the doorway. He tried to control his outburst, knowing that his temper was far too short, but the month's frustration had taken its toll. First Michael had managed to escape to the protection of the Southward Ice, and compounding that was the near-epidemic plague that was sweeping through the liberated cities of Cornath. He estimated that as many as one in four would die in the Cornathian holdings before spring. The disease had crippled his offensive capabilities, and in his heart he realized that by the time he stabilized his holdings, Michael would have fully recovered from the reversals, returning the balance of power to the level of a decade before, the only difference being that nearly half the total population of the Ice was dead as a result of the wars and plague. He had to control himself. Reaching over, he picked up the quill and stared at the messenger.

"Forgive me, my lord," the deacon whispered, "but he absolutely insists that he must see you at once."

"Who is he?"

"He won't say, my lord."

"Damn his soul, I'll see him in Hell if this audience is not important. And you'll stand alongside him, I swear it."

The deacon bowed lower, his knees trembling with fear.

"Damn you, go show him in."

"At your command, my lord." Bowing low, the deacon fled.

Several minutes passed before the door swung open to reveal a short, hooded form that strode purposefully into the room.

Zimri hesitated, his memory seizing on distant events. "You!"

"Yes, Zimri. I have returned."

Zimri approached the hooded form, his fists clenching up in rage. "Traitor! You betrayed your brotherhood, and me. Now after our victory you dare to return, most likely looking for some crumb of reward."

"You are wrong on all counts, my lord Zimri. First I am no traitor, for all along I have served the interest of Cornath, even after you led our Church to defeat. Second if you can call this fiasco a victory, then I must say that your reason has left you, and my mission is indeed useless."

Zimri was silent, torn between curiosity and the desire to see his old secretary in the hands of the torturers.

"Shall we not sit together and discuss why I am here?" his visitor asked. "If at the end of our conversation you are not pleased with my message, then you may do with me as you will."

Zimri nodded absently and beckoned to a chair by his desk. "Sit, Peter, sit and tell me what it is that has dragged you here out of some dark hole to torment me."

"After you, my lord," Peter said smoothly, pointing back to Zimri's desk.

Mumbling a quiet curse, Zimri returned to his chair and Peter settled down next to him. "Go on, then."

"I've heard the reports of your battle—masterful, absolutely masterful. Even in the court of Lismar they call you the Warrior See. I never would have imagined you standing on the forecastle of a fighting ship braving shot and arrow."

"It had to be done, Peter. If I had not led my men into battle and acted as Michael, I would still be in exile and Ormson would be sitting here in this room, rather than me."

"But of course."

"And, I daresay, if I had not done it, then you would be here nevertheless, dealing with him."

"Perhaps, but I prefer this arrangement."

"What is it that you want?"

"A situation that can be profitable to both of us."

"My dear Peter," Zimri replied coldly, "if it's profitable for you, then I'd sooner freeze in Hell than take advantage of it. You betrayed me by not bringing Ezra in on my side.

"If only you had done that," Zimri shouted, his face coloring with rage, "if only you had helped your Church in its hour of need, we could have defeated Ormson seven years ago.

"Why, Peter, why? Seven years of exile, seven years of freezing on the Westward Ice, watching my men die by the thousands. Why?..." Zimri's voice started to break, and he looked away.

"Because it was not yet time."

"Not yet time! Say that to all who've died. How dare

you come here with that message—I'm sickened by the mere sight of you. I don't want to listen to you any longer, and I can promise you your death will be hard, Peter."

"The past is over with, my lord," Peter replied smoothly, leaning forward so that he could almost touch Zimri. "Let's look at the present, which I daresay is every bit as perilous as what you have faced in the past."

Zimri was silent and looked away.

"It's true that you've defeated Ormson, but he is safe in the south. If a stalemate results, you know full well that Inys Gloi will regain the initiative."

"I know." Zimri's voice was edged with frustration.

"I propose to end this once and for all, within the year."

Zimri looked up at Peter and examined him closely. He could sense that Peter had come to him not as the inferior, but with a full sense of his power, and that he, Zimri, would have to hear him out.

"Go on, then."

"The Primate of Ezra, Palao du Lismar, has finally seen the peril of our present situation. He proposes a simple solution that will end this bloody conflict once and for all."

"And that is?"

"A full alliance."

Zimri sat up and gazed suspiciously at his old secretary. "Explain."

"It is quite simple, my lord. Palao sees that the crisis is at hand. Michael is secondary in his mind; it is Inys Gloi that we should all fear. Therefore he wishes to end this war the only way it can be ended, by bringing the full strength of Ezra into the conflict on your side."

"To do what?"

"Palao pledges the use of his fleets, unscathed by war for the last fifteen years. His heavy shock troops will be available for the final assault on Mathin."

Zimri stood up, unable to contain his excitement, and strode over to the window that looked down upon the city of Cornath. By all that was holy, a fleet that would take years to build was to be delivered into his hands overnight. In six months' time he could be at the gates of Mathin. A thrill of excitement coursed through him. The end was in sight at last! And then he looked back at Peter, who sat self-assured and complacent by his desk.

"At what price, my dear Peter?" Zimri whispered. "What is the price?"

"Ah yes, the price," Peter replied, smiling benignly at Zimri. "It is indeed a small price to pay."

"Let me be the judge of that."

"The payment is simple. Within the week you are to resign as Archbishop of Mor. After all, Zimri, you are rather unique holding both the Holy See and yet retaining the Morian Seat for yourself."

"And I am to appoint you as Archbishop of Mor?"

"But of course."

Zimri turned away. With only a handful of brother-hoods still in the Confederation, it would give tremendous power to Peter. He had considered such a move before, after Madoc's betrayal, but in the end there was some-thing about Peter that had prevented that final act of trust—and now it would be forced upon him. There was no choice, and he looked back at Peter prepared to accept the demand.

"There are several other points as well, Zimri. Ortaz of Lismar is to be appointed as Archbishop of Mord Rinn."

"What? That heretic dog, *head* of my Inquisitioners?"

Peter's smile disappeared for a moment. "I must say that I agree with you, but Palao insists on that condition as well."

"What of Demarn? He has served me loyally and well, what shall be done with him?"

"Get rid of him," Peter said quietly.

"But for what purpose must I do this?"

Peter was silent.

Zimri could read the distaste in Peter's expression. So

Palao wanted a balance against Peter, and someone that he was sure of. But Demarn had been with him throughout the exile.

"He has to go, Zimri, otherwise there is no deal."

The decision would have to be made. It could look like an accident or a hit by a raiding ship. Knowing the secret that Balor had told him about the nature of the plague, a simple exposure to the disease would be sufficient to clear the way.

"Anything else?" Zimri asked in quiet resignation.

Peter smiled expansively, sensing that Zimri would surrender to all points of contention.

"My appointment as Secretary to the Holy See, with full control over all the traditional offices of that position."

"And place you in the line of succession? No! Never! I'd sooner freeze in Hell than give you that power," Zimri cried.

"Do you and that . . . that scum, Palao, think me mad? The archbishoprics are one thing, but not the secretary. You'd have full access to my power, all my secrets would be known by the Ezrians, and in the people's eyes you would be next in power."

"Those are the conditions, Zimri, or 'my dear, Zimri,' as you are so fond of saying."

"How dare you address me like that!" Zimri screamed. "I see your colors! Oh yes, I've known from the beginning that you coveted the See. I would be writing my own death sentence. The body of Ormson would not be cold and I would be in the grave alongside him, and you would sell our brotherhoods to the Ezrians."

Peter sat in silence, an insolent grin lighting his features.

"You'll not leave here alive," Zimri cried. "I'll see you on the rack within the hour and send your broken body to Palao as my answer."

"Go ahead, Zimri. Just go ahead and sign your death warrant as well. I can already tell you Palao's plan if that is your decision."

So saying, Peter produced a heavy parchment from within the folds of his robe. The document was sealed with the ornate red mark of the Primate. He tossed it onto Zimri's desk.

"Read it later, but I can tell you what it contains. If you fail to agree to Palao's demands, he will offer a full alliance to Michael Ormson. The fleets which prepare even now to sail upon our side will instead go to Michael. All Ezrian bases will be opened to Ormson's fleets, thereby giving him access to the Northward Ice. I can promise you, Zimri, that Ormson will be back here in a year's time, and believe me, this time you will not survive."

"Damn you and your Ezrian scum forever."

"Damn us all you want, but in the end you will agree to the demands."

Zimri held the parchment in his hand and stared at Peter. "Get out!"

"Could you please make that clearer, my dear Zimri?" Peter said quietly. "Is it your wish for me to leave Cornath, or do you merely wish me to leave the room?"

"You know what I mean!"

"I think so. I'll call upon you tomorrow to start our planning for next fall's campaign."

Wearily Zimri stared at the man whom he had raised out of the gutter and trained for power. "See me tomorrow," he whispered.

Bowing low, Peter left the room.

The demands would have to be met. But there must be a way out, there was always a way out. Peter would not dare to strike until after the campaign. At least the new enemy would be by his side at all times. Once Ormson was finished, and Inys Gloi as well, there would be yet another challenge—assuming that Inys Gloi did not strike first, or that Michael, who had surprised him so many times before, did not again snatch victory out of thin air. He tried to relax.

Returning to the desk, he concealed the document from

Palao in the locked cabinet. Time later to examine the nuances of Palao's written demands. Reaching behind his chair, he pulled the chain signaling for a messenger. Within seconds a young acolyte was at the door, bowing low.

"Ah yes, find Demarn for me. Tell him I wish to discuss a mission with him."

# CHAPTER 15

"Seth, please don't go yet."

"But I must, Thomas. You know your mother doesn't approve my spending too much time with you."

"Where's my mother?"

Ah yes, where is she? Seth wondered. He knew, yes, he knew for certain where she was. A thousand-year plan was in jeopardy because of human frailties—Seth's falling under Michael's spell and refusing to strike, and Riadent's sleeping with Varinna. And Michael was behind that as well. Riadent feared Michael as much as Seth did, and in taking a woman who still loved Michael, he could somehow show his dominance over the Prophet.

"Why won't you answer me?"

"Because I don't know, Thomas."

"You're lying."

Seth turned to Thomas, and the look on the boy's face froze his heart. The stamp of Ormson was upon him, and in that young face he clearly saw the ghostlike image of his father.

Michael, how could I have betrayed you? Seth felt a tightness in his chest, as if his heart were about to burst from the pain in his soul. Why, Michael, why did I do it?

"She's with *him*, isn't she?

Seth was pulled back from his thoughts. "What?"

"My mother is with him again." Thomas whispered the words as if Seth and he were conspirators.

"What are you saying, boy?" Seth lowered his voice as well.

"It's just that I know." Thomas smiled vaguely and pulled away from Seth. The strange, haunting look disappeared and again Thomas was merely a little boy disappointed that a cherished friend was about to leave.

There was a knock at the door. Turning, Seth found it was Nathan.

"Come along, Thomas, it's time that we went to morning services."

Seth felt a twinge of jealousy as the boy walked to Nathan and took his hand. Nathan stared coldly at Seth, then after a moment a faint smile crossed his lips. Seth had another stirring of recollection as the two left the room.

Seth quietly settled to the floor and assumed the position of meditation. But in his heart he knew that the peace of contemplation would not be his. He was deep in the Sacred Monastery of Inys Gloi, but he was separated from his brothers forever. He was lost to both worlds: he had betrayed Michael; he was lost to the very order to which he had fled. He had nothing save the reminder of things past that Thomas conjured up.

All that he had lived for was in the end destroyed. Michael lost to his own power, Inys Gloi lost as well, and for Seth Facinn no life lay beyond those. Trapped, alone, he wept remorseful tears.

I must kill her now—while she still sleeps I must kill her, by all that is holy. Riadent stirred. Leaning over the bed, he contemplated the naked, defenseless body. It could be so easy; it would take but a moment to snap her neck clean. Yes, it could be done so easily.

Half a dozen times she had come to him, and after each act of love he had stood, contemplating her death as if such an action would be the proper penance for his fall.

Seth was right. In his heart Riadent knew that the Messiah created by the Prophecies of Inys Gloi was in fact a manifestation of a power beyond the control of Inys

Gloi. To sleep with Michael's woman returned him to human scale.

In the distance a single bell tolled. The call to matins. Was it already so late? In another month the Ice would be firm beyond the Broken Tracks, and then at last would come the time. Already the assassins were preparing to sail for Mathin and for Cornath. Soon Zimri and Balor of Cornath would die, and in Mathin Ormson and Daniel. Then would Thomas be brought forth, offering to all the peace of Inys Gloi.

Riadent had no further need of the woman. Her death was to have occurred by then, for the boy was beyond motherly care. Yes, he should do it now.

Quietly he crept onto the bed, preparing to strike.

Her eyes were open, looking into his. "You want to kill me," she whispered.

Riadent was silent.

"If you truly wish to kill me then go ahead." She stretched back her neck, offering him a clear target.

His hands started to tremble.

"You wish to kill me out of your guilt, but you won't," Varinna said quietly. "For if I die, then how will you triumph over Michael in the night? I came to love Ormson too late, after I was gone. You know that I love him still, and that Thomas is to me a daily reminder of that love. Yet I offered myself to you freely, needing the presence of a man in my arms."

"Damn your soul to Hell," Riadent whispered.

"It already is. But while I live my soul is mine. You know that you need me." Varinna extended her hands to him.

Riadent backed away.

"My lord, I know what you plan to do. I would be a fool not to know. You plan to act soon . . . very soon."

"In what way?" Riadent asked cautiously.

"Even now the weather is starting to turn. The Ice will form soon in the south. When the Ice is set for the winter,

Michael and Zimri will die. My son will then be the heir to both Cornath and Mathin. Inys Gloi will rule."

Riadent was silent.

"Michael will be dead and Inys Gloi will be free to walk the Frozen Sea, secure at last in its power. But the ghost of Ormson will still haunt you. I can exorcise that ghost. I can stand behind you, advise you, and help prepare the way."

"Already I think you know too much."

"I would be a fool not to know. I have lived in this fortress most of my life. I can sense the changes, the final preparations. For seven years you kept my son hidden. But now he is in the harbor every morning, learning the ships, observing the world. The signs are clear to me, and I am no fool.

"If you wish to kill me, go ahead," Varinna whispered. "But never again will a woman share your bed. I believe I was the first in your life. I am sure I will be the last."

"Get dressed and leave me," Riadent cried. "Get out of here, you slut."

"As you wish, my lord."

Embarrassed by her nakedness, he turned his back as she rose from the bed to don her simple fur-lined robes.

"Shall I return again tonight?"

"No."

"Are you sure?" She drew closer to touch him on the shoulder.

A tremble ran through his body.

After a long hesitation he finally spoke.

"The door will be unlocked," he whispered hoarsely.


"What are you doing here?" Varinna shouted, as the door swung open to reveal a dark-hooded form kneeling on the floor in the position of prayer.

Seth turned around to face her, and throwing back his hood, she saw his face streaked with tears.

Hesitating for a moment, Varinna looked back down

the corridor. Seeing that no guards were present, she retreated into the room, closed the door, and locked it.

"I'm sorry, Varinna. I thought that . . ." His voice trailed away to silence.

"You thought I was still with him?"

"Yes."

"You've known all along?"

"But of course."

"Any others?"

"I think Nathan, but I can't be sure. You two can't hide it much longer. As soon as he is aware that someone suspects, he'll kill you."

Varinna gestured for silence and pointed to a small doorway at the end of the room. Silently she crossed to the door and opened it, revealing a small meditation chamber within.

Seth followed her lead and closed the door behind them.

"As near as I can tell there are no listening holes here."

"There are not," Seth replied quietly. "Your chambers were once intended for Michael, if I had been able to bring him here as planned. Here the Master was to confer with Michael without fear of someone else's listening."

"Yes . . . Michael," she said absently.

"Why are you sleeping with Riadent?"

"To buy time for myself. I know that he planned to eliminate me once Michael was removed and Thomas was brought forward. Seducing him was a gamble, but I could see the lust in his eyes when he looked at me. I had to take the chance, otherwise I think I would already be dead."

"You might very well hasten your death as it is."

"Not yet, he is still too confused by my actions. But why he has not killed you is beyond me—your use is ended. You have failed, Seth Facinn."

"I think somehow it's because he can't admit that at the key moment we did fail. Perhaps I still might be needed in the transition when Thomas takes over, through my experience with Michael."

Seth started to choke on the last words and then turned away.

"You loved him, didn't you?"

"Yes, but I loved Inys Gloi as well."

"You know that the assassins will move with orders to kill Michael as soon as the Southward Ice freezes?"

"Yes."

"There is a way," Varinna said softly.

"What do you mean?"

"I intend to destroy this cursed order."

Seth looked around fearfully, as if through some supernatural means her words might be overheard.

"How?"

"I plan to escape with Thomas and go to Michael."

"But that's impossible. You'll never get past the outer gate."

"Perhaps, but I have nothing to lose—nor have you. Riadent will kill us both before the year is out."

Seth looked away from her. "You're asking me to turn traitor yet again."

"It is easy after the first time. I should know."

"But what good will it do in the end? Inys Gloi will still hold the key to power."

"By seducing Riadent I had a second choice in mind. His private chamber is adjacent to his sleeping area, is it not?"

"Yes."

"In there are hidden some of the documents relating to the daily functions of Inys Gloi. Am I correct?"

"Yes."

"What I am about to ask will result in my death, Seth, if you betray me."

"I know."

"There must be a list in that office of every assassin of Inys Gloi out on the Ice?"

"You're mad," Seth whispered. "You're bloody mad."

"I'm not mad I'm desperate to live. If I flee this accursed island, I will be hunted down by every agent of

Inys Gloi—even if I go beyond the Flowing Sea. I need protection. I will go to Michael but I must offer him something in return. I intend to find that list, the list of every agent Inys Gloi has placed. I will steal it and give it to Michael and then I shall be protected."

"And you want my help?"

"Either that or go out there now and denounce me; I can't take the strain of this much longer."

"For all I know you are in league with Riadent and this is merely a test; I should report you at once."

"If you wish, Seth Facinn. There's the door; go and denounce me. But I daresay he'll kill you anyhow in the long run, and there is Michael to consider as well."

"Yes, there is Michael to consider," Seth said quietly. "It always goes back to Michael."

He lowered his head, trying to remember the dream of an earlier time, but it would not come, for all had been washed away, lost forever.

"Salvation," Seth whispered.

"What?"

"Nothing, nothing."

"Will you help?"

"I believe the documents are there. I only saw him open the cabinet once and that was years ago. Around his neck he wears the signet of office."

"Yes, I've seen it."

Seth looked at her for a moment and she smiled knowingly.

"It is also a key. The ring fits into a carved socket in the wall behind his desk. That will open the cabinet wherein are stored the papers of immediate concern, too valuable to be left in a more open place. If what you seek is in his office, that is the only place I can think of."

"If not there then where else can I go?"

"You can't. There is one other place, the archives hidden in the base of the mountain."

"What archives?"

"Beneath the mountain a hidden stronghold is guarded

by those who take a solemn vow. Once they enter into the protection of the archive, they may never venture out again as long as they live. Therein is hidden the complete library of Inys Gloi. Such wonders to be found there of the Before—a complete history of our order going back twice two thousand years, and with it many of the Sacred Relics of that time—chalices, vestments, altar pieces, the Holy Shroud, relics of the Saints, pieces of the Cross."

"What is that?"

"Never mind, never mind, it's not important anymore. Besides, there are other things of far more interest. That is what I dreamed of showing Michael, for he would have had the power to reveal it all—to end the wars and to bring about the New Age as was prophesied. But it is lost, lost forever."

And Seth started to weep again.

"Could it be there, the list of names?"

"If it is, your quest is hopeless. Only Riadent can lead you in there, and the simple fact that you know of such things is death."

She looked at him quietly. "You tricked me."

"Yes, of course, Varinna. If you were a trap for me then quite simply I am now a trap for you. Your knowledge of our hidden library and what it might contain would be sufficient for Riadent to order your death, no matter what his personal desire."

She looked at him and laughed quietly. "We deserve each other, Seth Facinn."

"No, Varinna," he said quietly, "we don't deserve each other; we're merely what the world has become in the end. A place of deceit that Michael so desperately wanted to change."

"Yes . . . Michael," she whispered quietly.

"After stealing the documents, how will you get out?"

"That is up to you, Seth. There is no easy way out for me. On rare occasions I am allowed a walk with Thomas in the harbor area, but always with several guards nearby."

"Is Nathan one of them?"

"Yes."

"I see."

"Why do you ask?"

"Never mind for the present, just a thought, that's all." Seth hesitated for a moment then looked at Varinna.

"When they finally send the assassin team to Mathin, chances are they'll take a small but very fast four-man craft, for the team has to get in quick and without being detected. Our only hope is to grab the fastest ship, otherwise they'll run us down and kill us. When I think the right vessel is available, I'll give you less than twelve hours' notice to steal the list. Until then I'll not see you again, for our meeting might be cause for suspicion. Until such time, Varinna, prepare yourself. Go as frequently as you dare to the harbor and watch all that happens there. When our time comes we'll only have minutes in which to act." Seth turned and started back to the door.

"Seth."

"Yes?"

"*Can* we escape?"

"I doubt it." He smiled wearily and shook his head. "After all, what is there to escape to? Varinna, the Ice will see yet another war this winter, and endless wars after that, whether Michael survives or not."

"I don't care about that, or anything else. I want to live, I want to see Michael one last time to explain to him, and I want to save my son. If I have to go back to the gutter, so be it. I just want out of *this* madness."

Turning, Seth slipped from the room.

And where shall I go? Seth wondered to himself. After this, where shall I go?

# CHAPTER 16

With the dawn Michael walked through streets already astir with the preparations for yet another sail. His guard was doubled, at Daniel's insistence, and fanned out in every direction as they weaved through the back alleyways and out the north gate to the sloping hill that led to the Sacred Grove. Those who were closest to him were at his side, and as he scanned their faces, he felt a swelling sense of loss. So many were missing, so many were gone forever. Only a handful remained from the beginning, and on all their faces lay the stamp of the Ice and war. Their eyes had a distant look, as if already they were peering into the beyond.

Onward they walked through clearings that had once been forests and had so long ago resounded with the questions of his followers and the happy cries of a little boy long since dead. At the Grove, Michael stopped, and those around him gathered closer. He could sense their feelings—a desire to return to the past, when his simple words could shake the world with a vision of how all should be.

"And so, my friends, we gather here again as in the days of old," he said softly, and those around him stirred.

The wind whispered through the trees overhead as if driven by the first pale light of dawn, breaking on the eastern horizon. He looked past them for a moment, and many followed his gaze, as if he had sighted some distant apparition that was drawing near with a whisper of hope. Long he stood in silence watching the first red light of dawn as it swept down the hill, illuminating the ships arrayed in the harbor below. The fleet was assembled once again, the battered survivors of last season's defeat mingled with the ships that could be scraped up from the Southward Isles. In a desperate bid to match Zimri's fleet, nearly every vessel in the south had been impressed, but this time he would have no edge in numbers.

"I look at our city and the assembled fleet and I think how changed it is, how different we have all become since this adventure started. I look at you as well, and I see standing with us all those who are gone."

Some of the men looked around nervously.

"I can see Ishmael, who was here long before I ever sailed the Ice. And his faithful lieutenant Finson, who served by my side. And with them are all the others— Zardok and Cowan, Olin, Ormath, and ten thousand more. Gone in our cause, gone, but remembered still."

His words drifted away with the breeze, and many bowed their heads at his remembrances.

"So we sail forth again, and I called you here this morning—you, my oldest followers and most trusted warriors—for I wish to reaffirm in this sacred spot what it is that we are, and to tell you where it is we must go.

"Long ago we dreamed that we could end the cycle of religious wars by declaring our independence from them. But that could not be. For the nature of religious war is to prosecute it most violently on those who no longer wish to be a part of it. So in trying to end this madness, we have brought yet more madness upon the Ice. And in the weeks to come there shall be yet more war.

"Perhaps that is the way the world must be, but still I shall rebel at the thought of it, and I charge all of you now to remember the anguish of this moment as we again sail to battle.

"All of you remember this," Michael suddenly shouted. "Never forget this moment. Remember why it is we sail today, for I shall now tell you. It is not to spread a new cause. That was our first and biggest mistake. That was my mistake, which I shall always regret. In my desire for revenge I came to believe that the only way to end the religious wars was by force. The only way to bring the renaissance was through death. In that we have lost. But even if we should lose in the days to come, still I will tell you that we have won, for the knowledge we have created cannot be destroyed, even if each and every one of us dies and the city below us is burned to the ground. For too many people now know the truth, too many questions have been raised, and the system deemed perfect for a thousand years has been shown to be false. We have retreated only for the moment, but in the end we shall be triumphant in a way you cannot yet imagine."

He fell silent again, and the men waited for his commands. But instead he looked away as if lost in distant thought.

"I shall now tell you all," he said quietly, "for I do not want this to be lost. I shall tell you all that is true.

"Two thousand years ago ours was a world most of us could not dream of. The Earth was fair to behold, and the Ice was far away to the north. Look around you, for here on this spot was once a paradise of green forest and lush countryside where men could, if they desired, walk naked 'neath a tropical sun. And the Earth was full of life, teeming with creation beyond our wildest imaginings. And there was Man as well, arrogant in his power, crisscrossing the world with his ships and reaching to the skies with his buildings. And beyond all was his dream of power and his desire to reach the stars, where he believed yet more worlds such as this awaited."

All were silent, listening in awe to his words.

"So in their pride men went beyond this world with powerful engines, and walked upon a world that once was so close that it shone like the sun in the night. Yet, in a moment of supreme folly, Man overreached himself, and upon that world he built an engine ten thousand times more powerful that any built before, believing that it would carry him to worlds beyond. And in a moment the machine was no more, destroying itself along with the world that it rested upon, and from the wreckage of that world came the Arch.

"It was men who did that, nothing more!" Michael cried. "No God, no Saints, and no Prophet!

"The Arch is the remnants of that once-mighty world. And the wreckage of it rained down upon the Earth, destroying all. And in his final madness, Man turned against himself, unleashing weapons not unlike that great machine. And he made the destruction complete.

"Thus came the Night, and the world we live in today. And still we suffer from this. When a Saint falls from the sky, it is just another part of that old world falling from the sky. It is nothing more—no God, no Saint, just the result of the simple laws that govern an object's falling. Nothing more.

"And so, when that Night started, one church did survive, and for a thousand years it struggled to keep what knowledge was left, for Man still respected knowledge for its own sake and said that it was good. And at the end of the thousand years the numbers of Man started to increase, and looking back to that Time of Before, a great debate arose within the church and two things were said.

"A few stated that knowledge was good and that, using it, Man could rebuild his world. But the rest said that in knowledge Man had almost destroyed himself, and that therefore it must be hidden away until¹ some far-distant day when Man was ready to handle such things with care. And in the end, those who wished to hide the past and shroud it in mystery won, and all that was known of the Before Time was sealed away. The brotherhoods of the various churches were created to make sure that knowledge was suppressed and to create a religion that would fill the souls of men with other thoughts.

"It was upon that decision that the legend of the Messiah was created. For that church that had survived the Destruction lost its power to the new brotherhoods, and taking the stories of a Messiah from long before, they set about on a plan, believing that one day, when the time was right, by using a Messiah, they could retake their power and rule supreme. That order was Inys Gloi. And the orders that hid the knowledge were the brotherhoods of Cornath, Ezra, and Sol. The libraries of the churches hold vast storehouses of hidden knowledge, still ready after two thousand years to be used for the benefit of Man.

"Understand, my brothers, what I am saying. I am nothing more than a plot, a conspiracy set up by a jealous religion a thousand years ago. It slowly created the legends of a Messiah, the Promise of a Redeemer, and in reading the stars it foreordained a date for a Messiah to be born, and planned then to train that Messiah and use him so that they could once again hold a power they had held three thousand years ago.

"Thus was I given the mantle of the Messiah. But they had not counted on my will to resist them and to use that mantle instead to end the tyranny of religion.

"Understand and believe what I have said. And in the understanding remember that if only one of you lives to see next year, the story must be told. I was created by the old church as a weapon against the new. But that is not what I have become. If I am a Messiah for anything, I am a Messiah against ignorance and its handmaiden, religion, and nothing more."

He turned away from them with those words, and a clamor of confusion slowly grew behind him. Many had not heard or chose not to hear, and from some came wild shouts of confusion and dismay, while others stood in shocked silence.

Daniel, surveying the crowd, could barely suppress his anger, for in a moment Michael had denied all that had been cultivated for the last decade, and he knew that the words spoken here would soon spread beyond all ability to contain them.

Michael looked back at the men and smiled. "A day will come when you shall at last understand. All is now in order. The fleet is prepared and the plan is the same.

Eldric and his men shall cover the passes to the east. Morrison and Seay will take the Mathinian and Bathanian Passes. I shall hold the center, with the main fleet in reserve upon the Southern Shelf. The barrier lines are in place, and when the main van of Zimri has been sighted, they must be held at the passes until our main fleet with myself and Daniel in command can come up to engage.

"Are there any questions?"

"And what of Ezra?" Eldric asked, his voice edged with doubt.

"We shall soon see," Michael replied. "We know they've mobilized, but I have the assurance of Palao that if Zimri dares to venture onto the Southern Shelf, he shall sally forth on our side."

"Can you trust him?" Morrison asked.

Michael closed his eyes and smiled sadly. "There is nothing else we can do. But if Palao should come in, then the very order that they have created, the balance of power between the churches of old, will be broken once and for all, because in the aftermath only one of them will be able to rule supreme."

"But can you trust him?" another insisted.

"That is all we can do." He looked around at their uneasy faces, but there were no more questions.

"It is time," Michael said softly. "Good hunting to all of you. May the Ice before you always be clear. We sail within the hour."

The men turned and started to walk away.

"Eldric."

The old freebooter turned and looked at Michael.

"Could you come with me for a moment?"

With Michael in the lead, the two walked alone to the high stone chair of watching. Workmen were already busy around it, laying out a line of fortifications designed to protect the northern flank of the city. At Michael's approach, they respectfully withdrew so that the two might be alone.

"I'm going to ask you the same question you asked

me," Michael said, looking straight into Eldric's eyes. "Can I trust you?"

Eldric laughed softly. "What do you think?"

"No."

"If that's the way you feel, then kill me now," Eldric replied evenly.

"You know that's no longer my way."

"You're such a fool, Ormson. If I were you I would have fought it out in the north. For that matter, I would have killed Zimri eight years ago when I had the chance. The day you let him escape, I knew that you were mad."

"Or had a plan beyond your understanding."

"You're not dealing with plans, Michael Ormson, you're dealing with the lives of men. That is my responsibility now, the lives of my men."

"I'm forced to look beyond that. That has always been our failing throughout history. We've always looked to the immediate present, not planning or considering for those yet to come. That is what I am now forced to do."

"You haven't heard me, Michael. I have to consider the lives of my men. I've lost a lot for you, oh Prophet."

Michael did not respond to the sarcasm but merely smiled. "You've gained a lot too. We've used each other to our mutual advantage. I needed your men, your ships, and your fighting skills. You've received power and loot in return."

"Can you still offer me power? Can you still offer me loot? That is what I am forced to ask. Look, Michael, I grant that 'neath it all I have come to like you, and yes, even respect you. But I can't understand your strange detachment from this struggle. You seem already to have surrendered, to have given it all up, and you're leading those damn fools down there to certain death. What am I supposed to do? Tell me, what would you do?"

"That is why I ask you if I can trust you."

"Know that I plan to survive."

"I somehow doubt that you will. If you go over to

Zimri, in the end he will be sure that you are eliminated. Even if he doesn't kill you, your old comrade Norn will."

"That score is for me to worry about."

"I can assume that if Ezra goes over to Zimri, you will as well."

Eldric looked at Michael and smiled sadly. "You understand I must protect my people."

"I understand, but do you, my old friend? Do you understand?"

"Oh Angry Father of the Universe, we call to thee in the darkness. Why have You forsaken us? Why have You turned your back to us in our hour of need?"

Zimri looked down from the high pulpit, his gaze sweeping the assembled multitude that stood in silence for the ritual of the Supplication Night.

Every ship of Cornath had been impressed, not one vessel would be left in the north; all would follow him on the final campaign. Any man who could sail a ship or carry a weapon had been impressed into the final campaign. And as he looked out upon the tens of thousands, illuminated in a sea of torches, he again felt for a moment the surge of power that had once been the cause for his living, the dream of his life. But his heart was empty, devoid of all exaltation.

"Oh Father, who has forsaken us, hear those whom You have condemned to frozen death. Hear us and grant us reprieve. Return unto us the Garden of Paradise."

"Return unto us the Garden of Paradise," the multitude responded, "and end the torment of the Ice."

He looked to the sky again, crossed by the shimmering light of the Arch. And knew that the prayer was to nothing but darkness, like a thousand Supplication Nights before.

All was gone of his former dream, all was lost as they struggled on in a twilight nightmare of death. With the tens of thousands assembled he could imagine hundreds of thousands more, the phantoms of those whom he had driven to death in war and plague.

When will this end? Zimri silently wondered. When nothing is left? When not one of us remains alive? Is *this* what our dream of power has brought us to, Michael Ormson? You to end the Church, I to preserve it, and in the process we destroy it forever—so that nothing is left?

He looked out to his people lost in prayer and pain and knew that whatever else might transpire, the old spirit of the Church was dead forever. The people might feel triumph for the moment, but when Ormson was gone nothing would unite them. And what then of myself? Peter, Ortaz, and the envoys of Ezra stood at the base of the tower, and when the fleets sailed to the south, Zimri would reveal to his followers the alliance with the old enemy. An alliance that could be their only hope for victory.

"Holy Father, return unto us!" Zimri cried. "End the madness forever, we beg of thee!"

But no answer came, and as the hour of silent prayer passed away, Zimri knew that, as had always been, no God would reveal himself. And that yet again, Man was lost to his own designs.

They would sail in two days. And at the Broken Tracks the Ezrians would join them. But there was still one factor left unaccounted for.

"Why are you trembling, Varinna? You have nothing to fear from me tonight."

She tried to turn away from him but his arms held her tight, forcing her to look into his eyes.

"I'm afraid of you, Riadent, afraid of what's coming."

"What do you mean?"

"I've seen them in the harbor; you're preparing the assassins for Michael and Zimri."

"How do you know that?"

"The boat in the harbor, it's sailing to Mathin, is it not?"

"So."

"And once he is gone then you'll have no use for me."

"He looked into her eyes, looking for some hidden meaning to her words.

"Once Ormson is gone you'll no longer fear him or need me to hide that fear."

Riadent was silent.

"I need a drink," she said softly, "something to calm myself."

"You know where to find it."

Riadent lay back on his bed. The girl was right. Ezra was mobilizing and Zimri's fleet would sail in two days, at least he thought he would. But with the coming of dawn the assassins would move on Cornath to finish the job, ending the campaign before it started.

He watched her naked body as it drifted through the dark shadows of the room. And as he watched in the candlelight, he again felt the weakening of his flesh, the desire to possess her as a talisman of power against the darkness and fear.

She returned to the bed bearing the chalice filled with aromatic Yarwinder.

Settling beside him, Varinna bought the cup to her lips and sipped the wine.

"Does that help?"

"Yes, my lord."

She placed the cup by the side of the bed.

Reaching over, he touched her shoulder. She turned to face him.

"Do you still want me, my lord?"

Trembling, he reached out for her.

The first light of dawn flooded the room. Stirring, Varinna brushed Riadent's face, bringing him to consciousness.

"It will soon be time for the morning service, my lord."

"Yes, it's time."

Varinna smiled, and taking the cup by the side of the bed, she offered it to Riadent.

"Would you like some to clear your head?"

Without a word Riadent took the cup and drained it.

Smiling, Varinna stood and stretched, and hurrying to the foot of the bed, she recovered her gown and started to dress.

It will have to be done, Riadent thought while watching her. The boy is ready at last. I need her not. A kiss, an embrace, and a quick movement of the hands and it will be finished forever.

"Varinna," he said softly.

Turning, she looked at him.

"Come here and sit by me."

Returning to the side of the bed, she sat down.

"Let me kiss you one more time."

She hesitated.

"It's all right," he said almost gently, as if talking to a child.

She knew that this was the moment; he would end it here after all. "Why, Riadent, have I meant nothing after all?"

He looked at her, trying to focus. But she seemed so distant, so far away. "What's happening to me?" he suddenly cried.

He struggled to stand but collapsed back onto the bed, unable to move. "What's happening?" His voice was like that of a bewildered child.

She drew closer and smiled. "You were going to kill me, weren't you?"

"Varinna?"

"Yes, you were going to kill me, but I struck first." She watched his eyes grow wide with terror.

"Oh, it's not a poison, Riadent, nothing that simple. Merely a potion to sleep. You always had a drink when we awoke in the morning, and I prepared this last night, so you would not suspect. Oh, it won't kill you. In twelve hours you'll be awake, but by then the boy and I will be gone. And in my chamber I shall leave a note detailing all that you and I have done. What shall happen to you then, oh Master of Inys Gloi? What will your brothers say to you then?"

"Traitorous bitch," he whispered feebly.

"Aren't we all?" she hissed. "Aren't we all?"

Tearing his shirt aside, she pulled the talisman from around his neck. Riadent struggled weakly then collapsed back onto the bed. With frantic speed she dashed into the next room, and knocking aside Riadent's desk and chair, she inserted the key into the cabinet that held the most secret and treasured documents of the order.

"Good morning, Thomas. Out for your morning walk, I see."

Thomas nodded silently, examining the black-robed form whose single hand was extended in a gesture of greeting.

Nathan briskly stepped to Thomas's side and looked closely at Seth. "Strange to see you out here."

Seth looked at Nathan and smiled gently. "Thomas, have you been aboard that ship yet?"

Seth pointed to a small, sleek four-man sailing raft, whose sharply raked sails were silhouetted by the morning sky.

"Nathan, can I?" Thomas asked imploringly.

Nathan looked at Seth, clearly sensing something in Seth's tone—an odd touch of nervousness.

"Go on, Thomas, go aboard. Seth and I will be along to join you shortly."

The boy ran off, eager to explore something that in the past was strictly forbidden to him.

Seth came closer to Nathan and placed his hand on Nathan's shoulder. "Do you know what I have in my hand?" Seth asked.

Nathan stiffened.

"That's right, it's only a small pin, no longer than my finger. But if you make a move, if you try to cry out, its poison will be driven into the base of your skull."

"What do you want?" Nathan asked, trying to keep his voice calm.

"I think you're an agent of Zimri. At first I couldn't place you, then suddenly the memory came back to me. When I was in Zimri's prison, long years ago, you were one of the Inquisitioners, and that started me to thinking."

"Don't be foolish—many is the man who's come over to Inys Gloi from other orders."

"And many is the man whom Zimri has tried to place. Why is it that you were the only one to survive the wreck of our courier ship? Shortly thereafter Zimri was aware of the boy's existence. Oh, I've not told Riadent that, to be sure, for I've had my reasons, but through Michael I became aware of Zimri's knowledge and finally I put the two together. Now the question is, what has Zimri offered you in return?"

Nathan started to back up, but Seth tightened his grip.

"Don't make a move," he whispered. "There's more and I've not much time."

"Go on," Nathan whispered.

"Now let's look at this question. Assuming you are an agent of Zimri, his offering to you must be quite high indeed. Quite high, if you could bring the boy out, or better yet, simply kill him when escape became possible. Say, an archbishopric. Now, of course, Mor is out of the question; the First Choice is possible, but I would daresay Mord Rinn with its power would be more to the liking of one such as yourself."

Seth watched as Nathan's eyes widened ever so slightly. It was true! He had found the man's mark. He spared him a quick glance and looked toward the doorway leading into the citadel.

"I'm about to tell you two things. First you have been taken for a fool. Zimri has sold out to the Ezrians in return for their fleet. Part of the agreement was that an Ezrian has been secretly declared archbishop of Mord Rinn. Really, Nathan, you've been taken for the fool. Upon your return there will be no reward."

"You're lying."

"I wish I was."

A tremor ran through Nathan. The time was right. Seth looked back to the doorway. A white-robed form stood in the shadows.

"I'm about to walk over to that ship. Thomas is already aboard. You can betray me but I have left in a convenient place a note of my suspicions about you. Even if you kill me, it will still raise doubts about you as far as Riadent is concerned—and believe me, Nathan, everyone is expendable as far as Riadent is concerned. Once aboard that craft, I intend to hoist sail and take the boy and Varinna out of here."

"To where?"

"To Michael Ormson. If I've lied about Zimri, you still would have fulfilled your purpose to him by taking the boy out of Inys Gloi's hands, and you can have your reward. If I've told the truth, you'll be free to seek your revenge, for I am sure that there is a Secretary of the Church out there that could use your services. Now decide."

Nathan hesitated for a moment. It was all too fast, but he felt that Seth was telling the truth about both Riadent's possible reaction and Zimri's deceit.

"I'm with you."

"Right then. I want you to go aboard with the boy. Uncover the foresail as if showing it to him. I'll be over by the anchor line. When you're ready, run it up, I'll sever the anchor and we're off."

From the top of the high fortress the bell for morning services rang out high and clear. Fifty yards ahead of them the gate started to swing open, ready to admit the small raft that had come to the island during the night and had to wait for dawn's light to gain admittance.

"Thomas, hold the wheel steady and make believe that you're sailing the Ice," Nathan called, "while I unfurl this sail to show you how it's cut."

Going forward, Nathan watched as the first raft ran close-hauled past the steel gates.

A gray-bearded monk walked past Seth while on his way to morning services, and slowed at the sight of Thomas at the wheel and Nathan working a sail out of its casing.

"This is unwise," he said quietly. "Does Riadent know of this?"

"It is nothing," Seth replied smoothly. "I have his permission to show the boy the raft before it sails."

Turning away, but still looking suspiciously over his shoulder, the monk went on his way.

"Now," Seth hissed, "now hoist away."

Unhitching the halyard from its cleat, Nathan started to run the sail up.

The gray-bearded monk, hearing Seth, turned around, gave out a startled shout of surprise, and raced for the raft.

Pulling a dagger from the folds of his tunic, Seth sliced the anchor line away. The ship lurched forward as the wind filled the single sail running aloft, and Seth leaped aboard.

"Alarm! Alarm, close the gates!" the monk shouted as he sprinted to the side of the raft and leaped onto the portside outrigger.

Several monks in the harbor, turning at the shouts, started to race toward the raft, attempting to block its way, but the gate was still open wide.

"Thomas, you must trust me," Seth shouted. "Now lie down."

The boy started to whimper a protest, and with a quick backhanded blow Seth knocked him to the deck.

Grabbing the tiller, Seth guided the ship forward while kicking viciously at the monk who had boarded the raft, sending him over the side. Forward, Nathan still hauled down on the halyard, struggling with the cold-stiffened sail.

"The gate!" Nathan cried. "They're closing the gate."

With only seconds left, their only avenue of escape

was closing, as monks on either side struggled against the heavy, iron-shod barrier. Even as Seth watched, several monks rushed from a watchtower to lend their weight.

"We're doomed," Nathan cried.

Grimly Seth held the tiller. A crossbow bolt slammed down from the wall above and buried itself next to his right foot.

From a doorway by the gate a white-robed form suddenly hurried out. There was a flash of metal and one of the monks closing the gate fell over, spraying a crimson river of blood across the ice. With lightning speed the assassin turned and killed another monk, then, throwing the blade aside, ran toward the raft. The gate was still open.

"Varinna!" Seth shouted. "Quickly!"

Barely enough space was left to navigate as the starboard outrigger scraped along the edge of the closing barrier. Varinna leaped for the outrigger, slipped, nearly falling off, and then pulled herself aboard. Several more bolts rained down, and with a cry Nathan tumbled over backward, a quarrel sticking through his arm.

They were on the other side of the gate.

Clear of the harbor, the full force of the wind filled their single sail and the raft darted away from the wall. Lashing down the tiller, Seth directed Varinna to the mainsail halyard, and together they pulled it aloft. Filling the sail with the wind, the raft lurched forward, the apparent wind shifting forward as the vessel accelerated.

From behind they could hear a cannonshot, and the ice exploded with a thundering impact fifty yards to port, and after another report, a shell flew noisily overhead to burst with a blinding flash to starboard.

"We'll be out of range in a minute," Seth cried.

Looking to the still form of the boy, Varinna shouted a curse at Seth. As he quickly explained, she gave him an evil look while carrying her son to the small stern cabin. Going forward, Seth rolled Nathan over.

"We made it?" Nathan whispered.

"Clear of the harbor. By the time they set up pursuit, it will be too late. We made it, and this is the fastest thing on the Ice."

"Seth, come closer," Nathan whispered. "Kill the boy. That's what I was sent for. I only hesitated waiting for the moment of my escape. I was going to kill you the moment we were free. Kill the boy."

Seth shook his head.

"I know better than you. He's like his father, only worse, far worse. He's a menace to all, he is. He is a messenger from Beyond. Kill him, Seth." Nathan reached up imploringly, and with a cry of anguished rage, he fell back, slipping into unconsciousness.

Leaving Nathan's side, Seth stood up and went back to the tiller.

Varinna looked at the body on the deck. "Dead?"

"No, but he might very well wish he was. As long as either Inys Gloi or Zimri survives, he's as hunted as we are."

"Maybe we should kill him now."

"No, I think not, Varinna. Once we get to the Broken Tracks, I'll let him go. Someone like Peter might want him in the days to come, and I daresay Zimri will not appreciate Nathan's return."

There was another volley of shots, one spraying the deck with shrapnel, but the raft held true on its course of escape. And with the third volley they were safely beyond accurate range. In the distance Seth could see the pursuit ships setting out, but they were outdistancing them. Varinna, following Seth's orders, sheeted down the sails then returned to the tiller, which Seth now controlled, pointing the vessel into its fastest angle of sail.

"What did Nathan say?" she asked above the roar of the wind.

"Nothing important."

"He wanted to kill Thomas, didn't he?"

"Never mind."

She looked at him closely. "Will you?"

He shook his head.

"I think I fear that boy as much as Michael, but for once I will not betray anybody." He looked away for a moment. "Tell me what happened with Riadent."

"He fell for my plan, as I knew he would."

"Did you kill him?"

"No."

"But I thought you would!" Seth cried.

"Better to leave him to his own order," she said with a malicious smile. "What do you think they will say after our escape? And what will they do if Riadent reveals that I've taken the documents?"

"Then you got the listings?"

She nodded.

Seth felt an uneasiness about the affair. Riadent was still alive and would remain formidable if his order let him live. But for the moment there were more pressing concerns.

"We better sheet in tighter," Seth shouted above the rising wind. "Otherwise, we could be back in Riadent's hands." And so saying, the two set to the lines, while the raft shot across the Frozen Sea.

# CHAPTER 17

"HAUL IN THERE NOW, HEAVE AWAY ON THAT FORE-ROYAL sheet! Heave away there!"

Cursing with the effort, the crew tightened the sheet, causing the light frigate to inch up off its port outrigger.

"She's doing at least four the wind," Daniel shouted above the roaring gale as the *Bac Marcneach* raced northeastward, running abeam the wind.

"Must be near to forty leagues an hour," Michael replied as he and Daniel huddled in the scant protection of the windscreen.

The rigging shrieked overhead, counterpointing the deep humming resonance of the blades that cut across the mirror-smooth sea.

"'Tis not often that the Ice holds so smooth this far south," Daniel replied. He peered for a moment over the railing, then ducked back down, pulling his double-hooded parka even tighter.

Dreamily, Michael leaned against the barrier, letting his gaze wander across the smooth arcing curves of the tightly cleated sails, which harnessed the wind to their design. Two men struggled up from belowdecks, and sealing the airtight lock, they raced over to the pilots, relieving them from their half-hour watch. Staggering with the cold, the two pilots turned and, nodding to Michael, scurried below.

"Should follow them down," Daniel shouted. "'Tis death to stay up here too long."

Michael shook his head and pointed to indicate that

213

Daniel could leave if he wished, but he knew full well that the old warrior would not budge until Michael decided to return to the pile of reports and documents awaiting him in his cabin.

For two weeks they had been patrolling the Southern Shelf awaiting reports from the north, and what little that came was scant assurance. Zimri's scout and patrol craft had pushed them back from the Ezrian coast; indications were that the axis of attack would be there. But Michael dared not commit his fleet in that direction lest Zimri with a quick move swing to the west and storm the Mathinian Pass, thereby outflanking him and cutting him off from his base of operations. The crisis was building, and even now they were running a half day ahead of their fleet to the east, awaiting the next courier ship. She was long overdue.

Huddling lower and pulling up the bearskin cape around his shoulders, Michael let his mind drift away into a soft, dreamlike state—falling prey to the hypnotic trance of wind and speed.

So like the beginning, he thought quietly, when I stood watch alone in the chart marker's box. He let his gaze wander over to the small cubicle where a slender, shivering form stood alone, reading the charts and marking the conditions of the ice.

How he wished he could sail on like this forever, running freely across a northwesterly gale, standing watch, free of responsibility and the dread of what must come.

Daniel suddenly nudged him roughly, and gaining Michael's attention, he pointed aloft.

"Something's up," Daniel shouted. "Lookout's coming down."

Standing, Michael looked over the railing and swept the horizon with his gaze.

To the north was the faint outline of the Broken Tracks, rearing above the smooth southern plane. Astern four small escort ships trailed, and farther back two light frigates ran support, but he could make out nothing to forward.

The lookout alighted on the deck and ran to Michael's side. "Master, sail two points off the starboard bow."

"What is she?"

"Can't tell from this distance."

Daniel went over to the pilot's box and ordered the new heading.

Turning slightly off the wind, the frigate accelerated.

"There it is," the chart reader shouted. "There, almost dead ahead."

Within another minute the clear silhouette of the light corsair's three masts was visible to all, its billowing towers of taut blue canvas angled sharply against the afternoon sky.

"Who is she?" Michael shouted to the chart reader.

"Can't tell yet, but looks to be one of ours out of Mathin."

"Curious," Daniel said. "Mathinian ships are only as far east as the Gormathian Pass."

With less than a mile to go, the ship let off a volley of rockets that arched away with the wind.

"It reads 'run parallel with my course,'" the chart reader shouted.

Daniel looked at Michael, waiting for a response. The command was only given in haste, when something was pressing from behind.

"Follow that request," Michael replied softly.

"Prepare to jibe," Daniel shouted. "All hands, all hands!"

The cry thundered through the deck below, and even before the crews poured up on the deck, the *Bac Marcneach* shot past the courier ship.

"All hands stand ready. Helm over."

The two pilots pulled hard away on the wheel and the blades, answering to the tiller ropes, cut a sharp arc to starboard.

The frigate reached its angle of maximum speed and, passing it, slowly started to drop off its wind.

With a wave of the red signal pennant, the men uncleated the sheets and pulled the booms parallel to the keel.

"Jibe ho!"

With a resounding *boom* the wind caught the sails on the starboard side, bellying them out. Lines rattled through the blocks and the struggling crews worked to stop the swing and pull the sails back in for a close-hauled run. With lightning-like speed the ship shot away, so that Michael had to grab the windbarrier railing to keep from tumbling over. The courier ship was already a mile ahead of them, but its sails were out so that within several minutes the *Bac Marcneach* was pulling alongside. To the flanks the escort ships were executing the same maneuver and pulling closer, awaiting Michael's orders.

Ever so gently the outriggers of the two ships touched, and a great bearlike creature leaped down the corsair's support beams then crossed over to the frigate.

Eager hands reached out to pull him aboard, and even though the men had been dismissed, they crowded close around, curious to hear the reason for the strange maneuver.

"Vasilia of Mathin, two days out of the Gormathian Pass. Is this the Prophet's ship?"

"I am here," Michael replied, and the men parted, letting him approach.

Vasilia looked coldly at him, then with a quick gesture indicated that he would prefer to speak in private.

"Go on, they're good men here; I've nothing to hide from them."

"Master, I prefer not to—"

"I remember you, Vasilia, you've been with me since the Mathinian Pass. Now go ahead and report, I trust these men."

"It's finished, Michael, they're not six hours behind me and closing."

A murmur of dismay swept across the deck.

"Silence!" Daniel shouted, but the voices would not die away.

"Go on and report," Michael said. "From the beginning."

"All the eastern passes have fallen. We've lost, Michael, we've lost."

"Make sense, man!" Daniel shouted. "Stop raving like an idiot. How could we have lost? We know where they are and our fleet will smash them."

"Listen to me," Vasilia cried, tearing aside his face mask in anguish.

"We got a confused report at the Gormathian Pass less than an hour before they hit us from the southward side. Ezra's gone over to Zimri, they've doubled his strength, they have, and that's not the worst—not at all. Their fleet arrived off the East Ezrian Pass and Eldric was there, and the scum betrayed us. He opened the pass, he did, and went over to Zimri as well, with promise of pardon. The few Mathinians with him were slaughtered, and only a single raft of our men escaped to bear word to Gormath. Curse them, curse them all, Michael, they've doomed us, the bastards."

Vasilia broke into wild ravings and the deck echoed with shouts of panic and confusion.

Michael turned from his men, and pushing through the crowd, he went forward to the bow.

Daniel and several of the Companions followed him, half fearful of some dreadful act.

Concealed beneath his mask they could not see the strange, distant smile on his features as he looked out across the ice. And when he turned to face them he was quiet, as if removed from all earthly concern.

Confused, crying in anguish, the crew waited his command. In spite of his words at the Sacred Grove, many fell to their knees, as if he could by the wave of a hand render some great miracle that would bring amend to all pain.

"And so the final betrayal has come," Michael said softly. "For our cause was of this world, and we must therefore reckon with the frailties of men. Eldric has gone over and so has Palao, but little does he know what he will create.

"Press on all canvas!" Michael suddenly shouted. "We must return to the fleet. Order the four courier ships to the passes between here and Mathin, to pass the word."

"Do we fight them?" Daniel asked, his voice grim.

"No, Daniel, not this time. Zimri alone we might have faced. If Eldric was with us I would even have dared to stand against both Zimri and Ezra. But not now—they are too many, and there can be no surprise, as we have had before. They are like us now, Daniel. All ritual lost, any knowledge usable. We must return to Mathin. Back to Mathin, where it all started an eternity ago."

"My lord Zimri, signal from the van: 'Enemy rearguard in sight.'"

"Do you think they'll offer a fight?" Peter asked, looking forward to the line of ships on the distant horizon.

"Who can tell with the Prophet, my dear Peter? Who can tell?"

Turning from his secretary, Zimri walked to the bowsprit, letting the full force of the northwesterly wind pull at his ornate ceremonial robes. From horizon to horizon rode the armed might of the Holy Alliance. Far forward sailed the light frigates and heavy battle rams of the Cornathian brotherhood. Astern nearly a thousand assorted ships followed—four-man battle rafts, bombardment ketches, light and heavy corsairs, frigates, transports, and the massive bulk of a dozen battle cruisers, which were the sole remnants of a distant age of warfare.

Nearly a hundred fifty thousand men sailed with the fleet, most of them heavy shock troops for the siege of Mathin. Zimri knew he should feel an overwhelming sense of awe, for this truly was the largest fleet that had ever sailed the Ice. Never before had so many taken to the Ice in a common cause. Turning, he looked aloft, and *that* sight still filled him with awe . . . and a quiet fear of what such an act represented.

Floating high in the afternoon sky, a small kitelike object danced and darted at the end of a thousand-foot tether. Balor had told him of such a device and showed him a design from the archives from Before. With such a device, Balor claimed, a man could be pulled behind a ship into the sky by the force of the wind. Such an object was blasphemy, but by *ex cathedra* the Holy See could make any blasphemy orthodox, and Balor's argument was effective.

"Contrary to what we teach," Balor had whispered, "we both know that the Earth is indeed round. Therefore, the higher a man is, the farther he can see. Using such a device, a man can be raised four, even five hundred feet into the air—twice as high as a ship's mast. Therefore he can see far beyond the highest lookout and give warning long before the enemy sees him. If Peter had sailed with such a device before the Mathinian Pass, we could have avoided Ormson's trap. Take this and use it, Zimri, for the Prophet is wily and can still trap us. This can give warning long before we are seen, since the man who flies in such a device can spot the enemy and, using a weighted dispatch case suspended from a pulley block, can slide messages down the tow line to the ship's deck."

Several had died learning to master the technique of flying, but now half a dozen such devices were scattered throughout the fleet, and in the long pursuit toward Mathin had given fair warning of flanking raids before the attacks had even been launched.

The surprise would work for the coming encounter, Zimri thought, but a year from now what new miracle would he have to work to overcome the advantage? He watched for several minutes as the kite weaved back and forth on the end of its tether, wondering at the courage of the man above, who was held in awe by his shipmates.

"It is yet another sign, isn't it, my lord?"

Turning, Zimri saw that Peter had come forward to join him.

"Do you ever wonder where this will all end?" Peter continued. "A generation ago a fleet of but fifty ships inspired awe; now we have twenty times that number, and the very nature of our lives has changed forever. Where will this all end, my lord? What have we wrought?"

"There can be no end," Zimri said sadly. "Our forefathers knew that, and so did Michael, who broke the pattern of the past, casting all tradition aside."

"We should have killed him in the beginning, the way I wanted to."

"Let's not argue that now, Peter. How could we have known?"

"Inys Gloi knew."

"Yes, Inys Gloi. I wonder what they are making of all of this."

"For you have fallen victim to the ways of the flesh. Your name is anathema, your existence cursed, your path to salvation damned forever."

"He is doomed to torment eternal," the assembled host replied.

"You who were entrusted, you who were the culmination of a thousand years, the bringer of our Return, placed all in jeopardy—our dreams, our hopes, our Final Desire."

"He is doomed to torment eternal," came the response.

"We curse you forever, and now do remove from you the mark of thy most Sacred Office."

The man held between two blood-smeared monks tottered, his bloody robes soaked crimson from the dozens of wounds inflicted by red-hot pincers that had burned his flesh and seared his manhood.

The black-robed monk stepped from the assembly and approached the tortured form.

"Riadent, we curse you forever," he whispered, "all for that whore."

He reached into Riadent's robes and pulled loose the signet of office, its leather thong cutting deep into Riadent's flesh. He moaned softly.

"You stand before us accursed, your punishment clear. What atonement do you plead?"

Riadent looked at Jeremiah, the new Master, and with a pained, distant smile merely nodded his head. It was over, all over at last. He had awakened to find the monks gathered, hovering over his naked form, the nightgown of Varinna draped over him accusingly, and the signet by his side. He could have no explanation, no defense, only the agony of his shame and the two weeks of humiliation and torture.

"In the Name of Holy Church, in the Name of Inys Gloi, and all that was. In the Name of the Father, Sun, and Holy Spirit, and in the Name of all that could have been, I now condemn thee forever."

Jeremiah nodded to the blood-spattered Inquisitioner who stood behind Riadent.

"Finish it," Jeremiah whispered.

Riadent watched with ferretlike eyes as the Inquisitioner stepped in front of him. In his hand a steel rod shimmered red with incandescent heat. The Inquisitioner held it high, so that all might see, and a soft moan of anticipation ran through the assembly as they gazed at the twin prongs glowing at the end of the rod.

The Inquisitioner drew closer, filling his universe, the heat shimmers distorting, rising around him like an unholy veil.

Riadent tried to look past it, to fill his universe with a last vision—the smoke-filled chapel, lit by a thousand candles.

It came in upon him, the waves of heat closing over him. Instinctively he closed his eyes, plunging the world into blackness. He would not scream! No, he will not . . .

As the prongs melted into the twin liquid orbs that boiled and exploded from the heat, his screams echoed far behind the chapel, drifting out across the harbor beyond. The scorching fluid bubbled and hissed down his cheeks, and a gentle sigh of release could be heard from those who had gathered to watch.

Then rough hands reached for Riadent, tearing the clothes from his battered body. Through the overwhelming wave of pain came a distant voice.

"Cast him out into the darkness, to the Damnation that awaits him Forever."

Strong arms dragged him away from the altar, and they led him away as the assembled brothers intoned the words of excommunication.

*"Tarn nam hel du gruman acth . . ."*

From some hidden reserve of strength, Riadent threw back his head and shrieked, "He is truly the One, and we are His pawns. I'll be waiting for you in Hell!"

One of the brothers cuffed him across the side of the head and he fell silent, lost to his own agony.

Reaching the long staircase, they started down. Step by painful step they dragged him, and with every jarring blow he remembered how they had once felt upon bare knees or sandaled feet. He remembered how he had first ascended them on his knees to the Night of Initiation, and how a day had come when the brothers had carried him up those same stairs for his Installment as Master. Down through the fortress carved from a single stone the executioners dragged him, as the memories assailed him with their own special pain.

The door, they would soon reach the door and beyond that the gate, and even as he thought it the door swung open, and his flesh cried out in torment at the searing bitter cold. His useless feet dragged against the marble-smooth ice, and above the roaring of the wind he could hear the gate opening. As they passed through the gate, the full fury of the freezing wind tore into his flesh, so that he moaned a soft, pitiful cry. The two executioners stopped and lifted him erect.

"God curse you forever," one of them whispered, and with a violent shove they tossed him out onto the Ice.

As the bloody film that covered his body froze, Riadent barely heard the two monks retreating. The wind moaned a soft dirge.

Was it day? Night? He could not tell. Was the aurora out? Ah, how many times had he stood alone upon the pinnacle watching, watching and waiting for the signs—the memories, God, please stop the memories. Let me die empty.

He tried to stand but his body refused to respond. The shivering, uncontrollable and excruciating, started, and his wounds reopened. His fingers and hands were numb, and the firelike cold was creeping into his flesh.

"Come, soothe the burning," he whispered. "Come and soothe."

Again he tried to struggle to his feet; this time he succeeded.

"I am the Master," he shrieked. No, I *was* the Master—cursed, condemned, my name forbidden, my memory destroyed.

He tried to extend his arms to the heavens, tottered for several seconds, dreaming that he was soaring upward, then slowly he collapsed onto the Ice. Curling into a ball, he whimpered softly then whispered a blessing as the pain gradually drifted away with the wind.

It's not long now. Yes, he could remember watching this. Watching as a victim of his blade struggled feebly against the cold. He could remember so clearly now, how the boy still alive was tossed naked onto the ice and left to die. He had sat with him, driven by curiosity to see how a man dies from the cold, watched as the nameless victim struggled and cried, and finally grew still as his eyes froze over with the gaze of death.

But I have no eyes to freeze. Again he screamed. And his thoughts drifted away.

Terrified, he struggled back from the darkness, fighting desperately. No, not yet, not the falling away! Panic gripped him with its icy touch. It was drawing in upon him and he fought with the fury of despair as it reached out, drew him closer, and enveloped him in a warm blanket of sleep.

"They don't know," he whispered, not sure if he now felt remorse or triumph. She had taken it and they did not yet realize. He had fulfilled the final destiny, the final betrayal that, in the end, only he could see. Across a thousand years they had not realized this. He could see, yes, he could see it as it drew closer, a deepening of a darkness beyond.

"Yes, come, sweet death, come to me..."

"We found him just beyond the gate, Jeremiah. He didn't get far.

Jeremiah turned away from the executioner and smiled. "Take a raft. Load his body aboard it and drag the carcass far beyond the sight of this mountain. Bury him deep, and drive a stake through his body as a sign of our contempt. Bury him deep, I tell you—I never want his remains to be found."

"As you wish, my master."

Jeremiah looked up with surprise; he was still not used to the title. Yes, he was the Master now, with a legacy that would require all his effort. The boy was gone, and even now Zimri must be approaching the gates of Mathin. He had so little time in which to act, but the path was clear. He would assassinate them all, and then pick up the pieces.

"There it is, Michael," the pilot whispered. "The three sisters bearing to the north, Mathin is not a quarter glass away."

It was early afternoon. Looking back astern he could see half a dozen smudges of smoke on the horizon marking the latest casualties of a two-day fighting withdrawal. They had slowed Zimri's advance by not more than a day, but had gained time enough for the northward garrisons to evacuate.

"Mathin harbor in sight."

Barely a sail was visible before them, since the main fleet had arrived the night before—those that had not quietly deserted under cover of darkness and made course for the islands of Sol to wait out the battle.

"I can see it," a young Companion cried, "there—the hills of Mathin."

The ship grew silent, the only sound around them was the faint *hum* of the wind in the rigging and the rattle of the blades. The hundreds of men aboard ship slowly pressed toward the rail, standing behind Michael to gaze upon their city, as if seeing it for the first time.

Michael looked across the frozen sea and a flood of memories washed over him. In his mind he again envisioned the city as it once was, surrounded by the lush forested hills. He remembered every detail of that first approach to combat and the awakening to a bitter young woman of eighteen.

"Oh, Janis, are you with me?" he whispered. "Can you see this return, this coming back to where my life began?"

"What was that, Master?" the young Companion asked.

"Oh, nothing—nothing at all," Michael replied with a quiet smile.

"All hands prepare to loosen sail," Daniel cried. "All hands."

The men, each locked in his own memories, turned back to their duties and Michael stood alone, distant, and wondering.

No chants nor wild calls of delight arose from the ship's return to port, for each man's heart bore a sense of farewell. For one final moment they were ice runners, sailors of the Frozen Sea, free to float across the ice. Men hardened by a generation of combat, a generation of ceaseless strife, each knew a sense of regret and ending that brought a thickness to the throat. They, the crew of the Master, might never again hear the high-pitched call to battle, and go to the sea.

"Ease off your sheets there, all topsails and topgallants."

The speed dropped off imperceptibly at first, and then more and more noticeably, as the wind started to back off from the bow.

"Signal pennants. Mark steerage to starboard, trap line ahead."

The ship came up, pinching into the wind, and maneuvered past the outer trap line, half a league from the first ice wall.

"In the channel now, red flags to port, black to starboard."

Crossing into the channel, the ship passed thousands of laborers—old men, women, and even the smallest children, who, with the battle less than an hour away, still labored on the pitfalls and barriers.

A masked battery suddenly loomed up, so well camouflaged that Michael did not even notice it until they were alongside.

The hundred men manning the eight guns stood silent and grim, knowing that they had little chance of seeing the day's end. Michael rushed to the railing and raised his hand in salute, but they did not see him and he turned away.

"Ease off mizzen and fore mains, ease off all jibes."

The slackened sails arched out to port, snapping in the breeze, and the slowing vessel drove onward, powered only by the large mainsail.

They negotiated a twisting S-turn approach into the final run for the outer gate. Another masked battery was passed, this one protected by covered trenches and sally ports.

Some of the men raised their hands in a salute, and Michael responded with a gesture that many thought was not unlike the blessings of a priest.

Michael turned to the signal master. "Send up the red flares. Signal enemy approaching, prepare for attack."

Three rockets arced up from the deck and exploded in a flaming scarlet light. From all sides the people looked up then turned their gazes to the east. No sign was yet visible from that direction. The smoke of the last clash was too distant, the only sign of activity a half-dozen escort ships following in the flagship's wake. To the shouted commands of the barrier commanders, the people turned aside from their labor and by the thousands started back to the city gate.

The ship drew closer to the outer wall and passed the squat, heavy icetowers that bristled with the batteries taken from a frigate, the gun crews standing ready in position.

The last quarter mile of ice to the wall was a deadly maze of traps, sally ports, masked batteries, and tunnels. The gate to the outer wall was finally passed, and Michael surveyed the heavy ice wall that was rimmed with a hundred guns and an equal number of ballistae, onagers, and siege crossbows.

The next quarter mile was a replica of the last, with nearly the entire space between the outer and inner walls taken up by barriers, trenches, and masked batteries. At last the inner harbor was reached, to reveal a nightmare tangle of shipping that echoed with the cries of thousands of men preparing for the shock of battle.

Every ship of Michael's fleet was crammed into the harbor, so that barely enough room remained for his frigate to park. Once-proud vessels, veterans of a hundred fights, were being stripped, their guns placed in batteries to cover both the landward and seaward approaches. Over a hundred pieces still in reserve were placed to cover streets, alleyways, and points of possible breakthrough. Looking to the hills beyond the city, Michael noted where a dozen twenty-four-pounders had been placed in a makeshift fortress within the Sacred Grove to act as a high battery and to prevent the enemy's capturing the vantage point and using it as a place from which to shell the city.

The Companions, finished with their labors aboard ship, stood to in formation, awaiting Michael's command. Daniel came to his side.

"Master, it's time we left."

"Yes, yes it is, isn't it?" He looked around the ship one last time and walked over to the now-pilotless wheel. Absently he touched it, as if trying one last time to re-member, to touch the spirit of an ice runner and the thrill of the open ice.

"Yes, it's time." He turned away. "Come, let's go to the outer wall and watch the approach."

Reaching the outrigger support beam, Michael swung himself over the side and stepped onto the ice.

A hooded form, dressed in white and wearing a silver medallion, wormed through the press of men who had gathered around the ship. "Michael Ormson, Wenarth, the garrison master."

Wenarth had the distinct heaviness of the Zardok fam-ily and, as the oldest cousin, had assumed control of the family after Cowan.

"All is ready?"

"As you ordered, Michael. The double line of defense is finished, the fortress in the Grove as well. We've stock-piled enough rations to keep us until the Flowing Sea returns. When we received word of the breakthrough most of the noncombatants, at least those that were willing, were evacuated to Sol."

"Good, good. I'm going out to the wall; would you care to join me?"

"Master, you better come with me. There's something you must deal with."

"Can't it wait? Zimri will be here within the hour."

"Master."

Michael could sense a strain in Wenarth's voice. "What is it?"

"Not here, Master," Wenarth said in a soft voice.

Michael looked to Daniel, who nodded. With Wenarth taking the lead, they headed back into a city that echoed with the cries of thousands who knew that the remorseless enemy was finally at the gate.

Coming up past the warehouses, they stepped into the great square, which was covered by a dozen guns mounted hub to hub behind a barrier of rigging and bales of canvas, all frozen into a solid block. The front of the citadel had a false front of reinforced timbers designed to absorb all but the heaviest shot, and passing through a sally port, Michael entered the dimly lit interior.

"This way, Master," Wenarth called, leading them through the assembly hall and up into the private chambers.

Suddenly Michael was on his guard. Something was wrong. The sight of heavily armed guards at the top of the stairs reinforced a sense of foreboding.

"What is this, Wenarth?" Daniel did nothing to mask the threat in his voice.

"In there." Wenarth pointed to Michael's old chambers. "No one knows but myself and the guards."

Michael went to the door.

"Let me go in first," Daniel called. But Michael brushed him aside.

The door swung open and Michael stepped in, closed it, leaving Daniel outside. For several seconds he stood lost in darkness, as his eyes adjusted to the light. Then the ghostlike shadows started to come clear.

"You," Michael whispered.

"Yes, it is I, Michael Ormson. Seth Facinn, who was with you in the beginning." And from behind Seth stepped two others. "You already know Varinna, and this, Ormson, is your son."

"Signal 'Mathin harbor in sight.'"

A wild shout of anticipation went up from the assembled crew. The goal of a decade, at last within reach.

A flurry of commands was shouted across the deck as the crews stood to in prepartion for the assault.

"There is still time for a counterblow," Peter whispered.

"I think not."

"How can you be sure?"

"I can't, it's as if Michael has acquiesced to this final

turn of events. For the last year we have watched his power diminish in a manner which I first thought was a result of my skill, and then as the situation compounded, I felt was good fortune. But now I truly cannot explain this. Peter, here we are, before Mathin. The majority of his forces in hiding or, in fact, sailing at our side. Why, Peter, why?"

Peter turned to look at Zimri, whose sudden self-doubt was unusual. "But it is here, it is the truth."

"Is it?"

"Why ask now?"

Their conversation was drowned out for a moment as the signaler called out the communications from the advanced ships.

"Enemy fleet within the harbor, no resistance."

"What else could they do?" Peter cried. "Look at the power we have, Zimri. Look around you."

With a sweeping gesture Peter pointed across the Frozen Sea.

From horizon to horizon the ships were closing in, so that the patchwork sails of a thousand vessels blanketed the ice in multicolored hues. Plumes of icy spray arced behind the vessels, swirling across the breeze. Even above the roar of the wind, Zimri could hear the shouted chants as the men poured up onto the decks, eager for the battle. Columns of dark smoke marked several wrecks that were soon astern, the detritus of the withdrawing fleets final skirmishes. And as they swung close to a burning corsair, the assembled crews shouted hatred and abuse on the stunned survivors who huddled next to the flaming ship.

"Yes, what else could he have done?" Zimri replied.

Peter looked back to Zimri. "Think you that Michael has fled, that Mathin has been abandoned?" A note of concern tinged in his voice.

"No, Peter, I don't think so. Michael is there, he's waiting for us."

"Funny," Peter responded. "I remember a conversation with Michael, long ago. I told him that we would meet again, and that when we did, it would be to witness his death."

Zimri merely nodded and turned away.

Dozens of crew members were swarming into the rigging to catch the first view of the hated city, and within several minutes the men in the fighting top picked up the cry, and soon even those on the deck could see the low hills rising above the city. Onward they sailed, and with every minute the city came closer into view, while ahead the forward van slowed its pace.

"It's time," Zimri said, and looking back to the signal master, he called for the deployment to begin.

Six red flares rocketed off the deck of the ship, and the separate components of the fleet answered as planned.

Cornath's red attack fleet of light corsairs and frigates arched off to windward while the green fleet pinched up tighter to starboard, cutting out in a pincer movement to surround the island. One transport with a thousand men and half a dozen firegates cut across the eye of the wind and turned onto the opposite tack, to the north, to secure the Mathinian Pass so that supplies could be funneled down from Ezra and Cornath beyond. Their secondary mission, which only the squadron commander yet knew, was to destroy the monument to Michael's first victory, exhume the bodies of his men from the Ice and take them to St. Judean's Bane, so that no shrine would be left.

Eldric's fleet was pushed forward, the first shock of battle would be theirs. If left to the rear, this least trustworthy of allies might desert. In the forward position, under the guns of more trustworthy Cornathians, there would be no place to go but into the attack. Finally came the gold fleet of Palao, the heavy siege troops, equipment, and the elite shock troops of Mor. To them would fall the burden of the assault, once an opening was carved through the island's defenses.

"Let's go forward," Zimri shouted to the pilot, "and run along the wall. I wish to see what we face."

As the main body of the fleet dropped astern, the *Braith*

*du Mor* came up astern of Eldric's fleet, which was slowly probing forward. The range to the outer defenses dropped to under a league.

"There's the channel," the chart reader cried. "See the tracks, off to starboard."

Even as he spoke a ripple of fire slashed across the ice, and a half mile ahead a light frigate lost a blade and crumpled onto the ice.

"Hidden battery," Peter cried. "Masterful, masterful concealment, damn them."

Zimri watched as several light corsairs suddenly toppled over, falling victim to the outer edge of the trap line. Within seconds Eldric's fleet was turning, and then, with a blinding flash, the outer wall erupted, as a hundred pieces opened up with a scathing volley. Eldric's ships fired back at what had been their comrades just weeks before. All up and down the line the volleys roared and thundered, as shots shrieked, hummed, and fell among the massed shipping.

"Run them out!" the ship's master cried, and Zimri could feel the gun carriages rumbling beneath his feet. It was extreme range, but it was important that the fleet see the Holy See's ship engaged in the first volleys.

"Turn her to port," the master cried.

The ship heeled over and turned onto a course parallel to the wall. A heavy shot slammed across the deck amidships, cutting a bloody swath of destruction.

Zimri looked at Peter and laughed. "Wouldn't it be ironic if we were suddenly killed here, so close to the end?"

"Don't *say* that," Peter cried, making a sign to ward off evil.

"Aim for the masked battery," Zimri called.

Hurrying to the starboard side, he beckoned for a ballista captain to step aside. Grabbing hold of the machine's lanyard, he waited.

Another shot fired from the forward Mathinian battery struck the ship belowdecks.

"Steady there, steady" came the cry from the gunnery captain.

The range closed as they swept down across the killing zone of the camouflaged guns.

"Ready. Fire!"

The deck shook beneath Zimri's feet, and with a firm pull he snapped the lanyard back, releasing the trigger. A six-foot bolt slashed out of the ballista with a resounding crack, arcing up and away. All around him the men cheered, and in the smoke of battle the bolt was lost to view. Red flashes of fire rippled from the battery and the wall beyond, and another shot screamed through the rigging, severing lines and dropping the mizzentop sail in a tangled heap.

"Turn her away, Vinar. Let Eldric handle this exchange."

Zimri looked back to his cheering men.

"Prepare to unload. The siege of Mathin begins!"

# CHAPTER 18

DISTANT FLASHES RIPPLED ACROSS THE EVENING SKY. ROCKET flares slashed overhead, illuminating with garish light the field of mortal strife. Shouts of exultation, battle lust, pain, and fear echoed in the alleyways and the great square below, as the wounded were carried back from the walls and reinforcements were rushed to fill the gaps. Through the night Zimri's forces had driven forward with their maddening assaults, looking for the weakness, the one opening that would bring the assault to a quick conclusion without the agony of a siege. But Mathin had withstood the endless attacks.

He was exhausted beyond all caring, his parka and cape stained crimson from the blood of a bodyguard swept off the wall by the impact of a solid shot. Yes, they had held, Michael thought wearily, held out against the first attack, and now the siege would begin in earnest.

The door creaked open, but he did not turn.

"You sent for me?" Her voice shook. Was it fear or something else?

A sudden flash of light outshone the first light of dawn. Long seconds afterward a deep rumbling boom roared over the city. A ship's magazine going up. Hundreds dead most likely, all from that one flash of light.

He turned around to face her. "Why did you come back?" Michael whispered.

She stepped closer, and by the light of the fireplace he saw that she was trembling.

"Are you afraid?"

"Yes."

"Of me?"

"I don't know."

Michael looked away, not wishing to face what could be said. "The boy," he said, quickly changing the subject. "Is he resting?"

"Finally, but the guns kept him awake most of the night."

Yes, the boy. The way Thomas had stared at him, eyes wide in fascination and fear. What could he say to him? What could he say to his son? A son raised and trained by Inys Gloi to be his replacement. A boy who would not come into his own until his father was dead.

"The older he grew, the more he reminded me of his father," Varinna said softly. "He became a living nightmare for me, a constant reminder, my everpresent conscience."

"Is that why you returned?"

She drew closer.

"At first you were nothing to me. You were a victim, a vehicle of revenge against a world that destroyed my family, my home, and my life, so that Inys Gloi was all that I had. But afterward, when Thomas took on form, he came to be a living reminder of what my life should have been, and through him I dreamed a fantasy. That you were real, that what happened between us was somehow real and could endure."

Michael looked at her, searching for the truth.

"Don't look at me that way," she whispered. "I can't stand your accusations. I betrayed you and seduced you for Inys Gloi, but as the years passed that act has somehow taken on a different meaning."

"And what meaning did you find?"

"I dreamed that I was more than a whore of Inys Gloi. I dreamed that Thomas would be the only legacy I would have, and as his mother I would shape that life. I could not leave that final action to them."

"And what else did you dream?" Michael asked, his voice cold and distant.

"That something more existed between you and me than a cold act of lust and betrayal."

Michael turned away and looked back out the window. Varinna drew closer and stood by his side.

"At twelve I saw my family butchered and I was taken prisoner. The rape I experienced still burns through the worst of my nightmares. Two years passed as I lived the horror of a freebooter's slave, until one of them took me to Inys Gloi. There I was trained for their purposes, and at eighteen I was sent out to do the work that they looked upon with loathing but needed done nevertheless. I have had nothing, Michael, nothing at all until Thomas, and they were going to take that away from me as well."

"So why did you come here, into this trap? You could have lost yourself in Sol or one of the lesser islands."

"Because of you."

"You're idealizing—I was nothing to you. And you were an escape from the nightmares for me."

"I know that," she replied. "If I said I loved you it would be a lie, for when I slept with you there was nothing in my heart. But now there is. We have nothing left, Michael, except that which was created between us. That and a dream which grew in my heart over the years that you, of all the men I have known, were someone special. You were so vulnerable, even in your rage, and yet you commanded such power, as if it came from some inner source. Can't you understand what I'm saying?"

She suddenly cried. "I have had nothing—no love, no life, nothing but deceit. I wanted to create this one dream, this one fantasy, that something in my life had some meaning."

"And you want that in me."

"Yes."

Gently he extended his arm, and drawing her close, he held her at his side.

"I won't ask anything else of you," she sobbed, "just this, nothing more. I'm not Janis, and I never can be."

Together they stood in silence, and finally, after a lifetime of pain, she at last felt a growing sense of peace—even as the distant battle raged.

A flash of gunfire etched the room in light. Thomas stirred in his sleep and with a gentle sigh settled back into the feverish world of dreams. Standing by his side, Seth looked on and, extending his hand, pulled the blankets up over the boy's shoulder then settled back into his chair.

How familiar it all was, as if he had stepped out of the room but for a moment. How many times had he come here late at night to hold council with Michael, only to be directed to this room where the Prophet and Janis sat quietly hand in hand, watching their Andrew sleep in this same bed. And now here he sat, locked in the guilt of the past, feeling the cold edge of madness clawing at his soul.

Not a word had been exchanged between them, and the look of murder in Daniel's eyes mirrored the hatred that all in the room felt when the Companions gathered at Michael's side. All night he had waited for the calling. And in his soul he knew that it would soon come at last.

"My lord Zimri, all assaults have failed, and with heavy casualties."

"How bad?"

Grimath looked down at the tally sheets passed up the line from the various unit commanders.

"Nearly ten thousand dead and wounded since yesterday. We managed to pierce the outer wall twice, but were driven back."

"Any estimates on their losses?"

"We can assume that for the numbers Michael had, he lost far too many in the retaking of the outer positions."

The windowpanes of the ship's cabin rattled from a volley launched by the bomb ketches positioned nearby. Turning away from Grimath, Zimri watched the shot as it streaked up and away, to crash down into the enemy's outer positions over a mile away.

"Most of the men were from Eldric's command?"

"Yes, my lord."

"Good. Before this campaign is ended I want his power stripped from him. He betrayed Ormson after a decade of alliance; he'd do the same to us if he thought it would work."

Peter, who was sitting quietly in the corner, stirred from his nap and looked up at Zimri. "The same for me, if you could do it, Zimri."

Zimri smiled back and did not reply.

"Grimath, I want the heavy shock troops of Mor passed forward. For the present we'll pull Eldric off the line. No more assaults—we'll go to siege. Pass the word to Palao's men as well; I want their siege engineers to meet with me within the hour. We'll encircle Mathin with a barrier wall of ice and then dig trenches forward. I also want every gun stripped from Eldric's ships."

"He'll not like that, Zimri," Grimath warned. "You might have a fight on your hands over this."

"Damn him, he can't do anything about it. If he tries to cut his way out, we'll smash him and he knows it. I don't want his vessels armed. Take all the artillery, and as the siege lines are constructed, the artillery is to be placed as far forward as possible."

"As you wish, my lord."

"I'm going forward. Prepare my raft."

Grimath, bowing low, left the cabin. And Peter, rousing himself from his chair, stretched and walked over to the window.

"This one's going to cost," Peter said casually, while scraping at the frost on the window.

"We always knew that. Anyone who could desert Ormson already has. What he has left are the hard core, the fanatics who have been with him from the beginning. We have to keep on the pressure at all cost. If Ormson lasts till spring, he could turn the tables on us. If I fail in this attack, I doubt that your Palao will back me up next fall."

"How's that?" Peter asked cautiously.

"Inys Gloi will put the pressure on Ezra. They don't want a final settlement of this issue, that I am sure of. If we are forced to retreat we'll not get a second chance like this to take Ormson, and in the end there will be an agreement—the two of us existing on the Ice, and his heresy will spread of its own accord."

"Perhaps it already has," Peter replied.

"What does that mean?"

"Look at how we fight. For that matter, look at Grimath. A generation ago his ability to read would have been grounds for death. Look at the technology we use, the exploding shells, the telescopes, the lifting of men into the sky. They are but the tip of the ice representing the hundreds of changes."

"That can be suppressed once this is over."

"But what of how we all think? We have come to accept change and new systems as normal. That is the most dangerous thing of all."

What is he driving at? Zimri thought. But the conversation was interrupted by a call from the deck. The raft was ready.

Leaving Peter, Zimri pulled on his heavy parka and went out onto the deck. Pulling down his goggles as protection from the icy glare, he lowered himself over the side and stepped onto the sleek, high-speed raft that carried the dark-blue sails of Mor and was embossed with the emblem of the Holy See.

Catching the northwesterly breeze, they ran toward the outer wall, passing several battered assault units returning to the transport ships. Some of the men recognizing who was aboard the raft raised their voices in a loud call for blessings, and standing by the bowsprit, Zimri made the Sign of the Arch over the kneeling men as the raft shot past.

The thunder of battle was soon all around them as the

raft cut between the light corsairs and frigates that weaved in and out, closing in to the wall, turning to fire, and then retreating as they prepared the next volley. An occasional shot hummed overhead or bounded across the ice. The first bodies from the assault sprinkled the ice before them, and looking toward the outer gate, Zimri saw how the occasional prone forms soon became a vast frozen carpet of twisted, mangled flesh. Several gaping holes marred the outer defenses; taking out his telescope, he examined the line, noticing that even in the midst of the bombardment, men were working to repair the breaches as quickly as they were formed.

Approaching as close to the wall as the pilot dared, the raft turned down onto a broad reach and accelerated away, turning occasionally to avoid a body.

"Where is he now? Zimri wondered.

The field of meditation was disturbed at last. The boy had long since awakened to join his mother, and he had then gone alone to the meditation chamber, which had remained unchanged for eight long years. Throughout the day Seth had sat alone, fasting, waiting. He had closed the world out, joining his will into the whole, letting his vision return again to the crystal purity, and in that moment he had again seen into what must finally become.

He knew at last when Michael had entered the room, but there was no calling to him, and alone in his thoughts he had waited, until, with a quiet, gentle voice, Michael had entered his thoughts and called to him.

He opened his eyes, and in the light of a single candle, he beheld Michael sitting crosslegged on the floor in front of him.

"So you have finally returned," Michael said softly.

"And you, my master, have finally come to see me."

Without expression, or show of emotion, Michael nodded slowly.

"Ah, Michael Ormson, whom I once guided with such care, what have we become in the end?"

"Don't you know?"

"I'm afraid to think of that, Michael."

"I'm not."

"You know what's coming don't you?"

"Yes, but then in my heart, I knew *that* in the beginning, far more than you ever suspected. Why do you think I resisted you so at the start, Seth? Why do you think I tried to turn away from this path? Because even more than you, I could see what was finally to come. But the more I tried to turn away, the more I was forced to walk the path. Now at last, I've gained a freedom beyond. For I learned not to resist it, but to flow with it."

"But Zimri will defeat you, and soon. If I am not mistaken, last night's assault strained your defenses to the limit, and there is far worse to come."

"I shall win," Michael said softly.

Seth looked into his eyes for long minutes. He remembered so many times before... could recall when those eyes were twin mirrors of madness. But they were calm, almost serene. And Seth did not have the heart, nor the will, to challenge what he believed.

"Do you know why I came back?" Seth asked weakly.

"Yes, I know. For in the end nothing remained to you. I had destroyed Inys Gloi for you, and Inys Gloi in turn had destroyed me. Nothing was left. You could in the end serve neither, and without some cause, without something to serve and to dream about, you could no longer exist. That is why in the end you came to me."

Seth nodded and was shocked to realize that tears clouded his own eyes.

"When I returned to them, it was with an empty heart, purged of all desire. For I did not know how much I truly loved you, Michael Ormson. I had dreamed that you were the One. But it was the One as declared by Inys Gloi."

"And yet you were a fulfillment as well," Michael whispered, looking past Seth, as if to some distant unseen land.

Michael was silent for a moment, as if judging his thoughts, and then, smiling softly at Seth, he continued.

"There was a beginning, when Inys Gloi understood the nature of power and of our mortal histories. They understood that at the moment of crisis a man steps forward, unique among men, and that with a vision beyond normal men he leads his people into another epic. Inys Gloi understood this, and in their collective meditations they could see dimly through the curtain, and knew that I would be the one, a thousand years before my name was ever spoken.

"But they did not understand the final act; that was veiled to them by something beyond all our understandings. They did not realize that what prophecy creates oftentimes is an instrument of destruction, designed to fulfill a higher destiny beyond anyone's imaginings. That is the Michael Ormson no one, not even you, Seth Facinn, ever understood. I was created by Inys Gloi, and it was you who was the agent of that creation. But ultimately it shall be I who destroys Inys Gloi, who after four thousand years has lost all sight of what it should have been. They never knew that in creating me, they were preparing their own *final* end.

"For that is how it has always been. How many have gazed at the cradle never knowing that they were looking at the digger of their grave? That is your tragedy, my old friend. You thought that in serving me, you also served your first master. You believed that Inys Gloi was a partner in a Divine Mystery and you were its agent. But, Seth, the final tragedy is that this drama between you and me was indeed planned long before the seas ever froze. It is designed to sweep away all—even its own creator, and to replace it with the new."

Michael fell silent, as if the words he had spoken had drained him of all energy, and lowering his head, he sat motionless.

Finally Michael stirred again. "It is the end for us, Seth," he whispered.

"I know, Master."

Michael looked around the room that at his command had not been touched since the night of the deaths of Janis and Andrew. The walls were still scorched from the flame, and on the floor dark bloodstains marked where Janis had died.

"You knew what they planned, didn't you? And it was one of your people who blocked the escape door."

"Yes," Seth replied, his voice choking.

"I realized that long ago," Michael replied. "The night you introduced Varinna into my bedroom I knew that Inys Gloi had its hand in that act as well. Janis was luring me away from the path that I had to fulfill."

"Why didn't you strike me down?"

"For the same reason that I let you introduce the poison all those years, the same way you introduced the drugs for meditation. I somehow understood that it was part of the plan, a plan that even I can only dimly peceive at times."

"Can you ever forgive me?"

"You were my teacher, my guide. It was you who awakened me long ago. For the sake of that, I looked away. For without Seth Facinn, the Far Seeing, there would never have been the Prophet. But that draws to its end, Seth."

Michael started to stir, as if preparing to leave.

"The cycle of betrayal is complete," Seth whispered. "Don't leave me just yet. There is one last act yet to perform. Did Varinna tell you what she entrusted to my care?"

"No, but I half suspect."

"Inys Gloi still has its power—the power of fear. We used that for a thousand years to spread the word and to control. The reasons for that are ending. But Inys Gloi does not yet know that or understand."

Seth reached into his tunic and pulled out a sheet of folded parchment.

"Here is a list of every agent upon the Frozen Sea and

where they can be found. With one blow, Inys Gloi can be paralyzed forever. Take it and use it as you wish, Michael. For with their assassins gone, the Holy Island is open to assault."

Michael took the document from Seth's trembling hand and slowly rose to his feet.

Seth looked at his hand and then extended the stump of the other arm. "Remember how I once played the lyre, my friend?"

"It was beautiful, Seth. It sounded like a voice from beyond this world of tears."

Seth looked at the trembling hand and whispered, "It is complete, the final betrayal, the final redemption."

Michael knelt back down and touched Seth lightly on the forehead. "Go in peace," he whispered. "Go in peace and may the Ice and Sky before you always be clear, my friend."

Standing, Michael left the room, gently closing the door.

"So it is complete," Seth whispered. "Nothing is left, for all has been done."

He closed his eyes; the only sound in the room was the distant roll of gunfire thundering in the night. But his thoughts were far away, far away across a distant frozen sea, when the world seemed young and the dream was real.

His hand no longer trembled; it was still, as he had prayed it would be. Reaching into his tunic, he felt the cold steel hilt. It slipped free so smoothly, the gentle rasping of metal on metal echoing in the ghost-filled room.

He held the blade aloft, a gift from a Grand Master, on the Night of Initiation. He held it aloft and as he gazed into its mystery the dream became real. Michael Ormson was the One, the cry echoed down through the years carried on the voices of a hundred thousand.

"Michael is the One," he cried as a cold shiver of numbing pain coursed through his body.

"Michael is the One..." And drifting into the night, his spirit slipped away.

# CHAPTER 19

With the passing of each night Michael walked the battlements of Mathin, and each journey was more difficult than the last, as the outer wall disintegrated under the weight of the enemy bombardment. Even before Daniel he maintained an image of calm acceptance, as if all would come right in the end, but ever so slowly a grim resignation settled upon the garrison as their numbers thinned and the situation became more and more desperate. What had once been towering walls were now nothing more than frozen wreckage barely higher than the surrounding ice, and the siege lines of Zimri inched ever closer, until finally, the guns were firing at nearly point-blank range, blasting gaping holes into the fortifications, while overhead the mortar shells continued to rain their shower of death.

"My lord Zimri, a messenger has come from the third Morian regiment."

"Show him in," Zimri called, rising from his cot while trying to shake the sleep from his body.

A blood-spattered monk entered the room and bowed low for the blessing.

Rising, he faced Zimri and pulled back his mask to reveal gaunt, haunted eyes strangely alight.

"My lord, I've been forward, nearly to the edge of the Mathinian line. I think they're abandoning the outer wall."

Smiling, Zimri called to his servant to fetch his parka and cape. "How can you tell?"

"During the middle watch the reply from their guns slacked markedly. I ordered our weapons to fall silent and we could hear them pulling out."

"Have you sent your men in?"

"One patrol only, and they were repulsed."

"But you still think they're pulling out?"

"I'm sure of it, my lord."

"Let's go forward then and see. Order up your regiment—what time is it, by the way?"

"Just past matins, still a quarter of the night till dawn."

Zimri was soon out on the ice, his bodyguards fanning out into the shadows. Passing the outer siege line where the men huddled in their ice caves, Zimri descended into the communication trench that led to the forward position less than a hundred yards from the enemy wall. By the Archlight he saw the shadows of the battered line looming closer, and was soon shouldering his way past the assembled men awaiting his command.

The silence was eerie, surreal, after two weeks of incessant bombardment. Reaching the forward position, Zimri peered up over the lip of the trench and listened.

After several minutes he turned to the commander. "Order your men in but stop at the wall. If they've withdrawn in order, there'll be a hell of a reception waiting for you if you press forward."

With a nod of acknowledgment the commander turned to his signaler. "General assault, and pass the word to the commanders of the hundred to stop at the wall."

A single green flare hissed skyward, cutting its path beneath the Arch.

Drawing their scimitars, and with raised shields, they rushed forward into the darkness. To the few Mathinian witnesses, the blue-clad host seemed to emerge from the grave. Not a shot was fired, no call to battle was made. As the men charged past, Zimri leaned out over the trench, waiting for a possible trap to be sprung. After several long minutes a white flare rose above what had been the Mathinian line. The outer wall had fallen.

\* \* \*

"They're on the wall," Daniel whispered.

"I know. But we got out without losses."

"This puts their guns in range of the city."

Michael looked at Daniel and merely nodded.

A distant cry of triumph echoed across the ice as the enemy, realizing their victory, poured out of the siege line to occupy the outer position. Soon all could hear the guns being dragged forward, and before an hour had passed the first shot from the new positions arced overhead and crashed into the shipping massed behind him.

As the first light of dawn streaked the morning sky, the bombardment resumed. The alliance closed the ring on Mathin, concentrating its fire on the city gate, to smash the wall to frozen splinters. Throughout that long bitter day Michael stood with Daniel on the battlement as the concentrated fire of half a thousand guns was unleashed in an unparalleled bombardment.

Entire sections of wall disintegrated in an instant, dashing dozens of men to their deaths. Zimri unleased another weapon unknown before, as the mortars fired high over the wall. The shells split open upon striking, but rather than explode, a strange green cloud emerged. Any who drew close quickly turned away, shrieking in agony. Many were blinded by the smoke, and those unfortunate enough to survive were soon coughing out their lungs in a pink foam of death. Other shells streaked into the city as well and burst into flames on contact, so that before midday a fair portion of the city was on fire.

Desperately the defenders replied with every available weapon, sensing that the decision would soon be reached, and if they could break the back of the next assault the morale of Zimri's forces, and their supplies as well, would be exhausted.

Twice during the long, bitter day heavy assaults were launched on the gate, only to be smashed down before they had crossed a hundred yards of open ice. As the day passed into darkness the bombardment continued unabated, and beneath a rain of shells and poison gas the forces of Mathin gradually melted away, spilling their blood onto the Frozen Sea.

Returning to the city, Michael passed an endless nightmare of chaos. Entire blocks of the city had burned to the ground, wounded crammed every building. He was stunned to see women and young children bearing arms, rushing forward to the wall carrying shot and supplies to the beleaguered men.

Mathin was dying.

Varinna greeted him at the door of the citadel; her fear was evident.

"You're scared, aren't you?" he whispered.

A shell burst behind them in the square and the screams of the wounded echoed above the roar of battle.

She threw herself into his arms.

"I thought you were dead. I saw a group of Companions bearing a body off the wall and I thought you were dead."

Yes, he remembered that. Morrison, commander of a thousand, a veteran from the beginning, crushed by a block of ice.

She led him inside, and together they went up to the private chambers. Thomas stood at the top of the stairs looking down at them.

He was still so awkward around the boy, not knowing what to say to him, or how to act. For two weeks, during brief moments of privacy, he had sat and talked with Thomas, but how could he reach him, or reach into his own heart as well? In many ways he looked so like Andrew, and now as the boy stood above him, dressed in the white tunic of a Companion, he suddenly felt a surge of love for the young boy who was trying to hide his fear.

Michael knelt by his side. "Are you frightened, son?"

The boy nodded.

"So am I," Michael whispered, and the boy rushed into his arms.

"When will this end? When will they go away?" Thomas asked.

"Soon, Thomas, soon."

Gently he picked Thomas up and carried him to his room. Putting the boy down, Michael and Varinna sat by the side of the bed until finally Thomas drifted off to sleep. He could feel Varinna's hand slip into his, and with a gentle kiss to Thomas's forehead, Michael left the room.

"Do you know what's going to happen?" Varinna asked as they stood alone in her bedchamber.

"Yes."

"Will you tell me?"

"Not yet."

A thundering explosion suddenly ripped across the northern sky.

"The Grove!" Michael said in awe. "The magazine of the Grove just went up."

With a light as blinding as the sun, the entire hill above Mathin seemed to be bathed in fiery death. The concussion washed over the city, shattering what few windows were left. Pulling Varinna back from the spray of glass, Michael stood in awed silence as the trees of the Sacred Grove were consumed in flames.

"I must leave," Michael said sadly. "We have to prepare the landward wall for assault now that our flank is exposed."

"Can't you stay?" Varinna whispered, and looking into her eyes, he could see the longing. For two weeks he had come back to her night after night, but never had he passed beyond the simple hug or the gentle holding of her hand. He recognized that she wanted more, far more than he was capable of giving.

Smiling, he kissed her lightly and then backed away. "I'm sorry, Varinna, not now."

And he was gone.

\*   \*   \*

The men around him were grim, each wishing that the other would offer some word of encouragement. But none was given.

"Our casualties are appalling," Daniel said, his voice slurring from fatigue. "We have less than ten thousand men capable of fighting, we've lost half our strength in under a fortnight. Two thousand dead and wounded today alone, not counting those poor devils in the Grove."

"I've got every man standing to for a dawn assault," Findlan, the land wall commander, replied. "We should be able to hold on with luck, but another day like yesterday and I can no longer promise that."

Michael looked around the room. "You know what will happen with the coming of dawn. They'll have their guns in the Grove aimed straight down our throats."

"We could launch a counterattack on the Grove," Stanson suggested hopefully.

"Senseless," Daniel growled. "Even if we took it back we'd lose more than we can afford."

"Is there anything else we can possibly do?" Findlan replied, looking to Michael, as if he could produce another miracle.

Michael shook his head. "We must try to hold on; either that or, if you wish, I shall offer our surrender."

The men were silent and several minutes passed, until finally Seay spoke a gentle reply.

"Michael, the others deserted but we shall not. When you sailed, those left behind met to discuss this eventuality. The decision was unanimous. We fight to the end. Besides, what would Zimri offer us? He'll put this city to the sword, so if we are to die, we do it as free men."

Nodding to Michael, the commanders stood and, excusing themselves, left to return to their commands until Daniel was the only one left.

Raising his head, Michael looked into Daniel's eyes as tears filled his own. "Still they will die for me, Daniel. Why, why do they do this?"

"For you are the One," Daniel whispered. "Now if you

will excuse me," he said softly. "I must see to my family. I've not seen Epana and the girls for nearly a week. I think it's important that I spend this time with them."

Stepping to Michael's side, he gave him a rough embrace and left.

In another hour the assaults will begin, Michael thought. The moment has come.

In the light of dawn Zimri stood atop the shattered outer wall and looked back to the east. The sky was ablaze with flaming scarlet that pushed back the Arch into the twilight of the west. By the thousands the men were drawn up, rank after endless rank. The Morians stood shoulder to shoulder, their battle standards snapping in the morning breeze, their scimitars drawn and held aloft in salute, the cold steel sparkling in the frosty air.

Next to them stood their ancient foes, the freebooters of the south in a wild assortment of uniforms and the brown-clad monks of Ezra, who would advance with them into the fight. Every available man was ready, circling Mathin in a wall of death, and he alone would give the word.

The bombardment had died away; the only sound was the soft moan of the wind and the distant cries of the wounded. Looking toward the city, he saw it wreathed in smoke and flame as the fires raged unchecked. He could make out the defenders as well, ringing the battered walls, waiting for his command.

This was the moment long dreamed of, conjured in his mind a thousand times as he wandered the frozen north in exile. Never had one commanded an army such as this, never had one held such power on the Ice. He looked back to the men and waited. This was the moment at last, and his heart gave him its dark warning! Driving the thoughts away, he held onto the dream, wishing that it could be prolonged forever, but even as he dreamed the dream the sun at last broke clear of the horizon, flooding them in its dark red light.

Raising his clenched fist into the air, Zimri let a scream burst forth as if it were torn from his very soul. His arm dropped, and the echo of his scream was picked up by a hundred thousand voices. Scimitars flashed upward across a sea of men, and the host pushed forward, storming like a wind-tossed sea toward the walls of Mathin.

"Here they come!" the shout roared along the wall, as if the long-pent-up fury and tension of the siege was at last released.

"Gunners stand to, mark your range finding sticks at two hundred yards, stand ready!"

The host, a swarming sea of humanity, poured forward chanting their cries as every second brought them closer. Standing by the wreckage of the gate tower, Michael pulled his scimitar clear of its scabbard and held it aloft. Around him were gathered the bodyguards, and behind him in the harbor were the final reserves, the elite regiments of the Companions positioned to stop any breakthrough.

"Three hundred yards, stand ready now."

The roaring of a hundred thousand voices washed over them, drowning out all other sounds except the insistent roll of the great drums and the braying of the horns calling the men to battle.

"Look!" a Companion shouted. "There to the center, they're bringing up their batteries."

Giant sleds dragged by teams of a hundred were pulling up heavy siege guns to be fired at point-blank range.

"Get ready!"

All down the wall gunners stood back from their weapons, gripping the gun lanyards.

"Fire!"

A roaring wave of fire swept down the Mathinian wall and all vision was lost in the boiling clouds of smoke. Michael peered forward, and as the wind cleared a hole, he noted the devastation wrought as grape and chain shot plowed into the lines. Still they pressed forward.

One of the signalers tapped Michael on the shoulder

and pointed up to the hill crowned by the Sacred Grove. Even as he watched, one of the surviving spruce trees, which had stood for centuries, tottered and fell.

"They're clearing a field of fire," the signaler shouted.

A dozen guns on the hill were already tossing fire shells into the city, and the Cornathians were dragging yet more guns into position. Daniel was over there by the landward side holding the north gate, which was wrapped in flames. But there was no time to think of him now.

Another volley blazed down the length of the wall, but in the interval the Cornathians had pressed closer. With each volley the range grew less. A fearful toll of destruction bloodied the Frozen Sea, but still the enemy pushed in.

"Double shot," the section commanders called as the men frantically loaded. In spite of the proximity to their own men, the Cornathian and Ezrian gunners raked the ice wall, blowing out vast sections of the defensive position.

They were close now, too close. Michael hefted his shield, his men drawing close for the first shock of combat.

A surging wall of men rushed toward them. A cannon fired a load of double-shotted chain, which tore a gapping hole in the line. Crossbowmen fired, the arrows hissing into the densely packed formations.

Michael saw his man, an Ezrian priest, coming forward, waving a battle-ax on high. The blow came, splintering the top of his shield, sending him staggering. Recovering, Michael slashed low and missed. Screaming with demented fury; the axman got up and swung again. Michael jumped backward, blocking the blow. His blade flicked out, slicing into the Ezrian's mouth, cutting through teeth and bone. The body fell away.

Another was at his side, and he cut sideways with a vicious swing. All thought was gone, all memory replaced by the age-old instinct to fight. Companions calling his name drove forward, trying to form a shield wall, but the

Ezrian priests were upon them, battering down the defenses.

A blade sliced past him, laying open his parka. He could feel the warm river of blood swelling out of the wound. A crossbowman threw his body across Michael's, swinging his weapon by the handle, driving the assailant back. Recovering, Michael held his shield up as a shower of javelins rained down. The ice was slippery underfoot from the slushly rivers of blood.

He suddenly realized that their line was bowing under the pressure—in several places the Ezrians were already atop the wreckage of the wall. Calling for his men to rally, he held his scimitar aloft and drove back into the fray, cutting and hacking. With a wild, confusing push they regained the top of the position, driving past their own guns, where the crews lay dead and dying.

The first wave receded, and a wild shout of triumph went up. Even as the enemy pulled back, leaving a carpet of bodies, the next horror became visible. The sled-mounted guns had been dragged to the edge of the barrier trench. Before the last of their own men had withdrawn, the pieces opened up.

Entire sections of the wall seemed to rise into the air. Shards of ice howled around him, crushing all who dared to stand. Throwing himself behind a gun carriage, Michael cowered as the remnants of the wall disintegrated around him.

A Mathinian battery on a secure section of the battlements turned its pieces against the Cornathian unit and slammed it into submission, yet as quickly as a gun was disabled another was dragged into place.

For what seemed an eternity he endured the madness, as his command melted away. For a moment the gunfire slackened, and peering up over the wreckage, he saw that yet another wave was pushing over the bodies of the fallen.

"Here they come again!"

Wearily Michael got to his feet, and calling to one of

the reserve regiments, he ordered it into the ever-widening breach.

"Look out!"

The men around Daniel scattered as a ballista bolt nearly ten feet in length hissed past them, smashed through a heavily armored warrior, and threw him to the street below.

Blinded by a sudden wave of smoke, Daniel staggered back to the wall and traded blows with yet another assailant who had mounted the ladders that had sprung up all along the flaming gate.

With a cry of fury Daniel swung his ax down in a deadly arc, smashing the helmeted form with such a blow that a spray of blood poured out of the visor to freeze on Daniel's shield.

"They're pulling back!" came the cry along the defensive barrier, and with a yell of triumph Daniel held his ax aloft, shouting taunts of death unto the attackers who were retreating up the hill.

Suddenly overcome with exhaustion, the aging berserker slumped beneath the scant protection of the scorched wall. He knew that in a minute or two the batteries massed above would open up with yet another barrage, and after half an hour the assault would resume with fresh troops. So far they had survived half a dozen attacks by Morian, freebooter, and Ezrian troops.

"Messenger from Michael," one of the men called. A white-clad Companion carrying the short staff and standard of Mathin was visible through the smoke and confusion. Weaving past the wounded and dead, he reached the base of the wall and scrambled up.

"What happened to the two men I sent out?" Daniel asked.

"One died coming over to Michael's line, the other fell on the return."

"Can Michael spare the reinforcements?" Daniel asked between strangled gasps for breath.

"No, he's ordered that every fourth man from this position be sent into the center of the city as a reserve."

"By St. Dubay's teeth, I've got no reserve. We nearly lost the wall this last assault, and it's still an hour to darkness."

"Those are his orders," the messenger replied grimly.

Daniel stood up, cursing, and pointed down the length of the flaming wooden wall. "Look at this, damn you, look at it. I've lost half my men, I have, and still they keep coming."

The battery roared behind them, and Daniel ignored the shouted warnings as the shells slammed into the wall and burning buildings behind him.

"Do you see that?" Daniel cried.

"I have my orders and am expected to lead the men back."

Daniel turned to his aide. "Count off every sixth man."

"Michael said every fourth," the messenger shouted.

Daniel looked at the exhausted, trembling messenger. "This position will most likely fall with one more assault," he replied, his voice edged with bitterness. "I can't spare anyone; one sixth will do."

"The gate will most likely fall as well in the next assault; we need the reserves."

Exhausted, Daniel turned away. "Every fifth man then. Get them out of here quick, before the next attack hits."

Eldric looked into Zimri's eyes and spat at his feet. The Morian guards, cursing, half drew their blades, but with a barked command from Zimri drew back.

"You heard my order, you're to lead your men on the gate."

"Saints damn you to hell," Eldric whispered. "I've lost half my men today. God damn you, Zimri, there's thirty thousand dead and wounded out there—haven't you had enough for one day?"

"We've yet to take Mathin. He's ready to crack; one more assault will carry the wall."

"Send in your precious Morians, if it's so important! I'll not stand for it, I've had enough, I have. The agreement was that I open the pass and my ships provide support for the siege, nothing more. I should have stayed with Ormson."

"That's why you'll go forward," Zimri replied coldly. "I'll not have you come out unscathed in this."

"In fact you would prefer me dead," Eldric shouted.

"Precisely."

Norn, standing by Zimri's side, chuckled softly.

Eldric stopped his wild ravings and eyed Zimri coldly. "I never should have."

"You already said that. You betrayed a comrade of a decade and gave the balance to my favor. What is to prevent your doing that again, once this battle is over and the Ezrians and I are staring at each other? I daresay my good friend Peter has already been talking with you."

Eldric laughed defiantly. "But of course, the fat scum."

"Where's your lieutenant?" Zimri asked coldly.

"Dead, Ulvin's second now."

Zimri turned to one of his aides and ordered him to fetch Ulvin. "If you won't lead them in, Ulvin can."

With a shouted cry Eldric drew his scimitar and rushed on Zimri. Half a dozen crossbows snapped, knocking Eldric off his feet. Feebly he struggled and with a final cry of rage got up to his knees.

"I'll be waiting for you in Hell!" Eldric screamed.

Reloading, one of the guards walked up, placed the point of his notched bolt at Eldric's temple, and pulled the trigger.

From out of the press of men surrounding the drama, Ulvin suddenly advanced, led by half a dozen guards. As he approached Zimri he suddenly saw the body sprawled on the ice and hesitated.

"Your master has met with an unfortunate accident while we were discussing the next assault. Do you understand?"

Ulvin nodded.

"You are to lead your men in on an attack on the gate. Let it be known that if any hesitate or withdraw before being ordered to do so, my gunners will fire upon them."

Grim, Ulvin silently looked again at Eldric's body. Bending over, he pried the scimitar of command from lifeless hands.

"I know he died better than you will," Ulvin hissed, and turning, he pushed back to the front.

Zimri turned to face Norn. "You go with him as well."

Norn blanched and, like a hunted beast, looked at the ring of guards around Zimri.

"What went for Eldric goes for you as well. When this war is over, I want no freebooter scum left upon the Ice. You all had your chance with Ormson, but failed. Now decide. In with Ulvin or die here like Eldric."

Norn smiled softly, trying desperately to put on a show of bravado. "At least I had the pleasure of seeing Eldric dead."

Pushing his way past the guards, he walked toward the flaming caldron of Mathin and disappeared from sight.

Peter came up behind Zimri and watched as the freebooter disappeared into the smoke. As Norn departed, Zimri turned to Peter and smiled.

"Eldric mentioned that you and he had some rather interesting conversations."

"Oh really?" Peter replied, not betraying any emotion.

"Yes, but I must venture that it is of no consequence now."

As darkness gently spread across the evening sky, the battlefield fell strangely quiet. Dazed and exhausted, the warriors of Mathin looked out across the field of strife, hoping beyond hope that the assault was over. Between the two walls of the city a clear patch of ice could barely be glimpsed, so thick was the carpet of the fallen.

In the brief moment of respite, Michael walked the length of shattered wall giving calm words of encouragement or kneeling to bless a fallen comrade who in a happy day had stood by his side.

Nowhere had they faltered, nowhere had they given ground throughout that long, grim day of battle. But all knew they were at the end. The ranks were filled now with women, old men, the few children who had stayed in the city, and wounded who had staggered back from the hospitals to die on the battlements.

Suddenly from out of the gloom they saw the next wave coming. No longer charging or calling in exaltation, but advancing at a slow walk as if beyond caring.

Michael, stopping on the wall, watched as the column advanced toward the bitterly contested gate.

He knew those men—they were the freebooters, Eldric's own, and as the smoke parted for an instant he saw what drove them on, for sled-mounted guns and massed formations of crossbowmen formed to their rear.

Looking at the advancing formation, he could pick out individuals, could have called to them by name. No battle shouts rose from the Mathinian side; it was as if an involuntary, sad sigh drifted across the Frozen Sea as comrades prepared to slaughter comrades. Soon the clash of battle roared up around the gate, and the few surviving guns on the wall traversed their weapons to use what precious shot was left to plow bloody furrows into the advancing lines.

For what seemed like an eternity the battle raged, and with tears in his eyes Michael watched as some of the finest sailors on the Frozen Sea went to their deaths. In the gathering darkness he watched as his line bowed back to the breaking point, but still the Mathinians held. Pulling men off the wall, Michael sent them into the caldron; soon spaces of ten yards or more were without a single defender, but Zimri did not order the flanking assault that would have overcome the city's defenses.

Finally Michael understood. There would be no flanking attack that night; the Bathian freebooters would die before Mathin as payment for the betrayal. Into the first hour of night the battle raged, until the sounds of conflict gradually drifted away and only the screams of the wounded punctuated the night.

He walked the wall in the darkness. They were gone, all of them gone. The defense was merely an eggshell, bled white by the suicidal attack of the churches. No skill, little cunning had been employed, only a bleeding that had destroyed half of the churches' armies, but in the process had ground the Mathinians into dust.

Returning to the gate, he saw just how few were left, for exhausted beyond caring, the men were slumped onto the ice, incapable even of helping the wounded who cried for release. Looking out over the line, Michael saw the thousand running lights of the fleet and knew their exhaustion as well. Zimri would save the final assault until dawn.

Michael turned to the men. "Clear the fallen from the gate, and when you are done merely place sentries on the line. The rest of you return to the square."

The men looked one to the other.

"Abandon the wall, Master?" one of them whispered.

Michael walked up to the warrior and gently touched him on the shoulder.

"It is time to prepare." And without another word he turned and walked back into the flaming remnants of the city.

# CHAPTER 20

THE DARKNESS WAS COMPLETE. HE WAS WRAPPED IN SHADOWS of smoke and night. Beyond lay the city of Mathin, helpless, in flames, ready, almost begging, to die and have an end to it. But he would not deliver death tonight. No, suddenly he would not let it end, for he knew that all, all of it, would end with the passing of that city.

Peter was in the distance, walking just out of sight, waiting for his commands, but there would be none tonight. For he understood the Prophecy, "That the two shall be linked as one, and together shall come out of them the New Age."

Yes, the Prophecy. The flames soared high to the west consuming half a sky with their funeral pyre offering. And he knew his dream, and his soul were ascending with them. For after Michael there would be nothing. For close to two decades Michael Ormson had been the source of all his plans, the creator of his dreams, the creator of his power.

He knew that the power of the churches was dying in that flame. What *beauty* there had been, what power the churches once held in their rituals, plainchants, and services at dawn. How it had enthralled him and the world, letting them heal and forget the madness of the Before Time. And how, in the end, had they stifled and held in their arrogance all power. Power purely for the sake of power, and the continuation of it.

Gone, they were all gone now. He had slaughtered them upon a hundred nameless fields of strife, so that the mysteries were gone forever, the monasteries gutted and silent. One by one, he, Zimri, had unlocked the doors to knowledge, so that the mystery of the Hidden Brotherhood that Balor still watched over was no longer a mystery. Hundreds now knew of the secret treasuries of knowledge, for many had been enrolled to build the new engines of war. No longer could the churches lock the box of knowledge and hide it away. And when that was known, all the other things would be known as well—how the churches held their power, and how the leaders had perverted it.

"Legend, all legend," Zimri whispered. "Our power and yours, Michael Ormson—all built on legend.

"And like legends we will be swept away forever in the days to come when men study what has happened here. Yes, Michael Ormson, in order to defeat you, in the end I had to join you in all that you ever dreamed."

Zimri knew the purpose for his life was passing amid the flames of Mathin, for with the great enemy gone, a people exhausted by war would turn away from the legends and live but for one thing—a world where religion was no longer the key. Zimri knew the history of the Before, when after the great wars of religion western men turned away from the mysteries and unleashed the age of enlightenment, the age of discovery and of science. It would happen again, Zimri thought, and a hundred years from now they will not understand, they will shake their heads and wonder at our folly.

But here, for the moment, was his triumph, and try as he might, he could find no joy in the moment, only a sad, lingering pain. Even as he watched the city burn, a single form emerged through the smoke. In his hand was a white standard.

"Why are you doing this?" Daniel asked, trying to block Michael's path.

"Because I must."

"He'll betray you."

"I think not, Daniel. He will not steal his victory now that it is within reach."

"Let me come with you then."

"No, the envoy I sent declared I would come alone to meet Zimri between the two walls."

Daniel turned away from Michael.

"It's finished then," he said softly.

"Not yet, Daniel. One last act remains to be played." Stepping around Daniel, Michael walked through the shattered gate. The smoke from the fires eddied and swirled around him, so that at times it was hard to even see his feet as he stepped around the bodies of the fallen.

Suddenly a blue-caped form stood before him; he knew who it was. "Zimri."

"Yes, Michael Ormson. At last we meet, as I once said we would."

"And as I knew we would as well."

Zimri stepped closer, so that they could almost touch.

"Your time is at an end," Zimri said softly, without malice or anger.

"And your time as well, Zimri. For even if you did not, I realized that from the beginning."

"Yes, I think you did. You also said that you knew we would meet like this in the end—what did you mean?" Zimri set aside all caution since he knew in his heart there was no subterfuge.

"Just that," Michael replied with a smile, "just that, and nothing more."

"Surely you do not ask me to believe that you are indeed the Prophet?"

"But I do," Michael replied, looking into Zimri's eyes. "From the day that Seth Facinn first revealed to me who and what I was, I understood and knew that in the end it would come to this."

Michael fell silent, waiting for Zimri to respond, but nothing was said and so he continued.

"I knew that for some reason beyond my understanding, be it fate, chance, or some higher destiny, I was doomed to be the Prophet. For years I struggled against that, for in every path I looked I could see but one ending. That the churches and I would go down together in death. I tried mightily to turn away from it, but this destiny dragged me on. And you were its agent, Zimri."

Zimri, fearing to respond, merely nodded his head.

"For I had to give vent to the passion of a race that had lain dormant and idle for a thousand years. And though I called for peace, in the end *I* picked up the sword and used it. You, Zimri, gave me that sword. And even as I smashed down the churches, I knew they would spring back in the end to destroy me, and for that reason I let you live. For that reason and for the penance I took in response to my own madness, for I allowed myself to fall victim to the call."

"You were nothing more than the dream of Inys Gloi," Zimri responded.

"Ah, Inys Gloi," Michael replied. "Yes, and do remember that they were the founders of all the churches which took the power and drove the old order out. So in the end, Zimri, you might say that I was a creation of all the churches, for Inys Gloi is common to them all."

"If you knew this destiny, why did you allow me to win?"

"Inys Gloi expected me to consolidate my power, so did my own followers, and in the end when I died, there would be the new religion—the Prophet of the Ice. The Messiah of a New Age. And what am I in the end, Zimri? I am merely a man as thyself, and not divine as many now claim. And if I had triumphed with sword, then for two thousand years to come my word would be law, my name divine. Why is it that men must make a divinity beyond themselves? For do they not understand that the divinity is in fact *us*? That *together* we are divine, the creators of this dream which ultimately is an illusion, without meaning other than the fact that for the moment it is real."

Zimri looked away from Michael. "You *let* this happen?"

"Yes. I let it happen, yet at the same time I knew it would happen, for if there is a gift in me it's the ability to somehow see beyond. We all have that gift; I merely learned to use it.

"If there was a turning in my path, it was my love for Janis and the boy whom you killed."

There was a long silence, each expecting the other to comment, but nothing was said.

"I know why you did it," Michael finally stated, "and you unmasked my private dream that perhaps my life was indeed my own, to live quietly with contentment and love. But with their deaths and the madness in me that followed, I at last learned that my life was not mine, and I accepted what destiny offered. In that acceptance I understood too that in the end I must let everything be destroyed. For in that destruction your system would be finished as well, and out of it would come the synthesis of the new way. The path that man was originally destined to take. A path without constraint of religion or fear of divine anger. For in this war those who survive will have learned one thing above all else. The wrath of man and the pain he can create is far worse than any fear imagined about what comes after death. That in the name of religion, we have created untold suffering throughout the ages.

"I saw my men kill in my name while I was still alive and mortal. Think, Zimri, think what they would have done if we had triumphed and then I had died. They would have made me a God, as they have done to other Prophets and Messiahs in the past. They would finally have come to ignore the truth of what I really said, which was simply let each man live with his brother in peace. In my name yet more armies would have gone forth, swords in hand, eager to slay and torment all who disagreed.

"No, Zimri, that is not what I wanted. Therefore when Seth first introduced the slow poison to me, I took it and I allowed myself to be cloistered away. In fact, at times in my weakness I asked for death so that the burden would be lifted from me, but death, sweet death, would not come. Long I wrestled with my weaker desires to see triumph and power, and finally after the death of Cowan I saw at last what we had become, and there is where I called for the retreat."

"That was suicide," Zimri replied. "As soon as you showed weakness your allies fell away to me."

"Precisely, for they never understood. But in the end, Zimri, we here have triumphed. Look out across the field of battle—your army, along with the freebooters, is shattered. Those who survive tomorrow will return home, and in the end will ask why, why this maddening waste. I believe Rifton tried to warn you of that twenty years ago, that the people of the Ice had been pushed to the limit, but you would not listen. Now you will have my defeat, Zimri. Yet I, and all who are with me, have won."

"But your people in Mathin?"

"That is why I am here. If I surrender now, will you spare those who are left?"

Zimri shook his head. "I too must follow my destiny, Michael. I cannot let Mathin survive. Not after this. I cannot have a Mecca for a dead Prophet."

"Ah, I have also heard of that," Michael replied with a smile.

"But there is one thing you have not accounted for," Zimri said softly. "And that is Inys Gloi. They are the only ones untouched. They will be here after this war is over, and they still have the power to create fear and yet more legends."

Michael stepped closer to Zimri and touched him on the shoulder. "That is the final reason I am here. I wish to make an arrangement. An exchange of sentiment for power."

"And that is?"

"Two weeks ago Seth Facinn, who was of Inys Gloi, died by his own hand. But before he died he entrusted to me a document which I am prepared to give to you."

"And what is that?"

"A list. Upon that list is the name and location of every agent of Inys Gloi. I am giving you time, Zimri, for you know as well as I that the moment I am dead Inys Gloi will kill you and seize the reins of power."

Zimri looked into Michael's eyes and tried to hold his gaze, but in the end was forced to turn away.

"Think of it, Zimri, and listen to me. Mathin will fall in the morning, that we both know. When I am gone, take your most trusted men and your Black Brothers. Send them out and smash the means that Inys Gloi has used to protect itself, and then sail north to the citadel and lay waste to it. The siege might take years, but in the end you will have them and the vast treasure of knowledge that Varinna told me is hidden there."

"Varinna—when did she tell you?"

"She is in the city even now."

"And the boy?"

"That is the arrangement, Zimri. The document for their lives, and for the families of my followers."

"And start yet another cult? Never."

"She will have my orders and I know she will obey, for Varinna is weary beyond her years of this fighting. I have a light frigate in the harbor, stripped of its guns. Let it pass in the hour before dawn and the papers are yours. Do not let it pass and the list, the only one of its kind, will be destroyed in the fires of Mathin."

"I cannot," Zimri said coldly.

"They will sail to the Dead Lands, there to live or perish beyond the known world of the Ice. But you, Zimri, will have to contend with what comes after tomorrow."

"If what you said earlier is true, then you should give me the papers anyhow, since for your dream to be completed Inys Gloi must die."

Michael nodded slowly.

"That is true," he said softly, "but it is the only thing I have left to bargain with. That and the feeling in your heart that we are linked in this drama, you and I, and that in the end you can see how destiny drew our paths together."

Looking at Michael, Zimri could see that he was speaking the truth. Besides, it was Peter, not Inys Gloi, whom he would face once the battle was over.

Hesitantly Zimri extended his hand and touched Michael on the shoulder. "The ship will be allowed to pass."

Michael looked at him and smiled sadly.

"Do you remember that fleet you sent out years ago," Zimri asked, "the one commanded by Eldric's son, which was supposed to sail around the world?"

"Yes, why do you mention that now?"

"My patrols captured one of them last week. It was a single vessel that had deserted Jason Eldricsson's command. They've reached the Southward Shelf and there beheld mysteries beyond our imagining. Far away, thousands of leagues away, they traveled, finding ruins of the Before Time, races of people not imagined, civilizations unheard of. I of course arrested everyone aboard the ship, since they were loyal to you, but they stated that Eldricsson would return someday. I thought you might like to know that, Michael Ormson. Even as you die the Enlightenment begins anew, beyond any power of myself, Peter, or Inys Gloi to control." Zimri sighed softly and looked away.

Michael drew closer, and reaching into his tunic, he produced the papers of Inys Gloi and handed them to Zimri.

"Why give them now?"

"Because here at the end of all things I know you will keep your word."

Reaching up, Michael lightly took Zimri's hand in his. "Zimri of Mor, I must return to the city and prepare. The Blessings of your Saints be with you."

"And also with you."

"I shall be waiting for you, Zimri. We have been linked together and know that in the time to come I shall be waiting for you, for what shall you have in life, Zimri of Mor, after I am gone?"

"So here we stand at the end of all things," Michael said quietly, looking out across the assembled host that filled the square. "We have lived our dream of the moment, and it has been filled with triumph and with tragedy. And now it draws to its end. But know that even in what appears to be our defeat, we have won.

"For the age has come to an end, the churches themselves are transformed by their own actions, and the knowledge that has been released shall give man his destiny.

"I shall not give unto you a promise of what lies beyond this night, and I command any who still walk this Earth tomorrow to remember that. For I know that in the years to come legends will be born, and for those who are left I command that they tell the truth. I offer no promise other than the beauty of a mystery beyond our ability to perceive. I know not myself where it leads. Remember those words. If we can only accept the mystery within ourselves, we can learn to live our lives without fear of a legendary god or death. For each and every one of us has the power of god within him, and is in fact his own creator."

He fell silent and looked up to the stars, and all who watched him looked up as well. Some in their fear believed that in the end he would bring down a fire to smite their enemies, but there was no fire—only the cold tranquility of night.

"Perhaps there is where it shall one day lead, for the desire to reach the stars brought us once to the edge of destruction. Yet we should not turn away because of that failure, for in that end *THERE* shall be our destiny."

He looked back across the square.

"You know what tomorrow's attack will bring. I tell you freely that you can still save your lives. Simply drop your weapons and walk away, and when taken prisoner denounce me. After all, they are only words.

"For those whose children are still in the city, let them be taken to the stone fortress overlooking the harbor. Ten of the Companions have been assigned the task of surrounding that position after the city has fallen and the sack is over.

"Those who will stay, go now to your positions, for the attack will be soon."

Turning, Michael went into the citadel leaving the doors open. A sudden shout echoed across the square.

"He is the One. He is the One!"

Michael looked over to Daniel and smiled wearily. "My friend, I have one last task for you. Epana, your children, Varinna, Thomas, and the young sons of Cowan, along with as many others that can be placed aboard, are to sail within the hour. I expect you to go with them."

Daniel nodded sadly and with tears in his eyes walked away.

One final task to be performed, and walking up to the private chambers, he entered the room where she waited.

"We have little time," Michael said softly.

"I know." Advancing toward him, she leaned up and kissed him lightly on the mouth.

"Thank you for the illusion of the dream," Varinna said, her voice trembling. "I know I could never be Janis, but it was wonderful for the brief moment we had. I best get Thomas and leave." She started for the door.

"Varinna."

She turned and looked at him. Suddenly he swept her into his arms, hugging her tightly.

"Take my love with you. Raise my son and let him know the truth of what I dreamed."

For what seemed all too brief a moment they embraced. And finally she pulled away.

"It's getting light out," Varinna whispered. "It's time."

"I know."

Leaving the room together, they awoke Thomas, and

picking him up, Michael carried the still-sleepy boy down the stairs and out into the square. A small exodus of families walked down to the ice where the ship was silhouetted against the first faint indigo of dawn. Reaching the stern hatch, Michael looked into the eyes of Thomas.

"Take care of your mother. And remember me for what I was."

The boy nodded sleepily, and as Michael placed him on his feet, Varinna came close again and kissed Michael. "Farewell, my love, farewell."

Even as they disappeared into the darkness of the ship he felt he was walking in a dream. For a voice from long ago had whispered the same words, "Farewell, my love."

A soft crying drifted around him as families separated forever. Aged warriors stood rigid, the tears freezing on their tunics. Michael looked over to Daniel, who was leading Epana onto the ship with their two daughters in tow. For once there was no loud arguing and shouts of protest, and as Daniel disappeared into the darkness of the hold, Michael saw the heavyset woman throw her arms around her battle-scarred husband.

And so the moment came at last, and with shouted commands the sails were sheeted home. Cutting free the anchor lines, the frigate edged from the harbor and past the shattered gate. All were silent, expecting that in the end they would be betrayed. But no gun fired. And as the ship cleared the Morian siege lines, it inched on a full spread of canvas. Hiking up against the morning breeze, the ship was soon streaking on a broad reach, southward and away to freedom.

All in the harbor were silent, each locked in his own thoughts as the vessel disappeared from view. Silently the assembled host turned back to the defense of the city.

"A rare beautiful sight, it is," a husky voice said behind Michael.

Turning, he beheld Daniel smiling sadly through his tears.

"Daniel, what are you doing here?" Michael shouted.

"Now don't start that with me, young Ormson. Epana knew what I was going to do, and by my soul I think she was half glad to be rid of me. She'll take good care of my girls. Besides, with me out of the way the suitors will not be so afraid to come about. So I slipped over the side, I did, as the ship started out. By my pox-eaten soul, Michael Ormson, I was with you in your first fight, or have you forgotten? And damn my soul, I'll be by you at the end."

Michael laughed for the first time in days. And embracing Daniel, they went forward, to join the thin line of men on guard.

Even as they joined the men at the gate, Michael watched the Morian elite guard advancing in close order—the blue-clad host filling the ice from horizon to horizon. Looking around to his few battered men, Michael smiled with a distant, wistful gaze.

At last the great death was coming. The visitor whom he had feared for so many years was finally to embrace him. The host drew closer, and the ranks of crossbowmen stepped out from behind the Morian shield wall.

In the distance came the scattered roar of gunfire as the north gate was forced, but here on the Ice, the Ice that had been his home and his life, there was silence.

The crossbowmen paused, the front ranks kneeling.

"Shields up!" came the cry down the line.

But he let his drop to his side. They were no longer there. He could see beyond that now. The life of the Prophet was at an end, and after all, it was nothing more than a dream. Something lay beyond that—his own existence was free at last, free of the wishes and needs of others. He had succeeded in the end. The New Age and the Return of the Garden was at hand; men freed by his thoughts would bring it about, as the universal destiny had desired.

He could see them now as if coming out of a mist. Yes, he could see her at last, and the small boy laughing and running at her side.

"Janis!"

Casting aside his sword, he rushed joyfully to her embrace, never hearing Zimri's command to fire.

Even as he called for his men to fire, he turned away. The sharp hissing of a hundred arrows cut through the air and there was a silence, a deep stunning silence that closed over them all like a tomb.

Finally he looked. An aged warrior was bent over the body, cradling it gently. His men stood in silent awe, almost fearful of what had been done. The old warrior embraced the body, and wiping the blood from Michael's face, he kissed him gently on the mouth.

Suddenly there was a cry. They looked up, and there in the heavens was the Sign—a fiery arc of light cut across the dawning sky from west to east. Long was its passing, illuminating all with its light. Finally it disappeared over the horizon, where its light merged with that of the rising sun.

He knew that it could be explained, for Balor had told him how and why the lights fell from the sky, but somehow he knew that it was still a Sign.

The warrior, still kneeling by Michael, suddenly stood up. "He'll be back. He'll be back and his power will be that of millions!"

Lifting his battle-ax on high, Daniel rushed toward Zimri. The archers fired, piercing him again and again, yet still he pushed forward, swinging his ax and calling Michael's name.

The Morians rushed forward with a shout, obscuring Zimri's view. He saw the ax rise and fall, covered in blood, until finally it fell for the last time and disappeared beneath the press of charging men.

Column after column rushed past him, pouring into the city that was soon obscured from view by the thickening clouds of smoke. Eventually all that was visible were the flickering distant flames and the incessant flash of the guns.

From out of the smoke Peter appeared at his side and they stood together in silence, listening to the grim cries of the warriors rushing past.

The morning light was behind them, lending a soft red glow to the swirling smoke, and at last Zimri turned away from the city and started back to his ship. It was over at last, both for Michael and himself. Even in the moment of their victory he knew what was to come. The Age of the Churches was finished. Men would turn away from the fear and go into the new Renaissance of Man.

There would be struggles to come as the old order slipped away, lost in its illusion that it could hold on, for few yet understood what Michael had lived for. And in the times to come, many would remember only dimly what he had truly tried to say. But Zimri pushed that thought aside. He was still mortal and still the creature of a system that had given him power. And he would follow that path until, at last, Michael stood to greet him.

"I understand you've taken an individual named Nathan into your circle of advisors."

"Where did you hear that?" Peter replied.

"Oh, one of my men told me. My informant claims he recognized him."

"I've heard nothing of it," Peter said softly, looking at Zimri with a strange distant smile.

Zimri was silent for a moment, and then continued on.

"I want the city leveled," Zimri said, more to himself than to Peter. "The men are to be put to the sword, women if they surrender are to be spared. Any children that are taken will be placed in the monasteries and trained to serve our Church."

"And as for Michael?"

"His body is to be burned, his ashes scattered in secret. I want no shrine to be worshipped in the years to come."

"Did you fear him, Zimri?" Peter asked, looking into

the eyes of his old master, who was now his rival for power.

Zimri smiled softly and looked off into the distance.

"No, Peter, I never feared him, for I knew in my heart that in the end I would defeat him. No, I never feared him the way I now fear you."

The smoke swirled around them, so that Peter was for the moment lost from view.

"Me?" came a distant voice out of the mist.

"Yes, my dear Peter, you."

# About the Author

William R. Forstchen, who makes his home in Oakland, Maine, was born in 1950. Educated by Benedictine monks, he considered the calling of the priesthood but decided instead to pursue a career in history. Completing his B.A. in education at Rider College, he went on to do graduate work in the field of counseling psychology.

In 1978, William moved to Maine where he is currently an instructor of Ancient and Medieval History at Maine Central Institute, Pittsfield. He also coordinates activities as director of the Medieval Club, Live Dungeons, and Catapult Team Competitions at the school. His student teams recently set a new national distance record with a sixteen foot crossbow. William is owner of Northern Fantasy Game Company which specializes in play-by-mail games. The company will soon offer a play-by-mail game based on the Ice Prophet Trilogy. William lives with his wife, Marilyn, their dog, Ilya Murometz, and Anastasia the cat.

William's interests include iceboating, Hobie Cat racing, sailing, skiing, pinball machines, Zen philosophy, and participation in Civil War battle reenactments as a private in the 20th Maine Volunteer Infantry.